MW00941693

TRUTHS
UNSPOKEN

TRUTHS
UNSPOKEN

THE SOULS UNTETHERED SAGA · BOOK 1.5

K.J. MCPIKE

terracotta rose
PUBLISHING

For all the heroes of their own stories.

PLEASE NOTE

Truths Unspoken was previously published as:
Nemesis (The Astralis Series Book 1.5).

This is the same story, only slightly re-edited and
rebranded with a different title and cover.

PRONUNCIATION GUIDE

CHARACTERS

Xitlali = seet-**lah**-lee
(Lali = **lah**-lee)

Oxanna = ok-**sah**-n*uh*
(Oxie = **ok**-see)

Dixon = **dik**-s*uh* n
(Dix = diks)

Ulyxses = yoo-**lik**-sees
(Lyx = liks)

Salaxia = sah-**lah** k-see-*uh*
(Sal = sahl)

Xiomara = see-oh-**mah** r-*uh*
(Mara = **mah** r-*uh*)

Kala = **kah**-l*uh*

PLACES

Alea = **ah**-lee-*uh*

Lanai = lah-**nah**-ee

OTHERS

XODUS = **ek**-s*uh*-d*uh* s

Astralis = as-**tra**-lis

Astralii = ast-**tra**-lahy

Semmie = **se**-mee

Yavari = yah-**vah** r-ee

Awana = a-**wah**-n*uh*

Dear Lali,

~~I miss you.~~

I get that you hate me right now. Honestly, I hate myself for what I did, too. Looking back, I can't believe I ever thought lying to you was the best option. I guess that's why they say hindsight is 20/20.

But that's why I'm writing you this letter. I want you to know everything that happened—all of it, from beginning to end. Maybe then you'll see why I felt I had to do what I did. I know that doesn't change the outcome, but at least you'll understand my intentions.

In my twisted brain, lying was my way of protecting you, or trying to anyway. I didn't know what else to do, how else to deal with the damage I'd already done. I swear I never wanted to hurt you, but the whole situation was so messed up that I had already started hurting you before we even met...

ABDUCTION

Son of a—

I bit back a curse as I squinted at my target through the slatted closet door. She stood at her bathroom mirror, oblivious, and taking her sweet time smothering herself with every kind of lotion known to man while some pasty green mask dried over her face. At this rate, she was never going to sleep. Meanwhile, I was about to keel over. My legs threatened to give out after what felt like an eternity crouching between the plastic covers of dry-cleaned slacks and dresses, and I was slowly suffocating in mothball funk. Because, of course, she'd chosen to go through an elaborate beauty ritual tonight of all nights—right when I planned to strike.

The sad part was, I really had planned it. Obviously not well, but then, I'd never kidnapped anyone before. And it wasn't like there was a semmie handbook for those pesky times when you needed to snatch an ex-Astralis out of her home with your warped astral projection ability.

Trust me, I looked.

Watching her from across the darkened bedroom, I was tempted to appear behind her and be done with it. Her husband was snoring in their oversized bed, so he wouldn't see anything. I only needed two seconds to grab her. We'd be gone an instant later. But if she managed to get out a scream, then all of this would have been for nothing. After the hours I'd wasted to avoid involving her family, I wasn't about to have her wake them up now.

The hiss of running water made me perk up. Finally, she was rinsing off the Yoda facial. I shook the dark wisps of hair out of my eyes and shifted, ready to spring as soon as she settled into bed. The closet was just a few feet from where an upturned comforter invited her to climb between the flannel sheets.

But instead of stepping out of the bathroom after she dried her face, she opened the drawer beside the sink and pulled out yet another bottle of moisturizer.

I wanted to punch the wall. There was no way her skin could absorb anything else. How was it *that* dry in the first place? This wasn't the Sahara.

Desperate to ease the burden on my legs, I pressed my hands against the door frame in front of me. The molding creaked loudly in response.

I froze. *Way to go, idiot.* After all my preparation for this moment, I was going to screw it up by leaning on a rickety piece of wood.

Perfect.

"Yoseph?" The Lotion Queen poked her head out of the bathroom, the edges of her gold nightgown glowing in the light behind her. She looked toward her still-snoring husband like she wanted to wake him, and a string of profanities chorused in my mind. So much for keeping her family out of it.

You should have listened to Cade. I pressed my lips together to keep from exhaling my frustration. My Uncle Cade wanted me to snatch her from the dinner table last night and be done with it. We already had a makeshift cell inside an abandoned shipping container ready to hold her until she gave us the information we needed.

But I couldn't do it, not with her kids right there. Instead, I squandered most of the day memorizing the layout of this house so I could nab her when everyone was asleep. And I'd spent forever crouched in this closet just to make sure I didn't lose my nerve. I knew if I projected out of here, there was a good chance I wouldn't have the guts to come back and finish the job.

My target stepped into the bedroom, and I heard Cade's voice ring out in my head: *Compassion is only going to get in the way of finding your sister.* He was right—trying to keep the woman's family out of this was a waste of time. So what if her children heard her scream and didn't know where she was for a few days? Both of my parents had been dead for nearly fourteen years. Her kids could suck it up. I had to do this.

Now.

I stood so fast my shoulders bumped the hangers above me. My target's head whipped in my direction, freeing a strand of short brown hair from her frilly pink headband. Frowning, she stepped around the bed and inched toward my hiding place like a lamb approaching a lion.

My breathing sped up. If I waited until she was a lunge away, maybe she wouldn't have time to make a fuss. Then I wouldn't lose sleep tonight from knowing I traumatized her kids the way the Eyes and Ears had traumatized me.

Her silhouette crept closer. I turned my palm outward, holding my hand at the same level as her mouth in case I needed to muffle her voice. She reached to open the closet, and I smelled a mix of jasmine and mint through the gaps in the door.

Adrenaline rushed through my veins. My pulse pounded until I couldn't hear anything else.

Come on. Open it.

She hesitated at the last moment, glancing back at her husband, but I couldn't wait any longer.

I burst out of my hiding place. Terror ripped through her features as I looped my arm around her shoulders and smashed my fingers over her mouth. Squeezing my eyes shut, I pictured the inside of the shipping container just as she inhaled to scream.

We were gone before the sound came out.

2

CAGE

My target's legs buckled as soon as we appeared. I managed to catch her at an awkward angle with my arm pressed into her lower back, but her head nearly hit one of the ridges in the metal wall. I winced. That was all I needed, for her to crack her skull and get amnesia or something. Then I'd never find the rest of them, and I needed all five members of XODUS intact if this was going to work.

Rain pelted against the roof, a constant pounding that made the dim, hand-cranked light flicker as I strained to keep my struggling prisoner upright. She cried out, the sound little more than a puff of warm air against my fingers. Realizing I didn't have to muffle her voice anymore, I moved my hand off her face and hooked both arms under hers.

"Let go of me!" she shrieked. Her voice echoed loudly in the small space, but I wasn't worried about anyone hearing. I'd taken her from her home in Virginia to a

5

locked shipping container in an old junkyard on the outskirts of Miami. No one would be around to help her.

She fought against my hold as I maneuvered her toward the mat in the corner. I intended to set her down gently, but she twisted out of my grip and fell into it face-first.

"Who are you?" she whimpered, barely able to lift her head from the butter-colored foam. She blinked hard and gasped. "Why can't I see?"

Oh, yeah. I'd almost forgotten about the temporary blindness. It happened to Cade the first time he projected with me, too. He was a full-blooded Astralis like her, and it had taken him a while to get used to the way my ability worked. Instead of separating my spirit from my body like the two of them were used to, I projected my *entire* body, along with people and objects I touched. Just like all semmies—those of us with only one Astralis parent instead of two—my power came out *differently*.

"Why can't I see?" she repeated, trying and failing to push herself up. The gold satin of her nightgown had nearly ridden up over her ass, and I diverted my gaze to the wall above her. Rivulets of water trickled through the holes I'd drilled into the metal and formed small puddles along the plywood floor. The mat was probably getting wet, too, but I pushed away any trace of sympathy for the woman trembling on top of it. She deserved a lot worse than a soggy piece of foam after what she and her friends did to my uncle.

Still, her weak attempts to move and panicked blinks

made my stomach flop. I'd just plucked her from her home, like it was nothing. *Like the Eyes and Ears did to Kala.*

My shoulders tensed. No. I wasn't like them. I wouldn't be doing this if I had a choice. And I wasn't going to hurt anyone or run cruel experiments and tests like they were probably doing to my poor sister.

Heat coursed through my body at the thought. The woman in front of me was the reason I couldn't get to Kala in the first place. If she and her stupid little group hadn't teamed up to suck Cade's astral energy into a crystal, he and I could've gotten to Alea and rescued my sister a long time ago. Instead, we were stuck with no access to the Astralis realm.

"Hello?" My prisoner groped at the air. "What do you want?"

I only glared in response. Soon it would be Cade's turn to demand answers from her. Now that she was our captive, she would have no choice but to help my uncle and me find the others and undo the energy sink that had claimed his power. It was time to get started with our plan.

Closing my eyes, I projected to the house I shared with my uncle. He lay stretched across the leather sofa in the living room, his seven-foot tall body overtaking the couch so his feet dangled over the arm. He held a thick book in his left hand and a glass of red wine in his right. From where I stood, I couldn't see his face, only the back of his dark, cropped hair.

"Ah, the prodigal nephew returns," he said evenly, not bothering to turn around.

I ran my tongue along my teeth to stop the sarcastic response eager to fly out of my mouth. My uncle had a habit of saying things that didn't quite make sense. In truth, he'd always seemed a little eccentric to me. He came into my life when I was thirteen—barely over a month before my Grandma Naida died—and I noticed right away that he was a bit *off.* But he was kind enough to take me in, so I tried not to be judgmental.

Knowing he was waiting for me to come to him, I strode across the room until we faced each other. Only then did he lower the book. His light green eyes—just a few shades lighter than my own—assessed me. "You've finally finished the job?"

"Yeah." I forced down the tickle in my throat. "She's locked in the shipping—er, *the cage.*" Cade preferred that term for where we planned to keep our hostages. According to him, they'd acted like animals, and they should be treated that way.

A smile crept over his face, bunching the deep scar along his left cheek into a series of uneven ripples. "Brilliant." He set down his wine, the tumbler clinking against the glass of the coffee table as he stood. I watched the folds in his slacks loosen, the hems spilling over his black dress shoes. Given his height, it was a miracle that any pants were long enough for him.

"You got it done," he said, walking over to slap a heavy hand down on my shoulder. "I'm proud of you."

My head snapped up. "Really?"

"Well…" He pursed his lips. "It took you far longer

than it should have." His words deflated me, but I hoped he didn't notice. "Next time you'll do better."

I wasn't sure if it was meant to be encouragement or a command. Honestly, it didn't matter. I had to do better next time, or we'd never get his ability back.

"Are you ready to talk to her?" I asked.

"Oh, nephew." Cade's grin grew to reveal boxy, over-sized teeth. "I've been ready for twenty years."

3

REUNION

W<small>HEN MY UNCLE AND</small> I <small>SHOWED UP IN THE SHIPPING</small> container, our captive was leaning against the wall, still looking shaky.

"*Xiomara,*" Cade cooed in a falsely pleasant tone. "How lovely to see you again."

Even in the flickering light, I could tell her already pale skin had gone completely white. I guessed that meant her vision was back. "Cade," she gasped, the sound barely audible over the rain pounding overhead.

"Well, it's good to know you remember me." My uncle crossed his arms, the sleeves of his black dress shirt straining with the motion. "I had my doubts after you and your friends left me for dead."

"H-how did you find me?" Xiomara turned to me and swallowed. "And who are you?"

"Don't worry about him." Cade stepped between us to block me from view. I knew he wanted to keep the focus off me. Even in a situation like this where the person in question had no recourse, my uncle was trying to protect me, just like always. "This is between us," he said, reaching out a hand like he was going to caress Xiomara's face.

"Don't touch me!" She backed into the wall and side-stepped him, stumbling over the mat at her feet.

Cade laughed, but it wasn't his usual chuckle. It was a strange, maniacal sound. "Oh, Xiomara. You're as feisty as ever." He dropped his hand to his side and let out a long sigh, as if recalling a fond memory. "We'll see how long that lasts."

I rocked back on my heels, feeling like a creep watching some twisted reunion. After all the time Cade spent ranting about what this woman and her friends had done to him, I wasn't expecting him to smile at her like that. She'd ruined his life. Why was he so calm?

Xiomara was breathing like she'd just sprinted for miles. I counted five inhales before she asked, "What do you want?"

"You know what I want," Cade answered coolly.

Her breath caught, and she slid along the wall again, as if she were determined to be as far away from my uncle as possible despite the fact that her new prison was hardly six feet wide. "No," she whispered. "I won't. I *can't.*"

"Oh, I think you can, Xiomara. And you will." His gaze ran up and down her trembling body. Compared to Cade's huge frame, she almost looked like a kid. "Once you help us find the other four, of course," he added.

She shook her head, and her pink headband slid down to her brow. "Never."

That made Cade laugh again. "I figured you might say that." He turned to wink at me. "It's a good thing my nephew here has ways of making you cooperate."

"Nephew?" Xiomara's gray eyes studied my face for a long moment before widening. "*Kai?*"

I nearly choked on my own spit. How did she know my name? I knew she worked with Cade for a while in Alea, but he never said she knew about me.

"I thought for sure the Eyes and Ears…" She trailed off, the astonishment in her expression making me even more uneasy. Why was she acting like she was relieved I was okay? She took a step toward me, and I backed into the wall with a thud.

"Whoa, lady." I pushed my hands out in front of me. "I don't know what you're trying to pull, but don't think for a second that I won't hurt you if I have to." My voice came out sounding detached, and I told myself she wouldn't see through my bluff. After all, I'd snatched her out of her house; she didn't know what else I was capable of.

Her face fell, and she turned to Cade. In contrast to his alight expression, hers radiated pure hatred. "You're disgusting," she snarled, adjusting one of the straps of her nightgown. "Brainwashing your nephew to do your dirty work is low, even for you."

"Hey!" I pushed off the wall. "You don't—"

Cade held up a hand to silence me. "Forget it. Harsh as they may be, her words can't save her now."

My eyes narrowed to slits. He was right, but it didn't make her disrespecting my uncle any easier to handle. Wasn't it enough that she took his entire life away? I was the only person on his side, and now she was trying to turn me against him, too. She had some nerve.

Cade was the only family I had left in this world. He saved me from having to bounce between foster homes and took me in when there was no one else I could depend on. I wasn't about to abandon him now that he was depending on me.

"So." Cade arched a protruding brow at Xiomara. "If you are done trying to manipulate my nephew, let's get down to business. Where are the others?"

She ignored him and looked at me. "Kai, don't let him fool you. He's—"

"You don't want to test my patience," Cade warned. "Tell us where the others are, or things are going to get very ugly."

Her nostrils flared, and we all stood in a tense silence filled only by the patter of rain.

"Xiomara," Cade finally said, his frown from a few seconds ago replaced with a slow-moving smile. "I'm afraid if you don't cooperate, I'll have no choice but to send my nephew out to hurt your children."

She made a choking sound. "No! They have nothing to do with this."

"Then I suggest you do what we say," I snapped, willing her to cooperate. Even if she didn't know it, I was as desperate as she was to avoid bringing her kids into this mess. I'd wasted the previous day spying on her for that very reason. I couldn't justify harming them—physically or psychologically—when they had nothing to do with their mother's actions all those years ago.

"I don't know where any of the others are," Xiomara claimed. "I swear. I haven't seen them in years."

Cade tilted his head to the side, studying her. "You must have some idea where to find them, or at least where to look."

"I don't." Her face was insistent, almost convincing. But my uncle had already told me that she was a great liar. I hoped this was one of the epic performances he warned me about. If she really didn't have any information on the others, then we were right back to where we started—with no way to Kala.

I shoved my fingers through my knotted hair. "Do you have any pictures of them?" I asked, trying to sound firm. With a single photo of the group, this could all be over in a matter of hours.

She blinked. "Pictures? What good would that do?"

"Just answer the question," Cade commanded.

I held my breath as I waited for Xiomara's response. She stayed quiet, her gaze darting around as if she were looking for an escape.

Cade cleared his throat loudly. "This hesitation won't do. Time for a little encouragement." He pulled something out of his pocket and tossed it to me.

I caught the hard object instinctively. Looking down at my palm, I realized it was a folding knife.

My blood froze.

"Get the youngest one," he ordered.

"No!" Xiomara lunged in my direction, but Cade caught her around the waist.

"Go!" he yelled over the sound of her cries. Turning toward the mat, he let go of Xiomara. Her momentum made her stumble and fall into the foam. Cade whipped around to face me, his teeth bared. "Do you want to see your sister again or not?"

My fingers tightened around the cold metal in my palm. If this was the only way to get Kala back, I had to do it. I pressed the button to release the blade and forced my eyes shut.

"Kai, don't!" Xiomara shouted. I tuned out the rest of her pleas. Replaying Cade's mantra about compassion in my mind, I projected out of there praying I'd have the strength to do what needed to be done.

4

THREAT

I STOOD IN THE DARKENED HALLWAY WITH THE BLADE drawn. Sweat beaded above my upper lip as I scanned the empty corridor. Even though I'd memorized the layout of Xiomara's house, I didn't know which room belonged to which of her kids. The first door on the left was already ajar, as if telling me to start there.

Holding my breath, I eased it forward a centimeter at a time until I could see the bedroom behind it. Clothes and books littered the floor, illuminated by a small night-light that bathed everything in a soft blue glow. The bed held a collection of plush toys atop a lumpy, animal-print comforter. All that showed of the girl beneath the blanket was a mop of black hair and a skinny arm wrapped around a stuffed elephant.

The knife suddenly felt like a weight in my fist. Judging from the girl's tiny hand, she couldn't fight off a kitten. How was I supposed to hurt her? Just thinking about it made bile rise in my throat.

There had to be another way—something to scare Xiomara into cooperating. Maybe just showing up with the kid would be enough. If I appeared in front of Xiomara holding her daughter at knifepoint and then projected the girl out of there, it might scare Xiomara into talking. I wouldn't even have to do anything to the kid; any parent's imagination would come up with countless horrible possibilities. I knew all too well how morbid the mind could be, how torturous it was picturing the different ways someone could be hurting a loved one.

I stepped around a splayed hardcover and a pile of clothes to get to the girl's bedside. Her arm was perfectly positioned for a grab-and-go. One quick appearance, and I could bring her right back. She wouldn't even wake up until we were already out of here, and she would probably think it was all a dream. It wasn't like she'd be able to explain the situation any other way. No harm, no foul.

Provided you don't give the poor thing a heart attack.

I let out a soft sigh. Maybe I'd just tell Xiomara that she could either lead us to the others or watch us force her kids to help us. Wouldn't that be a sight? A bunch of semmies running around with untrained abilities, wreaking havoc on the unsuspecting members of XODUS.

Too bad none of her kids were old enough to manifest their abilities. During my spying sessions the previous day, I'd overheard Xiomara's husband joke that their oldest was "fifteen going on thirty." Semmies didn't develop their projection powers until sixteen.

Even if the kids were old enough, I couldn't do that to

them. Kidnapping them and threatening them until they mastered their projecting was exactly the type of thing the Eyes and Ears would do, and I refused to be like them.

The little girl flung her arm out in her sleep, and I nearly tripped over a notebook as I backed away from her bed. Her stuffed elephant fell to the floor, joining a sweater at the base of her nightstand. I stared at the toy, an idea unraveling in my brain. Maybe I could get Xiomara to crack without scarring a little kid for life.

I tiptoed forward to grab the elephant and quickly projected to the shipping container. When I appeared, Xiomara was swinging at Cade and screaming.

"Hey!" I shouted, my voice reverberating off the metal walls.

Xiomara whipped around, her hair wild and her headband now at the base of her neck. "What did you do?" She lurched at me but stopped dead when I held up the knife and stuffed animal.

Before she could say anything else, I stabbed the knife through the elephant's head and ripped the blade through its body. The stitching tore open with a pop, sending clumps of white stuffing tumbling to the floor.

Xiomara cried out, covering her mouth with both hands. Cade glared at me over her shoulder, his face telling me he wasn't impressed by my cop-out. But I couldn't stop now.

"Make me go to your house again, and it won't be a stuffed animal that gets a knife to the back." I shoved the toy's limp form at her. "Got it?"

She let out a sob, falling to her knees as she clutched the mangled toy. Tears filled her eyes, reflecting the flickering light.

"Last chance." Cade stepped in front of her and crouched so he could look her in the face. "Are we going to do this the easy way or the hard way?"

I held my breath, aware of nothing but Xiomara's reaction. I couldn't go back for that little girl.

Xiomara hugged the scrap of stuffed animal to her chest and sniffled. "Okay," she whispered, keeping her eyes on the floor. "You win."

"We win?" Cade pressed. "And what might our prize be?"

"I…" One of her eyes spilled over, and she brushed her cheek with the base of her hand. "I have a picture."

5

PHOTOGRAPH

IT WORKED. MY WHOLE BODY ARCHED FORWARD AS RELIEF flooded through me.

"Where is this picture?" Cade demanded, straightening his legs so he towered over Xiomara again. The light flickered behind him, making his broad shadow dance along the floor like a possessed spirit.

She sat back on her heels, refusing to look at either of us. "I don't know exactly. I'll have to dig around to find it."

"*Dig around?*" Cade laughed. "I don't think so. Tell us where it is, and we'll get it." His words wound me back into a cluster of nerves. I couldn't have my uncle tearing apart Xiomara's house in search of a picture. I wasn't going to risk him waking and terrorizing her family after I'd done everything I could to avoid it.

Xiomara pressed a trembling hand to her brow, still cradling the limp form of the destroyed elephant in her other arm. "I told you, I don't know where it is. Trying to explain where to look will take longer than if I look for it myself."

"You expect us to trust you won't try anything if we let you out of here?" Cade challenged.

"She won't," I jumped in, eager to keep him from joining any trip to her house. "Not when she knows I have easy access to her family." I held up the blade still clutched in my hand and shot her a dark look, daring her to disagree. "Isn't that right?"

"Of course." Xiomara dropped the remains of the toy as she got to her feet. "I-I won't try anything."

Cade's scowl returned, but I was sure he would be fine once we caught another member of XODUS. Taking Xiomara's wrist, I pictured the same room I'd found her in earlier. I let the image play through my head for an extra second to make sure her husband was still sleeping. For a brief moment, I wondered if he would wake up and see me threatening his wife.

I shook off the thought. So what if he did?

Setting my jaw, I followed the preview before I could talk myself out of it. The bathroom light was still on, casting a soft yellow triangle onto the wood floor. It was enough for me to make out the nightstands on either side of the queen bed and a long desk that covered most of the wall to my right. There were a handful of frames propped up on their surfaces, but I doubted any of them held the photo I needed.

The floor creaked as Xiomara started toward the closet, and her husband stirred. She and I went still as stones, watching the man roll over. He muttered something unintelligible, and a few seconds later he was snoring again.

"You should wait in the hall," Xiomara whispered so softly I could barely make out her words. "If Yoseph wakes up and sees you, this will take even longer."

I knew she was right, but the thought of leaving her unattended left a bad taste in my mouth. I scanned the room again. There was only one door to exit, and it was a two-story drop from either of the windows. She'd have no way out except to go past me. *Nothing to worry about.*

Reluctantly, I lowered the knife. "You have two minutes."

She nodded, and I headed out to the hallway. I left the door open, just in case she tried something crazy. There was no telling what someone would do when backed into a corner. I was a prime example of that.

Pressing my back against the wall, I blew the air out of my cheeks. I told myself whoever was in Xiomara's photo would be able to lead us to the other three. Maybe we'd get really lucky and the photo would be of the whole group. Then I could get all five women to undo the energy sink tonight and have them home before sunrise. Their loved ones would be none the wiser.

I heard something rip, and my heart took a nosedive into my feet. If Xiomara was tearing up the picture, I was going to lose it. Knife drawn, I rushed into the bedroom. She was hovered over the desk, scribbling on a scrap of paper.

"What are you doing?" I closed the distance between us in two strides. "Leaving notes wasn't part of the deal."

My free hand shot out to take the pen, but she pulled it back before I could reach it.

"I want to make it look like I left on my own." The desperation on her face shattered my resolve to stop her. "Please. I can't let my kids go crazy wondering if I've been killed." Her words sent a jolt through me, and a memory played in my mind like an old movie.

Mommy and Daddy lay still on the floor. I call them, but they don't move. Their eyes are open, but they don't blink. There are red stains on their clothes and all over the carpet, the furniture, the walls. Kala's pink lovey is crumpled in front of my shoes, but I don't hear her crying. She always cries if she drops her lovey. Where is she?

"Please," Xiomara said softly, snapping me back to the present. "They'll already be devastated enough."

A tremor moved through my throat. I knew the devastation of loss was nothing compared to the misery of uncertainty. Not knowing whether my little sister was alive was a slow, constant torture I was still enduring—one that I needed Xiomara's help to end.

"Kai, are you—"

"Just hurry," I managed to get out. Turning on shaky legs, I left the room before she could see how much her plea had affected me.

Back in the hall, I fought to calm my racing heart. Why couldn't I find even half the strength Cade possessed? He never would've let her get away with that note. He would've ripped the paper out of her hand and threatened to crack her husband's skull if she didn't get the picture right that second. Meanwhile, my knees turned to jelly at the mention of sad kids. It was pathetic. *I* was pathetic.

A cloud drifted away from the moon, letting a beam through the window at the end of the hallway. The blue-green glow landed on a collection of framed school portraits along the wall, and though I couldn't see the details of the kids' faces, I was sure they were all smiling —the vision of a perfect family.

I scowled. They had no idea what I'd been through, no idea that I was fighting so hard to get a piece of the life they probably took for granted. Why was I so worried about showing them mercy when life hadn't shown me any?

Xiomara murmured something as she stepped into the hallway, but I was too caught up in my thoughts to process what she said. "What?" I asked, turning to face her.

She shook her head. "Nothing."

I caught sight of the duffel bag in her hand and huffed. "Are you crazy? This isn't vacation time."

"I told you, I'm trying to create the illusion that I left."

I narrowed my eyes. *That's what you get for giving her an inch.* But Cade would never let me live it down if Xiomara brought luggage with her. It was bad enough she left a note.

"You're not taking that with us," I grumbled.

She opened her mouth to protest but thought better of it as she eyed the blade in my hand. With a sigh, she turned around and headed back into the room. I followed, noticing she had turned off the bathroom light so the only illumination came from the moon. She opened the closet and shoved the bag inside, taking a moment to unzip one of the pockets. When she turned toward me again, her arm was extended in offering.

In her grip was a small photograph.

6

WEAKNESS

I pulled the picture from Xiomara's fingers, unable to keep my own hand from shaking. Even with the moonlight coming in through one of the windows, it was too dark to make out the details of the image. As eager as I was to project to whoever was in it, I didn't want to turn on a light and risk waking Xiomara's husband.

Keeping the photo in one hand, I closed the folding knife and slipped it into my pocket with the other so I could take hold of her wrist. We appeared in front of Cade, who stood with his arms crossed. He tapped his shoe on the floorboards as our captive steadied herself on the wall.

"Got it," I said over the echo of the rain overhead. I waved the picture once, my heart thumping as I flattened it in my palm. With the flickering light, I could see the photo was clearly older than me. It was wallet-size and folded down the middle—right through what little could be seen of a redheaded girl's face. Beside the crease, a younger-looking Xiomara laughed, her likeness faded but still visible. It was the person I wanted to see who was little more than a curtain of hair and a blur of pale skin.

I growled at the image. "What am I supposed to do with this? I can't even see her face."

"Wh-what?" Xiomara panted, still holding onto the wall. She blinked at me as if she had no idea what I was talking about.

"Give me that." Cade snatched the picture from my hand, his hollow cheeks reddening as he examined it. Throwing the photo to the ground, he advanced on Xiomara until he'd backed her into the corner opposite where I stood. "Do you think this is a game?" he bellowed.

She winced and turned away, her face bunched as if she expected him to strike her. But he just flattened his palms against the wall on either side of her head and leaned in so close I was sure she could feel his breath on her skin.

"Make no mistake," he said, his voice barely above a whisper. "You will not leave this place until we find the others and undo the sink. It would serve you well to do as we say."

"That picture is all I have," she moaned. "It's a fluke it's even still around. My husband only kept it all these years because he likes how I'm laughing in it. There's nothing else."

My fists balled at my sides. She'd played me. She only mentioned the picture so she could leave a note for her family and pack her stupid little bag. And I'd been dumb enough to let her.

"Well, that's too bad." Cade pushed off the wall and gestured around the cramped container. "It looks like you'll be living out your days in here."

Xiomara kept her face turned away, and I took that moment to frown at my uncle. He couldn't be giving up that easily.

"Uncle Cade," I started, but he kept talking like he hadn't heard me.

"It is rather poetic really." He stared up at the ceiling as if it were a gorgeous sunset instead of a chipped white surface glowing in the quivering light. "Trapping you the way you trapped me in this wretched realm, keeping you away from your home the way you kept me from mine—it's a beautiful metaphorical take on justice."

Xiomara straightened up and tugged at the hem of her nightgown. "You're not the only one who ended up trapped here. The rest of us lost our abilities, too. We had to adjust to life here just like you did."

"Ha!" Cade dropped his chin and leveled his glare on her. "I'm no fool, Xiomara Vauhn. You *wanted* to escape from Alea. Your little crystal trick claiming your own astral energy was nothing but an unexpected perk. You were a traitor from the very beginning."

I looked between them, feeling the tension like a thick cloud. I had no idea what my uncle was talking about, but his words made Xiomara's shoulders shake.

"A traitor?" she spat. "Because I didn't hate semmies

like you did? If anything is poetic here, it's that you're depending on a semmie to get what you want!"

I couldn't stop my eyes from shooting over to my uncle. As soon as they reached his face, guilt stabbed at me. Why was I even entertaining the idea? Cade didn't hate semmies; he wouldn't have volunteered to take care of me if he did. He only worked for the Eyes and Ears briefly, and it was before he realized what they were really about. They were the ones who banned Astralii from having children with non-Astralii. They were scared because there was no way of knowing how semmies' powers would turn out.

But Cade had nothing to do with that. He was the only person in this world who cared about me, the only father figure I'd ever known. I wasn't going to let Xiomara make me question that, no matter what she said to try and turn me against him.

Cade stared her down for a long moment before speaking. "You have until tomorrow morning," he told her. "Come up with a way to find the others, or you will find yourself missing a child." He extended his wrist behind him, a silent instruction for me to take us home. I was all too happy to oblige. I needed to get away from Xiomara's mind games before my uncle caught me considering anything that came out of her mouth.

Once we appeared in our living room, Cade yanked his arm out of my grasp and whirled around to face me. "What was that stunt with the stuffed animal all about?" he shouted. "I told you to get the kid."

I bowed my head. Of course he was upset about that.

He always got upset when I let my conscience control me. He'd been trying to teach me to overcome it for years, but somehow it still managed to turn up at the most inconvenient times.

"Well?" he pressed.

I sighed. "I thought it would be more dramatic."

"Dramatic? I'm not stupid, nephew. I know exactly what you were doing. You're worried about her kids."

I didn't deny it. I *couldn't* deny it.

Cade kicked the leg of the sofa behind me, and I flinched. "You don't owe them anything," he roared. "You don't even know them."

"Exactly!" The word flew out of my mouth, harsher than I'd intended. I made myself look into his disapproving face. "They didn't do anything to deserve—"

He grabbed my shoulders so hard I thought he might dislocate them. "That's weakness! We talked about this. And in case you didn't notice, your little stunt didn't scare her. Why do you think she gave you a useless picture?"

"But—"

"Listen to me!" He shook me once, digging his fingers deeper into my skin. "How many times do I have to say it? Compassion will only get in the way of finding your sister. Do you want to get Kala back or not?"

I pulled out of his grip. Studied the carpet. I knew he was right, and I'd wasted enough time as it was. "I'm sorry," I mumbled. "I just didn't want to hurt a little kid. She's already going to wake up tomorrow without a mom." I fought off the onslaught of images from the day my own mother was taken from me. *Permanently.*

Cade exhaled loudly. "You can't torture yourself with imagined parallels. I know you want to be a good person, but there's no room for a morality struggle right now." I heard the thump of his hands dropping to his sides—the telltale sound of his disappointment in me—and I wanted to sink through the floor.

"I'm only pushing you because I want to save my niece," he went on. "I wish I could be the one to do it, but I can't. I'm depending on you. *Kala* is depending on you. You can't even imagine what the Eyes and Ears are doing to her."

He might as well have pulled the knife out of my pocket and stabbed me in the heart. Not only had I disappointed the person who'd dropped everything to take me in, but I was also failing my little sister. My chest tightened, and I had to focus to breathe. *In, out, in, out.*

I clutched the arm of the sofa. This was why I needed Cade. Despite his attempts to toughen me up, I was still too sentimental. But that was going to change. I silently vowed to prove myself, to do whatever it took to find the rest of XODUS. No more weakness.

"I'll do better," I said, still struggling to control the tremors racking my body.

Cade studied me, as if looking for proof of my claim. After my pitiful display tonight, I couldn't blame him.

"I mean it," I insisted. "What's our next step?"

"We wait. One night trapped in the cage away from her family and Xiomara will crack. She'll have something for us tomorrow. And if she doesn't…" His green eyes darkened. "You'll have to make good on that promise."

I frowned. "What promise?"

"To remove one of her children from the picture." He didn't seem to notice that I staggered backward. "We should get some rest," he said, his voice suddenly lighter. "No matter what happens, tomorrow's going to be a big day."

…I was never really going to hurt your brothers and sisters. In fact, I did everything I could to make sure that <u>didn't</u> happen. As much as I respected my uncle, I couldn't be okay with dragging innocent kids into our mess. That was a big part of the reason I was praying your mom would come through with a plan.

Obviously, I wanted to find the others so we could undo the energy sink, too, but I hoped it would make Cade ease up about going after you and your siblings in the process. In some ways, it did. Just not in the ways I was expecting…

7

PLAN

CADE AND I WENT TO RETRIEVE XIOMARA FIRST THING IN the morning. She was awake and sitting up on her makeshift bed when we got to the shipping container. Her short, dark brown hair was matted on one side as if she'd spent a good while lying down, but the bags under her eyes made me wonder if she'd slept at all.

Not that I cared. Thanks to her, I hadn't gotten much sleep either. My masochistic brain seemed to think it was okay to make me dream about her kids finding the note she'd left. Over and over, I'd been forced to witness the imagined scene of a devastated family sobbing in a big heap on the floor, and each time I woke up panting and sweating. I hadn't bothered glancing in the mirror this morning, but I wouldn't have been surprised if I looked just as wrecked as Xiomara did.

As soon as she saw us, she jumped to her feet. "I have an idea," she blurted out, tugging her nightgown down over her thighs. She probably had it rolled up in an effort to stay cool. The rain had stopped, and the tight space felt hot and sticky. "I have a way we can try to find Delta."

Her words lifted an invisible weight off me. Delta was the "D" in XODUS; the group's name was an acronym of all their first initials.

Grinning, I turned to look at my uncle. He had his back tucked into a corner, his gloating smirk aimed at our prisoner. "Is that right?" he replied. "Well, by all means, do tell."

"It's nothing definite," Xiomara said, wringing her hands in front of her. "But at least it's something to go on."

"Spill already." I mimicked Cade's pose, as if I could absorb some of his toughness by resting my back on the wall, too. The metal's warmth penetrated the thin material of my t-shirt immediately. "What's the plan?"

Xiomara let out a shaky breath and wiped a trickle of sweat from her temple. "Delta always talked about returning to her family's farm."

I felt my brow bunch. "There are family farms in Alea?" Cade told me everyone there lived in trees.

"Delta isn't from Alea," Xiomara explained. "She was one of the test subjects the Eyes and Ears kidnapped from this realm. They took her and her cousin, Brendan." Her voice quivered on his name, and something clicked in my head.

Before we started with our plan, Cade had given me the history of what happened with him and the members of XODUS. Xiomara convinced the group to steal my uncle's astral energy because she blamed him for getting her old boyfriend killed. She'd fallen in love with one of the test subjects in the lab, and Cade found out. Knowing the affair would taint the study, he reported it to his superior so Xiomara would be transferred. But instead of moving her to another department, they killed the guy to punish her, and Xiomara insisted it was all Cade's fault.

Was Brendan that guy? When my uncle said *test subject*, I never imagined it was someone they abducted from here. I had assumed it was a volunteer, like the people who signed up for clinical drug trials.

I turned to Cade, my jaw slack. "They kidnapped people?"

"Yes," he said, still looking at Xiomara. "They wanted to understand what made semmies' powers manifest differently. Part of what made Astralii think interbreeding was dangerous was the fact that they couldn't predict how semmies' abilities would turn out. So they wanted to see if they could manipulate non-Astralis DNA to mimic semmie DNA. Their goal was to cultivate astral projection abilities in those who weren't born with them."

"So Delta is just a regular person?" I hadn't even considered the possibility that any of the members of XODUS were non-Astralii.

Xiomara nodded. "I was charged with monitoring her and a few other test subjects while they recovered from the injections."

Injections? I shuddered, picturing Kala—at least how I imagined she looked now. What if she was dealing with the same cruel practices?

"Delta always blamed herself for the kidnapping,"

Xiomara continued. "Even though she couldn't have known what was going to happen, she felt guilty for convincing her cousin to sneak out the night they were abducted." Her voice shook, and I heard her swallow. "During her recovery, Delta always insisted that if they ever made it out of Alea, she would go home to South Creek. It's a small town in Arizona."

"So you think she's there now?" I asked, sharing a skeptical look with Cade. A gust of wind rattled the walls, making me wish we were having this conversation outside instead of in this hot box.

Xiomara shrugged. "It's worth a look, isn't it? Even if she's not there, South Creek is small enough that it shouldn't be hard to ask around and track her down. I'm sure we could find a family member, or someone who's in touch with her."

"Then that's where we'll start." Cade pushed off the wall and tugged his slacks from the backs of his thighs. I knew they must be sticking to his skin the way my clothes were sticking to mine. "We'll need a story," he said, running his hands along the sharp point of his chin. "We can tell people that Delta is Kai's birth mother."

My head jerked back. "What?"

"Yes, that will work," he muttered, more to himself than me. "Xiomara and I will pretend to be your adoptive parents. We'll say we're trying to support you in your quest to learn about your ancestry."

"Whoa, why are we bringing her with us?" I asked, jabbing a finger at Xiomara. After last night, I didn't trust her as far as I could throw her.

Cade sighed. "It will look a little suspicious if two men go asking around about a girl who vanished without a trace twenty years ago, don't you think? People are much more likely to trust us if we have a female with us." He gave Xiomara a once-over. "But not if we let you go looking like that."

I couldn't disagree. She was still in her sweat-stained nightgown, her flushed cheeks were streaked with the crusted remnants of tears, and her wild hair made it look like she'd spent the morning wrestling an alligator.

She glared between us. "Well, it was a bit challenging to clean up in this hole."

"We'll take you to our place so you can shower and make yourself presentable," my uncle announced. "Then we can see about the best way of getting to South Creek."

I nodded, trying to look confident despite my doubt. It seemed like a long shot to me, but I was willing to try anything if it could help get us to Kala.

8

GUILT

I took Xiomara and Cade back to the house, and my uncle instructed me to show our captive to the shower in the basement. The home we'd purchased last year came with an in-law apartment below the living room, but the thought of leading Xiomara down there was just plain weird.

Even if she was going to help us, she was still our prisoner. After last night, it was obvious she didn't take me seriously. Now I was supposed to show her around like she was a welcome guest?

Scowling, I opened the door to the basement and gestured for her to follow me down the steps. The in-law housed a queen bed tucked in the corner to the left of the staircase, a living area with a sofa and a couple overstuffed chairs, and a small but complete kitchenette along the back wall. Cabinets lined the space above the sink, and a refrigerator stood to the right of the tile countertops. The little apartment had everything except a private entrance.

I trudged through the unit, opened the bathroom door, and flipped the switch on the wall. The vanity lights flickered twice before coming on with a soft buzz. Remembering all the beauty products I'd watched her slather on last night, I turned to Xiomara and said, "You have ten minutes."

She nodded. "Okay. But I need to go home and get clothes."

"You've got to be kidding." Like I was going to take her to her house again.

"Well, I can't go in this." She gestured to her gold satin nightgown that had clearly seen better days. She had a point, but I still wasn't taking her home.

"I'll just bring you your handy dandy duffel bag," I snarled. Even if it was going to be helpful now, it didn't change how annoyed I was that she'd had the nerve to pack it in the first place.

Shutting my eyes, I pictured her bedroom and let the preview play through my mind. Her husband sat on the edge of their bed, his square-shaped glasses perched at the end of his prominent nose. He stared absently past the five skinny, dark-haired kids of varying heights standing in front of him with only their backs visible to me. One of two boys yanked a paper from the man's hand, but his blank expression hardly changed.

I snapped out of the preview and, suddenly, I was three years old again.

I stare at Mommy and Daddy. Something is wrong with them.

They lay on top of a big red stain on the floor, and they look like they are scared. But their faces don't change. I feel my toy fall out of my hand. Grandma Naida bumps into me, and her shopping bags crash to the floor, but I keep staring at Mommy and Daddy. Something is wrong with them.

Xiomara's hand touched my arm, and I jumped. "Kai, what's wrong?"

"Nothing." I pulled away from her, my heart thundering in my ears. Her family had found her note. That was why her husband appeared to be in shock—he *was* in shock, just like I'd been when I found my parents.

"Kai?" I felt Xiomara's gaze, but I refused to look at her. I wouldn't let her see how the scene at her house had gotten to me. That was probably her plan all along. If this was her trying to play me again, she wasn't going to win.

"Nothing's wrong," I repeated. "I'll be back with your stuff."

Previewing her closet, I saw that it was closed. Slivers of light came in through the slatted door, practically pointing to the duffel bag from last night shoved into the corner. I ducked to make sure I wouldn't hit the hangers and followed through with the projection.

I reached for the bag at the same time a tiny voice cried out, "Is this because I forgot to clean my room yesterday?" My hand froze in midair. "Tell her I'll clean it now!" The girl sobbed, the sound ringing in my ears. "I'll clean it now, I promise!"

"Sal, this has nothing to do with that," another girl's voice said. "Don't worry. Mom will come back soon.

41

Right, Dad? She has to come back." Her voice broke on the last word, and I was sure my ribs had collapsed.

Barely able to breathe, I wrapped my fingers around the bag's handle and projected to my room. The bag slipped from my hand as I dropped onto my bed.

Tell her I'll clean it now! I'll clean it now, I promise!

I pressed my fists into my temples. I only took Xiomara away from her family because I had to. I'd done everything I could to make it as easy on them as possible. But no matter how much I tried to reassure myself of that, I couldn't get the little girl's devastated voice out of my head.

9

SCOPE

While Xiomara cleaned herself up, I sat on one of the kitchen's bar stools with my laptop perched on the counter in front of me. According to my search results, South Creek was little more than a main road with a post office, a couple of stores, and a gas station. If Delta really had gone back, I doubted it would take long to find information on her whereabouts.

Maybe our plan would work after all.

"This picture of Main Street should be enough to get me there," I said, studying the image in the upper right corner of the screen. I swiveled my stool around to face Cade, who stood looking at the computer over my shoulder with a steaming mug in his hand. "I can stagger my previews to find a back alley or something so I can show up unnoticed." Even though it was draining and tedious, I'd used the technique before. All I had to do was find a new landmark in each preview to move in the direction I needed.

43

Cade took a sip of tea and glanced at the stove clock. "It's early enough there that most people won't be out yet. You shouldn't need any alleys to get the lay of the land without being seen."

"Good point." It was seven-thirty in the morning here in Miami, which meant it was only four-thirty in Arizona. I turned back to the computer, my stool sliding as I leaned forward to get a closer look at the details of the photo on the screen. A boxy brick storefront half covered with a black and white sign that read *Hank's General Store* took up the majority of the image. The store had two display windows on either side of the door, which meant I'd be able to look inside easily.

Perfect.

Committing the building to memory, I slipped into a preview. The sky was dark, a chipped street lamp providing the lone source of light. A scraggly-looking cat pawed at a plastic bag, but that was the only movement I saw.

I pulled out of the preview and stood up. "You're right," I told Cade as I closed my laptop. "It's pretty dead there. Won't take long to scope it out."

Cade nodded, swallowing another mouthful of tea. "Good. Xiomara should be ready by the time you get back."

I projected up to my room and slipped open my dresser's top drawer. Shoving aside my socks and underwear, I dug out the ski mask I kept for whenever I drained cash registers to replenish our funds. I knew the odds of anyone recognizing me from a security camera were slim, but I wasn't taking any chances. No matter where I was, there was always the risk of being spotted by spies for the Eyes and Ears. I knew they were always out hunting semmies and runaways, and if Delta and Brendan were kidnapped from South Creek, that town must've already been on their radar.

All the more reason to be careful.

Pushing the drawer closed again, I couldn't help but glance at the framed photo that wobbled on the dresser's black surface. The familiar charge went through me at the sight of the faded snapshot—the only family portrait I had. My toddler self grinned between my mother and father with my infant sister propped up in my lap. We looked like a happy little family, but no matter how many times I gazed at the photo, it never got any easier to believe that was actually my life at one point.

I ran my fingertips over the cool glass. "I'm going to bring you home, Kala." Remembering the disagreement I'd had with Cade the previous night, I added, "No matter what it takes."

Tugging the knitted mask over my face, I appeared in front of Hank's General Store. A breeze chilled my bare arms, carrying with it the smell of old cigarettes. I rubbed my hands along my biceps as I looked over both shoulders to scan the deserted street. Even the cat was gone, probably terrified from seeing me appear out of thin air.

I turned back to Hank's and cupped my hands around my eyes to peek through one of the display windows. Everything was sparsely lit, but I could see a row of quarter machines a few feet away—the perfect target to get me inside. It was always easier to project to things or people when they were just in front of me.

A second later, I was in the store. It was bigger than I'd expected, with ten numbered aisles and a fresh produce section. I just needed to find a bathroom I could use as my personal entrance. Restrooms were the best place to work with when appearing and disappearing in public. I had yet to see anyone notice me come out of one and care that they hadn't seen me go in. I was pretty sure most people didn't even register it.

I wandered deeper into the store with only the sound of my steps to keep me company. A sign that read *TOILETS* hung above the dairy section, its arrow pointing to a little hallway between the refrigerated display cases. Heading straight to the men's room, I reached for the handle.

It caught when I tried to turn it.

I cursed. Of course it would be locked. I tried the women's room with the same result.

Letting out a huff, I appeared outside the store and looked up and down the street again. Among the handful of small buildings, I noticed a run-down restaurant labeled as Pizza HuB. It was clearly a bad rip-off of *Pizza Hut.* The only changes they'd made were painting the rooftop orange and haphazardly painting over the lower-case "t" to make it into a busted-looking capital "B."

I shook my head. This town was a trip. I trotted down

the road in search of a place I could use for its bathroom. Even in the relative darkness, I could tell the asphalt beneath my flip-flops looked like it was a hundred years old. Its uneven surface hosted networks of cracks in every direction. When was the last time anything new had been added here?

Another burst of cold wind sent goosebumps up my forearms. The sensation was a weird contrast to the skin of my face, which was starting to sweat beneath my ski mask.

I spotted a gas station not fifty yards away, its sign for the public restrooms pointing toward the back of the building. Quickening my pace, I made my way to the men's room door. By some miracle, it opened.

My relief was cut short as the stench assaulted my nostrils. It smelled like a tomb filled with old diapers. Holding my breath to avoid gagging and the risk of contracting whatever airborne diseases were surely waiting for me inside, I flipped the light switch. It didn't take long to memorize the scratched mirror and stained sink. Just to be sure I had it, I projected home and back again.

No problem.

Making sure to lock the bathroom door from the inside, I appeared in my living room. Xiomara sat at the kitchen counter, her wet hair dripping onto the shoulders of her charcoal-colored blouse. She started when she saw me, and I pulled the mask off my face.

"Just me," I said, noticing the crumb-covered plate in front of her. Cade must've decided to feed her. I hadn't

47

even considered what we would do about that while we held her captive.

"Is everything all set?" Cade asked, sliding a plate into the dishwasher.

I nodded. "Yeah. All we have to do now is wait until the sun comes up in Arizona."

10

INSPIRATION

I STARTED DOWN MAIN STREET WITH CADE AND XIOMARA behind me. "The general store's this way," I said, strolling in the wake of a single blue car on the otherwise empty road. According to Google, Hank's opened at six-thirty, which seemed overly ambitious given that the town was still basically dead. But I wasn't complaining—our projection to the gas station bathroom went without a hitch since no one was around to notice us, and I was glad we would be able to ask the employees about Delta sooner rather than later.

I heard Cade mutter something to Xiomara. I couldn't make out his words, but she responded with a huff.

Whatever. I wasn't getting involved in their drama. Their shared history already made me feel like an afterthought, and their arguing only made it worse. I just hoped whoever we ended up talking to about Delta wouldn't pick up on the animosity between them.

A bell dinged as we entered the store, and a frail-looking old man with leathery skin and about five hairs on his head glanced up from mopping. "We ain't open yet." He jerked his head toward the wall to our right, where a giant red clock said it was six-twenty-eight.

Two minutes? Really?

The man resumed cleaning the floor near the cash registers, his forest green company shirt hanging from his thin frame.

"No matter." Cade moved past a display case of baked goods and stepped deeper into the store. "We're not here to shop."

That got the old guy to look up.

Xiomara held out her palms in a peacemaking gesture. "We were actually hoping you could help us find someone. A woman by the name of Delta Malueg."

The mop clattered to the floor, and the old man squinted at all three of us accusingly. "Is this some kind of joke?"

Xiomara frowned. "No, sir."

The man took a step toward us, pointing a bony finger in our direction. "Where'd you hear that name? What d'you know?"

"Nothing," I insisted, looking between Cade and Xiomara. "We don't know anything." *That's the problem.*

The man wrinkled his bulbous nose, his face reddening. "Whatever you're trying to do, it ain't funny. Get outta here!"

"What are you yappin' about, Bernie?" A short, stocky woman stepped out from one of the aisles carrying an armful of ramen noodle packages. Her auburn pony-tail hung over one shoulder and showed streaks of gray at her temples.

Muttering to himself, Bernie snatched up the mop and shoved it into the yellow plastic bucket. Water sloshed along the floor as he stormed toward the back of the store, the wheels of the bucket squeaking the whole way.

"Don't mind him." The woman waddled over to us and set her noodle collection between the cash registers on the counter. "He's a cranky old fart." She winked, straightening her own company shirt as she approached us. *Mel* was printed on her nametag. "How can I help you?"

Cade launched into the adoption story he'd come up with, explaining that we were looking for my birth mother. When he finished, Mel let out a low whistle.

"Is *that* why Delta ran away?" She shook her head, her mouth pushed into a thoughtful pout. "All this time we were worried sick, thinking something horrible must've happened to her, and really, she was just knocked up."

"Well, we don't know for sure that was the reason," Xiomara said. "Anything could've happened before she got pregnant."

Mel rolled her eyes. "Please. This ain't the type of town where people just turn up missing. Yet Delta and her cousin vanished into thin air the same night. He must've gone along to help take care of the baby. Or maybe he was the dad." She jabbed Cade with her elbow and belted out a laugh. "Wouldn't be the first time I'd heard that around here."

Xiomara cleared her throat, the daggers in her eyes ready to slice through Mel's round, pink face. "Is that really necessary in front of him?" She nodded in my direction.

Mel attempted to give me a sympathetic look, but her hazel eyes still sparkled with amusement. "Oh, sweetie, I'm just messin'. I wish I didn't have to be the one to tell you, but no one's seen hide nor hair of Delta for a good twenty years."

"What about the Malueg family farm?" Xiomara tried. "Can you tell us where that is?"

Mel scratched her head and rested her hip on the counter. "It's not their farm anymore. The Maluegs left a while ago."

"What do you mean they left?" Cade demanded.

Mel shrugged. "I mean they moved about ten years after Delta and Brendan disappeared." She sighed and scanned the rows of shelves with a distant look in her eyes. "I don't blame 'em. Tragedy like that's hard to recover from if you stay in the same place, especially with the candlelight vigils on the anniversary of their disappearance. They still do 'em every year."

Xiomara sucked in a sharp breath. "Thank you for your time," she said out of nowhere. "We'd better get going." Before anyone could react, she was already turned around and heading for the door.

"Sorry I couldn't be more help," Mel called after Cade and me as we followed Xiomara out of the store.

Once we were on the street, Cade caught up to Xiomara and spun her around by the arm. "What was that about?" he snapped. "She might know where we can find a picture of—"

"We won't need a picture," Xiomara interrupted. "I know where we can find Delta."

11

PROSPECT

Cade let go of Xiomara's arm. "What are you talking about?" he hissed, glancing at the store behind us as if Mel might overhear him from inside.

"I just remembered Delta has a special ceremony for Brendan every year on the anniversary of his death," Xiomara said breathlessly.

"Okay…" I pushed my hair out of my face, but the wind whipped it right back, flattening it to my forehead until the ends poked at my eyes. "And that helps us how?"

"I'm sure she'll do it this year, too." Xiomara's expression stayed firm, not a hint of doubt shadowing her features. "When she does, I'll know exactly where to find her."

"And where might that be?" Cade asked.

"Muir Woods, near San Francisco."

"You think she's still going there after twenty years?" My voice made my words sound more like a challenge than a question. I couldn't help it. While I knew how doing special things for birthdays and anniversaries seemed to help in coping with lost loved ones, I had a hard time believing Delta would continue a tradition two decades after the fact.

Then again, Grandma Naida had baked a cake every year on Kala's birthday, as if my sister might just waltz into our house to share it with us. Maybe Delta was the same way.

Xiomara wasn't deterred by my negativity. "Delta was always a very sentimental person," she said. "I'd bet my life she'll show. And she's our best shot at finding the others. She's the only one who knows how to trace astral energy."

Cade inhaled sharply just as a thunk caught our attention. We all turned to see an elderly couple making their way toward us, the man's wooden cane striking the sidewalk as they approached the storefront. I doubted the pair had anything to do with the Eyes and Ears, but they reminded me that we shouldn't be talking about this in public. Anyone could overhear us.

"Uncle Cade," I whispered. "Maybe we should have this conversation at home."

He nodded, and the three of us headed back toward the gas station. We made sure to wait until the elderly duo had been inside the general store for a few minutes before we all piled into the bathroom and projected home.

Back at the house, Cade picked up the conversation right where we left off. "What do you mean Delta can trace astral energy? Only the highest Astralii know how to do that."

Xiomara made her way over to the patterned chair and sank into the seat. "They forced Delta to program crystals for them once her ability manifested. The team in charge of her realized she could project her thoughts into people's minds and her intentions into crystals. You know as well as I do that stronger intentions make more powerful stones."

I looked between them, struggling to keep up. Intentions? Powerful stones? I hardly understood anything about crystals, other than their capacity to trap astral energy. Cade had never gone into more detail than that. It didn't seem necessary before, but now I kind of wished he had told me more.

"Come to think of it," Xiomara said, "this ceremony might be our only chance to find Delta if she's still wearing the block."

"The *block?*" Cade slapped a palm to his forehead. "She wears a *block*, and you're just telling us now?"

"I forgot until I thought about our ceremonies."

Cade swore and started pacing the length of the counter that divided the living room from the kitchen. I looked back and forth between him and Xiomara, waiting for one of them to explain what they were talking about.

Neither of them noticed.

I sighed and plopped onto one of the bar stools. "What's a block?"

"A set of stones that repels astral energy," Xiomara replied.

"*Repels* it?" I gaped at her. That was another thing to add to the list of astral energy manipulation topics I didn't know about. What else could stones do with astral energy?

"When we got back to this realm, Delta was understandably paranoid," she said. "She created a collection of programmed stones that she could wear to prevent any Astralii from kidnapping her again."

The last part hit me like an invisible fist in the gut. I couldn't imagine the trauma Delta had been through—the same trauma Kala was probably going through as we spoke. I took a deep breath. I couldn't start feeling bad for Delta when she was part of the reason my sister was still suffering.

"Why does it matter if she can repel astral energy?" I asked.

"Because your ability comes from astral energy," Cade barked, still pacing. "Even if we managed to find a picture of Delta, the block will prevent you from projecting to her."

"Oh." I slumped on my stool, my back bumping the edge of the counter. Of course there would be something else to complicate things; I couldn't catch a break with a net the size of Texas.

"That's why we have to go when she's there to do the ceremony," Xiomara said. "I'm telling you, she'll be there."

Cade stopped dead in his tracks. "Fine. When will this little ritual take place?"

Xiomara's expression turned to ice. "On the anniversary of the night Brendan died. You should remember it well."

"Watch it," Cade growled, triggering another tense look between the two of them.

"Wait." I stiffened. "If Delta is wearing a block, how am I supposed to project to her?"

Xiomara stopped glaring at Cade long enough to look at me. "You won't project to her. Just take us to Muir Woods. If we get there before she does, her block won't affect your ability."

Cade still looked furious, but as far as I was concerned, this was as good a plan as any. "So when will Delta be there?" I asked.

"The day before…" Xiomara swallowed. "I mean, February seventeenth."

I nearly fell off my stool. "That's—"

She nodded. "In two months."

"Great." I ran a hand over my face. Waiting until then would be agony.

"I know it's a long time," Xiomara said, "but it's the only way to know for sure where Delta will be."

"So we're just supposed to sit around twiddling our thumbs for two months?" I spat.

"Of course not." Cade's voice came out so loud it startled me. "We'll continue looking for the others."

"Based on what?" Xiomara challenged. "I told you, I don't know anything else. I want to get this over with as much as you do, but I can't give you information I don't have."

Cade's smile didn't reach his eyes. "I'm sure you'll come up with something before February." Though the look on Xiomara's face didn't give me much confidence, I really hoped my uncle was right.

…He was wrong. Nothing we tried worked. I swear, I never planned on keeping your mom for so long. I thought it would be a couple of days—a week, tops. But time kept passing with no progress, and we couldn't let your mom go home when there was a risk she would set up a block like Delta's.

I still felt horrible, though, especially after witnessing your family's reaction to her good-bye note. The guilt ate me alive, so much that I convinced Cade to let your mom stay in the in-law apartment in our basement. I told him it was too big a pain to keep projecting back and forth to bring her food and take her to our house to clean up, but the truth was that I just wanted to make her as comfortable as possible while we kept her captive.

When it was finally time to go after Delta, I thought for sure we were going to start making progress finding the others. Unfortunately, things didn't go as planned…

12

ESCAPE

XIOMARA AND I SAT SIDE BY SIDE AT THE BASE OF THE redwood, both of us silent as the morning sky. *She's going to show. She's going to show.* I tried to will it into reality, even though my hope was dying a slow, painful death.

Delta was supposed to start the ceremony around sunrise, but the sun had been up for hours. It shone through the thick canopy of leaves above us, all cheerful and annoying. It probably would have been pretty any other day, but today I just wanted to get out of here— preferably with Delta on hand.

If this didn't work, I didn't know what we were going to do. Nine weeks had passed since I'd first nabbed Xiomara, and we'd made exactly zero progress with finding the other members of XODUS. Christmas and New Year's came and went, both marked with failure. Everything we tried only led to dead ends.

We managed to find Delta's family shortly after our first visit to South Creek, but we left with nothing more than a few choice words from her mother for *stirring up old crap,* as she so eloquently phrased it. From there, we tried tracking down the others' previous employers and friends. We even turned to stalking Ursula's ex-boyfriend, which took twice as long because Xiomara couldn't remember if his name was Brian Connor or Brian O'Connor. That little pain-in-the-butt "O" added what seemed like another million guys to the list. Then, when we actually found the right one, he was useless. He'd married a woman who made him get rid of all traces of his ex-girl-friends, and he hadn't spoken to Ursula in years.

We were so desperate that Xiomara tried drawing the others to see if I could use her art to project to them. I was pretty sure none of us really expected the drawings to work, though they did look almost real. Still, it was another bust to add to a list that seemed like it might never stop growing. At this rate, it would take a miracle to get all five women together to undo the energy sink.

Xiomara sighed, as if she'd been mentally tallying our failures, too. I fidgeted against the tree trunk at my back. It was uneven and uncomfortable, even through the thick fabric of the oversized coat I'd borrowed from Cade. Living in Hawaii for ten years and then moving to Miami hadn't exactly given me a need to buy outerwear, so my uncle let me wear one of his peacoats to keep me from freezing to death in the February air. He refused to get rid of the coats after we moved—something about them being the first nice things he could afford in this world. I'd teased him for being so excited about a buy-one-get-one-free deal that he ended up with two of the same coat, but at this particular moment, I was grateful for it.

Cade was hiding nearby. Xiomara claimed Delta would never agree to help us if she knew my uncle was involved. Just in case Delta refused anyway, he was waiting with the gun I'd stolen from a convenience store almost a year ago. We'd made a pact to use it only in the case of confronting the Eyes and Ears, but Cade didn't want to take any chances with Delta. After making no progress for the last two months, I had to agree.

In truth, the gun was more for scaring than for hurting. It was only a .22 handgun and unlikely to do deadly damage. Even so, I hoped there would be no need to pull the trigger. After all, a well-placed shot *could* still kill someone.

The sound of snapping twigs made my breath catch, and I felt Xiomara tense beside me. A moment later, a short, slightly overweight frame stepped into view.

"Delta!" Xiomara jumped to her feet.

I quickly got up, too, unable to believe that after all the recent letdowns something had finally worked.

Delta staggered backward, clutching the leather bag slung over her arm. "Who are you? How do you know my name?"

"Del, it's me, Mara."

"Mara?" Taking a small step forward, Delta leaned toward us and squinted. Sunlight sparkled in the collection of shiny black stones woven into a net-like pattern on top of her head. Was that the block? Through the gaps in the headdress, I could see her short hair was dyed a light shade of blue. Her pale hands trembled as she brought them to her mouth. "Is that really you?"

"Yes," Xiomara said, dusting the leaves off the back of her pants. "It's me." She inched forward, but Delta dropped her bag and barreled into her old friend to give her a tight hug. They embraced for a long moment before Xiomara dipped her head in my direction. "You remember Kai, don't you?"

"*Kai?*" Delta studied my face, and her eyebrows shot up. "Kai *Awana?*"

My mouth fell open. How did she know me, too? Did *all* the members of XODUS know who I was?

"It's him," Xiomara confirmed with a tight smile.

"Oh, Kai!" Delta rushed toward me as if she wanted to embrace me, too. I staggered back, stumbling over an exposed tree root. No one had hugged me since Grandma Naida, and it was a reflex to avoid physical contact. Cade said hugs made people weak, and that was the last thing I needed.

Delta stopped short. "I'm sorry. You probably don't remember me. I knew you when you were little. Before…" Her face fell. "I always assumed they kidnapped you, too."

I swallowed. So she knew about Kala.

"I thought the same thing." Xiomara glanced back at me. "But we ran into each other recently, and I realized Kai was never taken." I looked quickly between the two of them. I really hoped Xiomara had come up with a more believable story than *we ran into each other.* But Delta didn't question it.

"Del," Xiomara continued. "They didn't get Kai, but they got Kala. That's actually why we're here. We need your help."

Delta blinked and cocked her head to the side. "Help?"

"I want to do everything I can to help get Kala back," Xiomara lied. I had to give her credit, though—she did sound convincing. "The problem is, I can't do much without my ability."

Understanding washed over Delta's face, and the loving look she'd been giving me morphed into fear.

"I know it's a lot to ask," Xiomara went on before her friend could respond. "But you understand crystals better than anyone."

Delta shook her head, her fearful eyes darting from tree to tree, as if one of them might dole out punishment if she agreed to help us. "I taught you everything I know, Mara. And I can't get your power back without the others."

"You can trace them," I jumped in. I couldn't stop myself. We'd agreed to let Xiomara do the talking, but I needed to know if this woman could help us or not. "You can trace astral energy, can't you?" Delta looked like she might cry, but I pressed on. "Please. We've tried everything to find them."

"I couldn't trace the others even if I wanted to," Delta said. "Their astral energy—*all* of our astral energy—got trapped inside the crystal, too. Trying to trace it would only lead to where the crystal is buried."

Xiomara's fingers clenched and unclenched at her sides. "Well, have you stayed in touch with any of them?"

"I haven't talked to any of you in over a decade," Delta whispered. "I'm sorry, but I can't help you."

Cade cursed loudly behind us, his voice breaking through the quiet of the forest. Delta's head snapped up just as he stepped out from behind a tree with the gun pointed right at her.

"Cade," she choked out, nearly falling into the dirt as she staggered away from him.

"What are you doing?" I shouted, glaring at my uncle. Why was he showing himself now? There were still a ton of questions I wanted to ask Delta before letting her know Cade was involved. Now she was going to panic.

Delta turned back to Xiomara with accusation written all over her face. "You tricked me."

"I'm so sorry, Del," Xiomara whimpered, the tears in her eyes glistening in the sunlight. "I never would have brought you into this, but he threatened my children."

"And now I'm threatening you." Cade waggled the gun and moved toward Delta until she backed into one of the tree trunks. "These two may buy your helpless act, but I know you can find the others."

Delta took in a shaky breath and squared her shoulders. "I will never help you."

"Is that so?" he challenged. "Will you help your mother? You know we found her not too long ago. What was her name?" He glanced over his shoulder at me, a hint of a smile turning up the corners of his mouth. "Ah, yes. Dolores. She was a lovely woman, wasn't she, nephew? Why don't you bring her here and see if we can change Delta's mind?"

"Kai, no!" Xiomara pleaded.

But it was too late. Now that my uncle had revealed himself, we would have to make Delta cooperate somehow. I pictured the short, plump woman who'd told us off for asking about her daughter weeks ago. I could still see her face clearly in my mind, but the moment I tried to project, something slammed into me with the force of a speeding bus.

My spine connected with a redwood trunk, and white spots swarmed my vision. Gasping, I collapsed to the ground. Shouts broke through the ringing in my head, followed by retreating footsteps. Someone tripped over my foot and fell across my body, sending another shock of pain through my legs. The gun went off, and one of the women screamed.

"Stop her!" Cade's voice rang out over the scuffle.

"Delta!" Xiomara called. "Wait! Please, wait!"

No! My heartbeat thundered in my ears as I realized what was happening.

Delta was getting away.

13

SEARCH

CADE SHOUTED AS HE SCRAMBLED TO HIS FEET BESIDE ME. Another gunshot fired, and I forced myself to sit up just in time to see my uncle running in the opposite direction, following Xiomara through the trees.

I pushed onto my feet. The ground swayed beneath me, and I stumbled into one of the massive redwood trunks. Catching myself with a scrape of my palm against the rough bark, I staggered in the direction I'd seen Cade and Xiomara run. I prayed they'd caught up to Delta. If she got away...

Shaking off the thought, I chased little more than the sound of snapping twigs. Sweat ran down my temples as I crashed through branches and underbrush. I leaped over a fallen tree and wove my way between the clusters of trunks until I came to a clearing divided by a small wooden fence. Xiomara and Cade stood panting on the other side, each of them scanning the area in different directions.

There was no sign of Delta.

I leaned on the top of the fence, fighting to catch my breath. "What…happened?" I managed.

"He happened!" Xiomara stabbed a finger at my uncle, clawing her hair out of her face with her other hand. "What were you thinking? I told you not to let Delta see you. You're forcing me to help you, but you're not listening to me!"

Cade's eyes narrowed, his chest still heaving from the chase. "She wasn't telling you anything." He jerked out of his coat and draped it over his arm. Under it, he was dressed in a black button-up shirt and black slacks, looking as if he were headed to a job interview instead of trying to chase someone through the woods. "I took matters into my own hands. How could I know my nephew would launch himself across the forest?"

"I didn't *launch myself*," I said, finally able to stand upright. "Something hit me."

"That would be the block I told you about." Xiomara shot Cade a poisonous look. "Why did you tell him to project?"

I shook my head. "But I wasn't trying to project to Delta. I was trying to get to her mom."

"Delta must've been standing too close, or between you and your target." Xiomara threw up her hands. "It doesn't matter now. She'll never take off the block, and she sure as hell won't come back here. We're never going to find her or the others because *someone* doesn't even have the patience of a toddler!"

Though I hated to admit it, Xiomara was right—Cade had screwed up our one shot to get Delta.

"So now what?" I asked, the inside of my skull pounding.

"We find her." Cade shoved the gun into the waistband of his pants. "She couldn't have gotten far, but the longer we stand here, the further away she gets. Let's split up. The first one who finds her, get that damn block off of her."

The three of us headed in different directions, and I scanned the forest as I walked. Though I slowed my pace, the twigs underfoot made it impossible to move without making noise. If we didn't hear Delta, she must have resorted to hiding. I paused, letting my eyes roam through the plethora of trees. Some of the trunks around me were hollowed out. Delta could have easily slipped inside one to stay out of sight, but I knew there was no way we could search all of them.

Cade's shout made my heart skip. I bolted toward the sound of his voice, afraid to project and get knocked on my ass again. I didn't hear Delta's cries or any sounds to indicate he'd found her, but he must've called us for a reason.

It didn't take me long to reach him. When I did, he was kneeling on the ground and zipping up a tan bag.

Delta's purse!

Xiomara burst through the trees to my right. "Did you—"

Cade put a finger to his lips and held up the bag. "There's no sign of her," he practically shouted, as if he wanted Delta to overhear. Grabbing up his coat with his other hand, he stood and continued speaking as if he were making an announcement to all the creatures of the forest. "But we need to head home. The park is going to open soon, and I don't want anyone to find us here."

I knew that was code for *we need to get out of here and search this purse,* though I wasn't sure why it had to be a secret. What did it matter if Delta knew we had her purse? I was sure she would figure it out eventually.

Xiomara nodded, seeming to catch on to Cade's plan. "Let's get going," she said, matching my uncle's excessive volume. She and Cade started toward me, each with an arm outstretched.

I took a step back. "No way. I'm not projecting and hitting that block again." The memory alone made me wince.

Cade sighed and dropped his arm. "Then let's head to the entrance. From there, we can get out of here." He passed Delta's purse to Xiomara and whispered, "You take this. We don't want anyone questioning if I stole it."

Hurrying through the woods, we found the trail back to the entrance and ducked into the restroom near the parking lot. Once we'd gotten home, Cade snatched the bag from Xiomara and haphazardly dumped its contents onto the carpet. He fished Delta's wallet from the pile of tissues and wrapped candies, unsnapped it, and slid a small plastic card from inside.

Her ID.

"Is her address on there?" I breathed.

"Of course. That's why we're not still out there

searching for her." Cade tossed the card to me with a flick of his wrist. I caught it and quickly read the print next to the picture of Delta.

> *DIANNE JOSEPHINE MELBOURNE*
> *192 MELROSE CT.*
> *PHOENIX, AZ 85007*

She'd changed her name, but she still lived in Arizona. I frowned. Her mom said she hadn't seen Delta since her disappearance all those years ago. Why hadn't Delta gone home like Xiomara thought she would? Why live so close to her family but never go and see them?

"What if she doesn't feel safe enough to go home after your little stunt in the woods?" Xiomara sank to her knees in front of the sofa and studied the contents of Delta's purse on the floor. "I told you she's paranoid."

Cade waved her off. "She'll have to come home eventually. We'll be waiting there when she does." He turned to me. "Find a landmark in Phoenix. We'll figure out a way to her house from there. She won't be able to get there for at least a couple days, especially if she doesn't have her ID. In the meantime, we can see if she has any photos of the other three."

I nodded, setting Delta's license on the coffee table. I knew it would be hours before we could get to her house. Even if I found a landmark online, and even if by some miracle it was close to where Delta lived, I would have to find a time when no one was around to see me show up. Not to mention, I would have to go through the whole process of finding a public bathroom or some other private area to bring Cade and Xiomara with me. But it would be worth it if there were photos of the others.

Not if we have no hope of getting to Delta anymore.

I swallowed my doubt. Cade was right—Delta had to come home sometime. I just hoped it was sooner rather than later.

Delta's house was an eyesore. There was flower print everywhere, from the wallpaper to the sofas to the curtains. The whole place had a fake perfume smell that made me want to gag. How did she stand it?

"You take the first bedroom," Cade instructed Xiomara. "Nephew, you take the second. I'll take the living room."

I followed Xiomara down the hall and turned into the doorway on the left. Scanning the collection of photo albums that lined two sets of white shelves, I realized I wouldn't be able to do much in the way of searching. I didn't know what any of the others looked like. Pulling out the first album, I decided I could at least rule out landscape shots or ones that didn't include females. Then I'd just collect anything that could potentially show Ori, Ursula, or Solstice for Cade and Xiomara to go over.

As I flipped through the crinkly plastic pages, I pulled out every photo that showed any girl who could have been a member of XODUS. Soon, the pile of pictures was starting to take over the floral comforter on the twin bed.

We were well into the evening when Xiomara cried out, "I found one!"

Tossing aside the photo in my hand, I barged into the other bedroom with Cade right behind me.

He plucked the image out of her hand before I could and held it close to his face. His mouth curled into a smile as he handed me the picture. "Say hello to Solstice."

14

HEARTLESS

MY PULSE POUNDED AS I STUDIED THE REDHEAD IN THE photo. She sat beside a younger-looking Delta in what appeared to be a restaurant booth. Xiomara was in the picture as well, perched opposite Delta. Neither looked as sour as Solstice, whose blue eyes were so light they didn't seem to fit her dark scowl. Or maybe that was supposed to be her sexy face. Either way, I was glad she wasn't grinning so big it distorted her freckled features.

Memorizing the shape of her nose, mouth, and jaw, I turned my focus back to her eyes. They were the key to projecting to people, especially when they had aged. Once I was sure I had her face down, I held my breath and pictured her in my mind.

A flash of images came together. Bubbles dripping down white tile walls. Hands shampooing wet hair. Water running off ivory skin. *Lots* of ivory skin.

I snapped out of the preview before my body could follow it and let out a few choice words. Of course

Solstice would be showering when I finally found her. Kidnapping Xiomara while she was in a flimsy nightgown had been bad enough. I was starting to feel like a pervert.

"It didn't work?" Xiomara dropped onto the twin bed, clutching the wildflower-print comforter with both hands.

I tossed the picture onto the dresser beside me. "It worked. I just saw her." *Way more of her than I intended.*

"Well, why didn't you bring her here?" Cade demanded, a network of creases forming above the bridge of his nose. "What are you waiting for?"

"She was in the shower." I avoided his gaze, inadvertently meeting Xiomara's instead. I didn't like the way her eyes softened, the skin beneath them inching up as if she just watched a kid take his first step.

"You've got to be kidding me." Cade's voice came out eerily soft as he ran a hand down his face. The white, jagged line of his scar practically glowed against the rest of his reddened skin. "*That's* what's stopping you?"

I gaped at him. "What was I supposed to do? Nab a naked chick?"

"Why not?" He threw his arms out wide, nearly taking up the full width of the bedroom. "Let her be humiliated. She deserves a lot worse than embarrassment."

Xiomara's snort told me I wasn't the only one appalled by what he was suggesting. I didn't care what Cade said; I wasn't about to kidnap anyone bare-assed. I had some standards.

Knowing my uncle wouldn't drop it, I reached for

ways to stall. "I just…I want to get a good look at her apartment." As the words came out, I realized it really would be a smarter plan. We'd found a picture at Delta's place, after all. Who was to say Solstice wouldn't have photos of the others, too? It would be foolish not to look into the possibility. "She might have something useful," I pointed out. "I want to make sure I can go back."

Cade's only response was to further narrow his eyes.

"At least someone is being rational," Xiomara murmured.

"I'm sure she'll be done in a few minutes," I added, hoping Cade wouldn't react to her dig. I couldn't handle more of a strain between them. Being in the same room with them had become unbearable over the last two months.

"A few minutes?" Cade stalked over and grabbed me by the shoulders. "You have to be stronger than this!" He shook me as if it would drive his point home. "We're never going to get out of this nightmare if you insist on trying to make it *convenient* for the people responsible. There's never a perfect time to—"

"Leave him alone." Xiomara's hand appeared over his shoulder, her long nails digging into his shirt as she tried to pull him away from me. "He's not a heartless monster like you." Cade shook her off just as I jerked out of his grasp. My own momentum carried me backward, and my legs hit the edge of the chair behind me, sending me straight into the deep-set seat.

Cade shoved Xiomara into the wall and pinned her

there, his face twisting into a sneer as she cried out. My eyes caught the butt of the gun still tucked into the back of his pants, and I jumped to my feet. With their tempers flaring, I wasn't going to risk him pulling that thing on her, even if it was a low-caliber weapon. We still needed her help to undo the sink.

I pushed my way between them, forcing Cade to break his hold on her. Before he could react, I grabbed her arm and projected to our in-law apartment. Xiomara started to speak, but I appeared at the top of the stairs and locked her in the basement without a word. Even with the door closed, I could hear her calling my name.

I ignored her. Whatever she wanted to say, I was sure it was some kind of appeal to my conscience. She had a bad habit of trying to make me feel guilty at every opportunity, as if I needed her constant reminders that I was doing things I didn't want to do. But she would never understand. No one understood me except Cade.

Too bad he's going to rip you a new one the minute you go back to Delta's.

Pressing my forehead into the door, I shut my eyes. The longer I stayed here, the angrier my uncle was going to get. While I admired his ability to overcome guilt, sometimes I just wished he would listen to reason.

He probably wishes you would, too. I sighed. Cade did have a point—there was never a *good* time to abduct someone. The only real excuse to avoid it was the risk of exposing ourselves, and he knew as well as I did that no one would see me if I grabbed Solstice out of the shower. This was why he was always telling me that my morality was holding me back. The only reason I hadn't followed through was some self-imposed code of conduct.

Why couldn't I just let it go like he could?

With another sigh, I straightened up and projected to Cade, bracing myself for his wrath. Sure enough, he sat on the arm of the sofa with his arms crossed, looking at me like he regretted the day he agreed to adopt me.

"Now you're defending her, is that it?" he snarled. "Did you forget who *really* has your best interests at heart? Who's *really* ready to do what it takes to get your sister back?"

The last jab made me wince. "I wasn't defending her," I argued. "I locked her back in the basement so you and I could talk without her getting in the way."

"There's nothing to talk about." He slid off the couch and lumbered over until he was towering over me. "That's the point. Instead of talking, you should be *acting.*"

I tensed my jaw. "Fine. I'll go get Solstice now. Should I take her to the cage or our basement?"

That at least got Cade to pause. His face lifted in thought. "Better make it the cage. We won't mention Xiomara yet. Solstice will be more likely to cave if she thinks she's in this alone."

"Done."

"Wait." Cade held out his wrist. "Take me there now. I don't want you and Solstice making nice without me, or you'll be defending her next."

I refused to take the bait. Wordlessly, I projected him to the shipping container I'd first used to kidnap Xiomara. It smelled musky, and the hand-cranked light had long since gone out. The only illumination came from tiny rays that squeezed through the holes I'd drilled into the walls. Turning the handle on the man-made light to bring it to life, I eyed the mat in the corner. Somehow, despite it being inside a sealed space, it looked dirtier than the last time I saw it.

"Don't make this an all day thing." Cade rolled up his sleeves. "I'd rather not cook to death in here."

Ignoring him, I closed my eyes and slipped into a preview of Solstice just as she finished pulling up the side zipper of a sky-blue dress.

Thank God she has clothes on. I followed the preview and appeared behind her. At first, she was too busy digging a bottle of prescription pills out of the medicine cabinet to notice me. She shut the glass door at the same moment I moved to grab her, and we both caught my reflection. My overgrown black hair was wild, my green eyes shadowed by thick, dominant brows hardened to make me look every bit the heartless monster Xiomara insisted I wasn't. But she was wrong. This was who I'd become—who I had to be.

Solstice opened her mouth to scream, but I clapped a hand over her face. Wrapping my other arm around her shoulders to hold her in place, I felt my shirt soak through where her wet hair pressed against my chest. The jolt of cold distracted me long enough for her to get out a muffled, throaty sound. I tried not to think about who she

81

might have alerted. I couldn't worry about her loved ones right now.

Taking a moment to memorize the jewel design along the mirror so I could come back, I took her to face my uncle.

15

ALLIES

CADE NODDED APPROVINGLY AS SOLSTICE DID THE SAME doubled-over wheezing thing Xiomara had done the first time I brought her to this makeshift cell. I didn't try to catch Solstice, though; that would have guaranteed more goading from Cade. I stepped aside and let her stagger backward until she fell onto the mat with a soft thump.

She cried out and grabbed at the air, struggling to get up. Cade watched with a gleeful expression, like this was entertaining or something. I knew he'd been waiting for decades to exact his revenge on these women, but the look on his face triggered a twinge in the pit of my stomach. This wasn't supposed to be fun. As eager as I was to get this over with, and as grateful as I was that we'd finally gotten Solstice, I wasn't enjoying any of this.

Then again, I hadn't gone through what my uncle had because of these women. Maybe I'd be singing a different tune if they'd ruined my life.

Using the ridged wall to claw her way to a standing

position, Solstice moved her head from side to side blindly. "Who are you?" She was breathing so hard she could hardly choke out the words. "Wh-why can't I see?"

"You've got bigger problems than temporary blindness." Cade pulled the gun from his waistband and aimed it at her. A tremor moved down my throat, but I told myself my uncle knew what he was doing. He was probably skipping right to threats because Xiomara and Delta didn't volunteer any information when we simply asked.

"Cade?" Solstice rubbed her eyes with the backs of her hands, and I wasn't sure if she'd seen him or if she still recognized his voice after all this time. "H-how did you find me?"

"That doesn't matter." I straightened up to sound stronger. Maybe if I started acting more like Cade, we would start progressing faster. "What matters is that you're going to tell us what we need to know."

Solstice blinked in my direction. "Who's with you?" She squinted between us until her eyes settled on the gun Cade had pointed at her. She let out a soft gasp, and I knew her vision was back. "What do you want?"

"You know what I want," Cade said. "Did you and your little friends really think you could take away my astral energy and get away with it?"

"Cade—"

"Save it," he barked. "If you don't want me to shoot you right here and now, you'll lead us to the rest of them."

Solstice snorted and lifted her wet hair so it no longer clung to her bare shoulders. "As much as I'd love to see those skanks go down with me, I can't help you. I cut off contact with them a long time ago."

Cade took the safety off the gun. "You're lying."

"Afraid not. So I guess you'll have to shoot me." The conviction in her words pushed the air out of my lungs. I told myself it could've been an act to save the rest of them, but I still had to fight to keep the panic out of my voice.

"I'm sure you have something," I insisted, more for myself than her. I couldn't handle another dead end. "Old photos or—"

She let out a sharp laugh. "Are you listening to me? I don't have anything. I want nothing to do with their lives."

"Do we need to pay a visit to someone you *do* care about to get you to cooperate?" Cade threatened.

"Ha!" Solstice's face twisted in disgust. "You think I care about anyone in this godawful realm?"

"Look," I said. "Either you help us, or you never see the outside of this box. How about that?"

"Then I guess I'll be getting even paler soon." She crossed her arms and leaned a hip against the wall. "I can't help you."

I kept my face expressionless and turned to my uncle. "Let's go back to her apartment. There has to be something there."

But Solstice didn't even flinch as we vanished.

It took all of five seconds to gather that Solstice wasn't big on photos. From the looks of her bedroom, she wasn't big on much at all. The walls were bare, and there wasn't a single frame or photo album. Other than a full bed, night table, and small bookshelf that housed a few trinkets and candles, the rest of the room was nothing but carpet and white walls.

I followed Cade down the hallway, noticing it was just as bare as her bedroom. The hall gave way to the living room, which housed some blue and white couches and a fireplace. My eyes caught on an oversized framed photo on the mantle at the same time Cade noticed it.

"There." He pointed to the image of a teenage-looking Solstice hugging a blonde kid who couldn't have been older than three. Cade and I both smiled, and I knew he was thinking the same thing I was thinking. Solstice may have claimed she didn't care about anyone, but she clearly cared about whoever that boy was. If we could get him, we could make her admit anything.

I stepped forward to get a better view of the photo. From the looks of the young Solstice in the picture, it must have been taken quite a while ago. "Do you think I could project to him?" I asked, suddenly skeptical. "Solstice looks so much younger in this picture—that kid could be like twenty by now."

"Well, we won't know until you try."

I sighed. The only other person I'd tried to project to based on a childhood image was Kala, and I'd never been successful. Cade said it was because the picture and the handful of memories I had of her were from when she was a baby, and she'd changed too much since then. What if it was the same story with this kid?

Like he said, you won't know until you try.

I studied the photo, taking note of the boy's bright blue eyes. Focusing on his image in my mind, I waited for the projection to take over. But there was no rush of images behind my eyelids. Only blackness—just like when I tried to project to my sister.

"Nothing," I muttered. I looked around, as if another option might magically appear in the bare room. As annoying as it had been seeing the perfect little collection of framed photos in Xiomara's house, I was starting to wish Solstice was more like her.

Wait…

"Do you think Xiomara knows who the kid is?" I asked. "She and Solstice were friends at one point. Maybe she could help us find him."

Cade's face lifted. "Great point, nephew." Those three words felt like my biggest victory in months. Maybe he wouldn't regret keeping me after all. "Bring her here," he said.

Within a couple minutes, I projected to the basement, gave Xiomara a brief explanation, and brought her back to Solstice's living room. Thankfully, she'd grown accustomed to projecting with me, and I didn't have to wait for her to get her bearings anymore.

Wasting no time, I pointed to the picture. "Who's that kid?"

Xiomara squinted at the image. "That's Daniel."

Yes! She does know who he is. My eyes shot over to Cade, but he was still focused on Xiomara.

"Okay…" He rolled his hand impatiently.

"He lived in the community with the rest of us in San Francisco. He wasn't a semmie, though. His mother had him from a previous relationship. It was Daniel's younger brother who was half Astralis. Anyway, for some reason, Daniel latched onto Solstice, and Solstice had a soft spot for him. She said he reminded her of her nephew. After we were stranded here, he was the only one who could make her smile."

"Then we have to find him," Cade said.

Xiomara frowned. "You can't *find* him. He's dead."

My gulp was audible. "What?"

"He died a couple years after we met him," Xiomara explained. "Cancer. Getting stuck here was really hard on Solstice, but losing Daniel…" She sighed. "Solstice was never the same after that."

A lump formed in my throat. I told myself I didn't feel bad for Solstice—she didn't deserve any sympathy—but the kid…the poor guy didn't even make it out of his childhood.

Maybe Kala didn't either. The thought came crashing down on me like a rogue wave, leaving me struggling to breathe. Nothing happened when I tried to project to Daniel because he was dead. What if the fact that I couldn't project to Kala had nothing to do with how much she'd changed physically? What if she…

The room seemed to shrink. My legs felt like flimsy twigs as I grasped the arm of the sofa. I bought into

Cade's theory about Kala's changed appearance without question, but how could he possibly be sure? What if something had happened to her? We had no way of knowing. What if Cade only made that up so we'd get his ability back? What if my sister—

"What's the matter, nephew?" Cade's question broke through my thoughts, and he was next to me an instant later. "Are you okay?"

Looking at his concerned face sent a surge of guilt through me. He'd moved heaven and earth to find me, taken me in without a second thought. And how did I thank him? By questioning his motivation. What was wrong with me?

I shook my head. "I'm fine." *Kala is alive.* It had to be true. I'd been through way too much in my life to be dealt another blow. There had to be some balance.

Xiomara edged toward me. "Kai, are you sure?"

Pushing my face into a hard expression, I nodded. "I'm just trying to figure out how we're going to get Solstice to talk now that we know we can't use him." I tossed my hand toward the photo on the mantle.

"Talk about what?" Xiomara asked. "I'm surprised she hasn't already led you to everyone else. She wants to undo the energy sink more than anything."

16

DESPERATION

Xiomara looked from my shocked face to Cade's and back again. "I'm serious," she said. "Solstice begged us to undo the sink for years. She'd do anything to get her ability back."

"Oh really?" Cade straightened up, his head nearly touching the stucco ceiling. "Then why is she refusing to help us?"

"She didn't refuse." I groaned, feeling my hope crumble around me like a cheap cracker. "She never said she *wouldn't* help us—only that she *couldn't*." I dropped onto the blue and white plaid sofa I'd been gripping for support. "She said she doesn't know anything."

Xiomara pulled her grown-out bob into a small ponytail and held it in place with her hand. "Well, she wouldn't lie about that. If she said she doesn't know anything, then she doesn't."

"This is such bull!" I shouted, fighting the urge to kick

a hole into the wall. "What kind of friends don't keep in touch?"

"It's been twenty years, Kai." Xiomara let her arm drop to her side, releasing her hair so it fell back along her chin. "I cut off contact to keep my family safe. I'm sure the others had their reasons, too."

"We don't care about their *reasons*," Cade spat. "If you came up with leads, Solstice can, too." My heart sank at the idea of spending more months running off on wild goose chases. I didn't know how many more I could take before I snapped.

Xiomara dropped onto the sofa next to me. I shifted away from her, but she didn't seem to notice. "Nothing came of those leads," she reminded my uncle. "At some point, you have to accept that your plan isn't working. What if we're still stuck a year from now? Two years? We can't keep doing this forever. I have to go home. My children need me." Her voice wavered, and damn it, it got to me. Not because it hurt Xiomara to be away from her family, but because I saw how it had devastated her kids.

"Oh, but we *can* keep doing this forever," Cade sneered. "If I'm stuck somewhere I don't want to be, what makes you think I have any problem subjecting you to the same misery?"

Xiomara dropped her face into her hands. I felt like doing the same thing. I didn't want to spend the rest of our lives trying to round up the other three members of XODUS either. There had to be another way for us to get to Alea, even if it meant we'd have to give up on restoring Cade's ability.

"Between you and Solstice, I'm sure you can figure out something," Cade insisted. "And we're not going to rest until you do." Moving over to where Xiomara and I sat, he held out his wrist. "Take us home, nephew. And bring Solstice to meet us. Anything she remembers about Ori and Ursula could help—old jobs, places they used to go, whatever it may be."

I did my best not to let my face show that I was losing faith in Cade's approach to saving my sister. He'd mentioned other Astralii hiding in this realm before, and at this point, it seemed like we would be better off trying to find them. Somehow, I would have to convince my uncle that it was time to explore other options.

I just didn't know how to say it without making him feel like I was betraying him. I owed him so much, and I wanted to do my part to repay him. I'd hoped it would be through helping to get his astral energy back. He deserved to be happy, especially after everything he'd been through in his life and what he sacrificed for me. But how long were we going to keep running in circles before he accepted that we would have to try something else?

My eyes shot to Xiomara, who was sniffling next to me on the couch. We couldn't keep her hostage forever just because Cade was too stubborn to let her go home. Even if she deserved it, her kids didn't.

"Well?" Cade shot me a look. "Are we going?"

I suppressed a sigh. Now wasn't the time to bring up my doubts. Xiomara would surely jump on my band-wagon, and Cade was already hurt that I'd projected her away from him earlier. The last thing I needed was to make him think I was teaming up with her to point out the flaws in his plan. He and I would have to talk later.

I cleared my throat and nudged Xiomara. She didn't even look at me; she just let her arm flop in my direction. Her lack of enthusiasm pretty much summed up my own feelings, but I projected both of them home without complaining. Then I went to get Solstice from the shipping container, making sure to warn her that she needed to close her eyes to avoid the temporary blindness.

When we showed up in the living room, Xiomara looked like she might faint. "Sol?" she whispered.

Solstice's head snapped up, and she swiped a hand across her eyes. "*Mara?* What are you doing here?" Her face tensed, as if she'd just answered her own question. "You led them to me, didn't you? It wasn't enough that they caught you—you had to throw me under the bus, too?"

"They threatened my children," Xiomara shouted.

Solstice's eyes spit fire. "Always an excuse with you. I see you haven't changed at all."

I looked between them, too caught off guard to speak. What was with the hostility? They were supposed to be friends. I turned to give Cade a questioning look, but he met it with one of his own. Apparently, he hadn't been expecting this either.

"Don't you get it, Sol?" Xiomara sounded more exhausted than angry. "They want to find all of us so we can undo the sink. Once we do, it will free all of our astral energy. Then you can go back to Alea, just like you wanted."

"As if you did this for me." Solstice scanned the granite countertop that lined two sides of the kitchen, and I couldn't help but notice that her eyes paused on the front door across from it. "Of course you'd drag me into this and not the others."

"Trust me, you were my last choice."

Cade's groan quickly turned into a roar. "We're not here to listen to you argue!"

Both women ceased talking, and I took advantage of the silence. "The sooner you come up with a plan, the sooner you never have to see each other again," I said. *Please, just come up with something that has some promise.*

Xiomara sighed, pressing her palm against her forehead.

"Oh, are *you* frustrated, Mara?" Solstice jeered. "Give me a break. It's your fault we're in this mess. You should have let me out of this realm after your stupid plan backfired."

"We both know going back would've been too dangerous."

"Maybe for you. Arlo never had any issues with me. He would've taken me back."

"Yeah, so he could kill you himself."

"Enough!" Cade glared between the two of them and spun around to storm into the kitchen.

I frowned after him. "What are you doing?"

"What does it look like I'm doing?" He pulled a bottle

of rum out of the cabinet. "If I'm stuck depending on these immature fools, I'm going to need a drink."

A drink? If he was resorting to alcohol, he had to see this wasn't working—that this wasn't *going to* work. Whether he liked it or not, it was time to start looking into a Plan B.

17

OPTIONS

Solstice shifted on the couch, tucking her legs under the skirt of her dress. "Are you sure we can't trace the others?" She jabbed Xiomara with her elbow way harder than necessary. "Just try."

Cade shot her a look as he jammed the lid back on the dry erase marker. He stood next to the giant white board we'd propped up using one of the bar stools and the kitchen counter. Xiomara, Solstice, and I sat on the sofas, and the two of them had been calling out names for my uncle to add to the list of Ori's and Ursula's old friends and acquaintances. It was like some messed up version of a grade school exercise, but with hostages—and a gun waiting on the dining room table.

Given that my uncle was on his fifth rum and Coke, I wasn't so sure having a weapon anywhere near him was a great idea, but he insisted we needed it in case Xiomara or Solstice tried anything. The gun was a couple feet away from him, so he could reach it before them, but I could project over and grab it before him if I had to. I just hoped it wouldn't come to that.

Xiomara ran her hands over her cheeks. "I told you what Delta said. Tracing our astral energy won't get us anywhere."

"What if Delta's wrong?" Solstice threw an arm toward the board. "We don't exactly have tons of choices."

That much was true. We'd spent the last three hours tossing around ideas, and the best thing we had come up with so far was to have Solstice call Delta's cell phone. It hadn't been hard to figure out the number—we used the phone we found in her purse to call mine so we could see the number we needed. Solstice left a voicemail saying Cade and I had come after her at work and she needed Delta's help to put a block on her apartment. We just had to hope Delta would get a new phone and use the same number—and that she would call Solstice back.

"Maybe we should at least give it a try." I looked around to each of their drained faces. "You know, just to rule it out."

Xiomara sighed. "I don't even remember how to do it. Delta only went over the theory with me once, a long time ago."

"Well, you're the only one she showed any crystal stuff," Solstice grumbled. "So you're basically our one shot."

"Drop it." Cade swirled the ice in his drink, making it clink against the sides of the glass. "It won't work."

"Neither will tracking down friends and employers from two decades ago," Solstice shot back.

Xiomara's head thumped softly against the wall behind her. "Fine," she huffed. "If Kai takes me to a crystal shop tomorrow, I'll try. But I wouldn't bank on it."

I wouldn't bank on it. That seemed to be the theme of the night. I stared at the dry erase board as if the names on it might magically start forming a coherent plan. I could feel myself getting more and more antsy about trying to convince Cade to look into alternatives.

"What if you tried projecting to this?" Solstice tugged down her bottom lip. The deep pink skin was marked with a black X.

I frowned. "What's that?"

"It's a tattoo we all share." Xiomara pulled at her own lip to reveal an identical mark. The defeat in her expression lifted as she let it pop back into place. "Can you project to symbols?"

I got to my feet and moved over to the opposite sofa where Solstice sat next to Xiomara. "I can try."

Leaning down to examine the symbol inside Solstice's lip, I realized it wasn't a normal X. Instead of straight lines forming the inside angles, they were rounded. It almost looked like someone took a hole-puncher to four sides of a square. I studied the odd shape, not sure I wanted to know what it was supposed to mean. I closed my eyes, envisioned the symbol, took a deep breath, and...

Ended up previewing Solstice. *Of course.* Pulling out of the preview, I blew the air out of my cheeks and met the redhead's eager gaze. "It just leads me to you," I mumbled.

"What did I tell you?" Cade drained his glass, and I cringed. I really hoped he didn't go for drink number six. Then again, maybe it was better that he was drinking. Maybe he'd be more open-minded when I pleaded my case about giving up on getting everyone from XODUS in one place.

"I guess that makes sense," Xiomara said, though her disappointment was palpable.

I was sure mine was, too. I turned back to the board and inhaled slowly. We were getting nowhere, and the sooner I got Xiomara and Solstice out of here, the sooner I could talk to Cade about trying a new approach.

"Look, it's almost a quarter to midnight." I gestured to the stove clock. "It's been a long day. If the best we can come up with is projecting to tattoos, we clearly need to try again with fresh brains tomorrow."

I glanced at my uncle. *Provided you're not hungover.*

Xiomara got to her feet, her jeans creased along the zipper from sitting for so long. "Can't argue that." She walked over to me with her wrist outstretched.

I reached for Solstice, too, but she crossed her arms. "I'm not playing slumber party with Mara," she snapped. "Just take me home."

"Not happening. You're going downstairs, too." Taking her arm, I projected her to the basement with her ex-friend. Solstice doubled over when we appeared in the in-law, and I knew she'd forgotten to close her eyes.

I started to pull away from Xiomara, but she tugged

on my arm. "Kai," she whispered. "Will you do me a favor?"

I furrowed my brow, equal parts offended and curious at her request. Did she think we were friends now? That we did each other favors? The fact that she thought I was soft enough to even consider asking made my jaw twitch.

Before I could respond, she held up her index finger and rushed around Solstice's hunched form to the bed tucked below the stairs. Lifting the corner of the mattress, she pulled out a folded piece of paper. "I know you won't let me go home," she said as she came back toward me. "But will you take this to my daughter?"

"What is it?" I took the paper from her. *Lali* was printed across the top in tiny scrawl.

"It's a letter."

"Oh, can I write letters to my loved ones, too?" Solstice sneered, finally standing upright. "Let's all play pen pals."

"Shut up, Sol. You don't *have* any loved ones." Xiomara turned back to me. "It's just to explain what's going on."

"Explain what's going on? Like that you were kidnapped?" I scoffed. "I don't think so."

"No, it's not that. It's—"

"*Ohhh.*" Solstice clicked her tongue. "I almost forgot. Your little abomination of a daughter's birthday is tomorrow, isn't it? She was born on the anniversary of the day you expelled me from my home."

"Shut *up*, Sol," Xiomara shouted. "This doesn't concern you."

Solstice let out a bitter laugh. "You should have told your daughter she was a half-breed from the beginning. You should have told your clueless husband, too, but you love pulling people into your messes before they know what's happening."

"You knew what you were doing," Xiomara fired back. "You were *happy* to punish Cade because he never reciprocated—"

"Don't you dare!" Solstice dove at Xiomara with a newfound strength, but I stepped between them just in time.

"Stop it," I yelled, holding Solstice back as she thrashed. I was already regretting bringing her into this. It would be a miracle if she and Xiomara didn't kill each other during the night. "You two are worse than toddlers."

With a final death stare, Solstice jerked out of my grip and stormed into the bathroom, slamming the door behind her.

That was it. I was going to convince Cade to switch tactics if for no other reason than to keep my sanity. Realizing I'd dropped Xiomara's letter, I knelt to pick it up. I'd intended to hand it back to her, but she gasped excitedly.

"Thank you!" she cried. "Lali's bedroom is the first door on the right. You can just drop off the note and leave."

"I didn't say I'd do it." I hadn't even had time to register the request before Solstice flipped out.

"Please, Kai. Lali needs some preparation for what's

going to happen to her. She'll have no idea what's going on or why she suddenly has an ability or—"

"Wait." I held up my hand, finally processing what she was saying. "Lali turns sixteen tomorrow?"

Xiomara nodded. She went on talking, but I wasn't listening anymore. My mind was too busy racing through the possibilities. I hadn't wanted to involve Xiomara's kids, but if her daughter was going to come into her power right when we had run out of options, it had to be a sign. Maybe she could help us.

Maybe she was exactly the Plan B I was hoping for.

…Lali, I need you to know that I never would have gone after you if I felt I had another option. It was just, the way things were going, I was desperate. I couldn't ignore that there was a chance you would be able to get us to Alea, especially after it was looking like we'd never be able to undo the energy sink.

But after everything I'd done to mess up your family, I knew the least I could do was try and recruit you in as moral a way as possible. And trust me, I did try to do it the moral way. It just wasn't as easy as I'd hoped…

ALTERNATIVE

"Uncle Cade!" I rushed up to where he sat on one of the bar stools sipping from his newly refilled rum and Coke. "I have an idea."

His eyes didn't move from the dry erase board, now flat on the granite counter. "You know, I'm getting quite tired of those words. They rarely seem to get us anywhere."

"It's not about finding the other members of XODUS," I said. "It's about getting to Alea without them."

He inhaled part of his drink, coughing and spluttering as he set it down on the counter with a clank. "What?" he wheezed.

I slid onto the stool next to him and quickly ran through my hope of recruiting Lali—provided she had an astral form. If she did, there was a good chance she could help us reach Kala. Cade had originally hoped I would be able to get to Alea on my own, but I couldn't reach the portal because I couldn't travel—meaning fly in astral form. I didn't *have* an astral form. That was why we'd resorted to trying to get Cade's ability back in the first place. But if Lali could travel, we could skip undoing the energy sink altogether.

"We just have to figure out how Lali's ability works," I concluded, pausing to catch my breath.

"Just show up and nab her. Seems simple enough to me."

I glared at Cade. Lali had nothing to do with what her mother did. She deserved a gentler approach, especially since I'd already caused her enough trauma. But I knew he wouldn't see it that way. I had to go with a point he couldn't argue.

"Her power will have just manifested," I tried. "She'll need a clear head to learn how to control it. If I just up and kidnap her, her emotions are going to be all over the place."

Cade ran his tongue along his teeth. I knew he couldn't dispute the logic—he'd seen firsthand how hard it was for me to learn to control my own projecting. Even with a level head and him there helping me, it still took all of my focus to manipulate my emotions in order to trigger my projections.

"She'll need a teacher," I went on. "Someone who can walk her through learning her trigger like you did for me."

He lifted his drink again. "Fine. Try it your way." Before I could enjoy my small victory, he added, "Maybe you'll start listening to me once you see that it's not nearly as efficient."

"Efficient?" I eyed the dry erase board on the counter. "That ship has sailed. We need a new approach." He grumbled at me, but I kept going. "Tomorrow's Thursday, so Lali has to go to school, right? I'll pretend to be a new student—"

"Now you're getting carried away. We took you out of school for a reason."

I sighed. Cade pulled me out of school after Grandma Naida died, preferring to homeschool me instead. I'd been more than happy to oblige, and I was still glad I didn't have to deal with obnoxious classmates and going to point-less classes every day. But my uncle was missing the point.

"I'm not really going to enroll," I said. "I just need an excuse to talk to Lali. It's not like I can randomly approach her on the street. If I pretend to be a new student, I can act like I'm trying to find a classroom and take the conversation from there."

Cade rubbed a palm along his buzz cut. "Let's make sure her ability is even worth it before you show up at her school."

"How?"

"We can observe her while she sleeps."

My nostril twitched. I'd felt like enough of a creep spying on Xiomara during her little beauty routine. Lingering in someone's room to watch her sleep was on another level.

"Semmies have a tendency to trigger their abilities in

their sleep, especially before they gain control," Cade explained. "The mind is most open in sleep. Don't you remember your sixteenth birthday?"

How could I forget? The morning I turned sixteen, I woke up on my favorite beach in nothing but my boxers. Thankfully, Cade had explained the whole semmie thing to me by then, so it wasn't as terrifying as it could have been. But it was still humiliating, and it took me forever to get back home.

After walking for what felt like an eternity, I'd stumbled upon a stranger who was kind enough to let me use her phone to call Cade. My guess was she wanted to get the kid in his underwear out of her space as quickly as possible, but I was just happy to talk to my uncle. He coached me through what I needed to do, and I found a secluded place to practice projecting until I got home.

A sigh made its way through my nose. Cade had been there for me that day when no one else was—when no one else *could be*—just like he had been for the last three and a half years. I'd always be grateful to him for that, even if we disagreed on how best to recruit Lali. But at least he was working with me now. I could agree to watching her sleep if that meant we would learn about her ability without terrorizing her.

"What time is it?" Cade glanced over his shoulder at the clock on the stove. *Eleven-fifty-eight.* "We should get there as soon as she turns sixteen, in case she projects right away."

"Will her ability manifest right at midnight?"

"I don't know." He got to his feet and pushed a wrist in my direction. "But I'm not going to miss it if it does."

"Okay." I stood up, happy to hear he was onboard. "I still haven't gotten a look at her or her room, but Xiomara said it's the first one on the right."

"That's fine. We'll just listen outside her door to make sure she's asleep. Now let's go."

The floor moaned under our weight as soon as we appeared in the hallway. I cringed, remembering how a creak had given me away right before I kidnapped Xiomara. It was like this house was determined to thwart my plans.

The sound didn't faze Cade. Illuminated by the moonlight pouring in through the window at the end of the hall, he started toward the door closest to the stairs. Right before he reached it, I heard the knob turn from the other side.

Spinning in a half circle, I flattened my back against the wall just as the door flew open. "Mom!" a girl's voice called out. "You—" Her words cut off, and I knew she'd seen Cade.

Damn it! Still out of Lali's line of sight, I waved a hand to get my uncle's attention. He staggered toward me, and I grabbed his wrist just as something snapped inside the bedroom.

We didn't stick around to see what it was.

Once we arrived in our living room, I threw Cade's arm back at him and shouted, "Why didn't you duck out of sight when she opened the stupid door? Now we're screwed. *Again.*"

He looked at me with a stunned expression, and I wished I could take back what I'd said. It wasn't fair for me to yell at him. He had been right in front of her room; there wasn't time for him to react.

"I'm sorry." I tugged at my hair. "I'm just frustrated." *That's putting it mildly.* My hope of keeping Lali as level-headed as possible was officially shot. Our chances of getting her to help someone she caught sneaking around her house in the middle of the night were probably pretty slim, too.

The knob to the basement door rattled, and Cade whirled around. I heaved a sigh. I couldn't handle more drama with Xiomara and Solstice. I'd dealt with them enough for one night.

"I'm going to bed," I muttered as Cade reached to open the door. I projected to my room and flopped onto my mattress. Now what were we going to do? I was sure Lali was on high alert after seeing Cade, so I could rule out trying to catch her projecting in her sleep.

I stared at the gray paint of my ceiling. Maybe I could still find her at school in the morning and figure out a way to talk to her privately. She'd seen Cade, but I was pretty confident she hadn't seen me. If I could find a way to talk to her, she didn't need to know I had anything to do with the man in her hallway.

"What do your tattoos *really* mean?" Cade's shout carried up from downstairs. "You know where the others are, don't you?"

"I told you everything I could think of," Solstice cried. "I don't know anything else!"

I rolled my eyes and tugged a pillow over my ears like a kid trying to tune out his parents' arguing. At some point, my uncle needed to accept that we'd exhausted our options for finding all the members of XODUS. But until then, I was stuck figuring out other solutions by myself.

Okay. Game plan. I had no idea where Lali went to school, and I still hadn't gotten a good enough look at her to be able to project to her.

The photos in the hallway outside Xiomara's bedroom popped into my mind. Maybe I could find a good picture of Lali now, and then preview her every few minutes until I got a decent look at her school tomorrow. From there, I could show up near the building and catch her in the hallway or something.

I lifted the pillow from my head and tossed it aside. Before I could slip into a preview, I heard Cade shout, "Two!"

Frowning, I turned to look toward my door just as an explosion came from downstairs.

My whole body turned to stone. Was that…

The gun.

Cade had left it on the table.

19

TEMPER

No! No, no, no! The word echoed in my mind as I raced out of my room. I was halfway downstairs before I remembered I could project. When I appeared in the dining room, Solstice was swinging her fists at Cade, her red hair loose and flying around her shoulders.

The air gushed out of my lungs at the sight of both of them. *Alive.* Cade had Solstice pinned against the dining room table so she practically sat on one of the bamboo place mats. He was the one holding the gun. But why would he fire it? Was he trying to scare information out of her?

"I may need you," he growled, still unaware of my presence. "But I don't need you to have all of your body parts intact." He pressed the gun into her leg, and my stomach rolled.

"Uncle Cade! What are you doing?"

He looked up at me, and Solstice took advantage of his distraction. Knocking his gun-wielding arm aside, she kneed him in the groin. He let out a grunt and dropped the weapon as he doubled over.

Solstice fought to get around him, and I realized she was trying to get to the gun. I projected to it and snatched it up off the floor before she could.

"Everyone, just calm down!" I begged.

At that moment, Xiomara banged on the basement door, screaming from the other side. That was it. I couldn't take anything else tonight. I shoved the gun into the back of my shorts, grabbed Cade's arm, and projected him up to his bedroom before he could protest.

I pointed to his neatly made bed. "You're drunk. You need to sleep it off before you do something we'll both regret."

Still hunched over, he all but fell onto his mattress. I felt my face twist as I watched him. When did I become the adult in this equation? He was normally so collected and in control. I guessed all the recent letdowns had gotten to him more than I'd realized. He wasn't invincible after all.

Folding one side of the blanket over him, I appeared downstairs again in time to see Solstice yank open the front door.

Son of a—

I dove forward, barely catching it with my foot. The bottom scraped across my exposed toes, and I swore at the top of my lungs.

"Let me go home," Solstice cried. "Please. I have to get away from Cade. He's insane!"

"He's not insane." I wrestled her away from the door and shoved it closed. "He's drunk. And desperate."

"He's going to kill me!"

I threw my head back, feeling my patience deteriorate. "He's not going to—"

Solstice raked her nails across my arm and lunged for the door again. Biting back another string of curses, I wrapped my fingers around her arm and projected her to the basement before she could get away. She collapsed to the floor in a heap, but I was beyond the point of caring.

Xiomara finally gave up pounding on the door at the top of the stairs and raced down to us. "What's going on?" she cried. "Is Solstice okay?"

I waved her off. "She's fine." *Sort of.*

"I heard a gun." Xiomara cast a sidelong glance at Solstice's curled up form. "She was trying to force her way upstairs when Cade dragged her out to the living room. He locked the door before I could go after her, and then they were arguing—"

"Yeah, well, she's fine," I snapped. "And I've had enough for one night." With that, I projected to my room and locked the door behind me. As if I didn't have enough reason to pursue an option that didn't involve holding these women captive, now I had to deal with Cade nearly shooting one of them. The sooner we got them out of here, the better.

Pulling the gun from my waistband, I stormed over to my closet. I quickly ejected the magazine and cleared the gun before shoving it and the ammo inside my hamper. No one needed to know where either was for a while.

Sliding my closet closed, I spun around and pressed my back into the door. What a mess. It was barely a quarter after midnight, and my newfound hope had already been squashed.

No. I could still salvage my plan. I just had to find a photo of Lali in her hallway tonight so I could preview her first thing in the morning and scope out her school. Pulling my phone out of my pocket, I switched it to airplane mode so it wouldn't ring and give me away while I used its flashlight function in the dark hall. The way things were going tonight, I wasn't taking any chances.

I previewed the hallway to see if the coast was clear.

It wasn't. A little dog had its nose pressed into the wood floor right outside Lali's room.

Great. There was no way I could get a look at any pictures without the dog barking and freaking Lali out even more.

Pulling out of the preview, I threw my head back and let out a long, satisfying string of profanity. It was tempting to kick the half-open drawer built into my bed frame, but I resisted the urge. My toes had taken enough of beating after Solstice smashed them with the bottom of the door.

I needed to regroup. I glanced at my open bathroom and decided on a hot shower. Peeling off my clothes as I went, I stepped onto the cool tile floor and turned on the water. Soon steam fogged up the room.

Taking a deep breath of warm air, I moved into the stream. The hot water rolled down my body, and I ran through my plan for the next day. If I wanted to show up at Lali's school and talk to her before class, the timing would be tight. I'd have to try and find a picture as soon as she left her house, which meant I'd have to preview her every few minutes even earlier than I thought. Once I had a picture, I would preview Lali and find a landmark at her school.

I sighed, letting the water run over my hair and flatten it along my forehead. I'd be doing twice as much previewing as I thought. It would be draining, but I could make it work.

Unless…

I could just linger until I heard everyone leave her house. Thankfully, I'd mapped out the whole place the day before I kidnapped Xiomara, and I knew the front door was through the kitchen. I also knew there was a pantry not too far from that. Maybe I could hide with the cereal and canned vegetables and listen until everyone left. As soon as the house was empty, I'd be able to knock out the rest of my plan without a problem. Then I wouldn't be totally drained from incessant previews, and hopefully, I wouldn't look like hell when I first approached Lali.

You're getting carried away. Cade's earlier claim played through my mind, but I refused to listen. Even though I didn't know exactly how Lali's ability would manifest, I had to believe it would be something useful. Maybe it was irrational, but after the day I'd had, I needed something to hang on to. And I wasn't going to let it go without a fight.

20

SNOOP

I PRESSED MY EAR UP TO THE PANTRY DOOR AND HELD MY breath. Dishes clattered, chairs scraped across the floor, and muffled voices came from the kitchen just around the corner. It was breakfast time, and Xiomara's family was pattering around, oblivious to my presence as I waited for an opening. The minute they left the house, I would be off like a shot to find a picture of Lali and head to her school. But for now, I was biding my time.

At least the pantry didn't smell like mothballs.

"Where are the bagels?" a boy asked.

"Sal ate the last one yesterday," an identical voice answered. I assumed it was his brother, but they sounded so similar, it was like the kid was talking to himself.

"I didn't realize we were out." Judging from the deep bass tinged with exhaustion, that answer came from their dad. "I'll get some more tonight, D-Rex."

D-Rex? I hoped for the kid's sake that wasn't his actual name. It was questionable even as a nickname.

The trio of voices chattered for another few minutes, and I shifted my weight. Listening to them go about their daily business made it easier to convince myself the family was fine, that all the guilt I'd carried with me for holding their mother captive was unnecessary. I was sure they missed her, but they sounded happy enough. It wasn't like they were fetal and sobbing all day like my dreams wanted me to believe.

"Happy birthday, Lalisaurus," the dad called out, pulling me out of my thoughts.

I stifled a snort. What was wrong with this guy? What would make anyone think *Lalisaurus* was an acceptable nickname? D-Rex was bad enough. But at least now I knew Lali had come downstairs.

"Thanks," she replied. I strained to listen, on the off chance she mentioned anything about a weird experience last night. If she had projected in her sleep, I was sure she'd write it off as a dream. With any luck, she'd write off seeing Cade disappear into thin air as a dream, too. That was, if she slept at all after seeing a seven-foot intruder in her hallway.

"Happy birthday," the twin voices chorused.

"Thanks, guys," Lali said.

"What are you gonna do, Dad?" one of the boys asked. "Lali's gonna be behind the wheel soon."

"Don't remind me," the man grumbled. A moment later, he added, "That thought will keep me up at night."

Lali responded with a fake laugh, and a boy called out, "Hey, don't touch the 'do!"

"Just be glad I don't *cut* the 'do," Lali retorted.

A hollow ache spread through my chest at the back-and-forth between them. I wondered if Kala and I would've interacted in a similar way if we'd grown up together—if we still could once I found her.

Suddenly the pantry door pushed into me. I jumped back, and my hand slammed into something on the shelf. I heard whatever it was hit the floor, but there was no time to pick it up. I vanished before I could be spotted.

Appearing in my bedroom, I blew out my breath. Why was I such a failure? I'd been so lost in thought that I hadn't even noticed footsteps approaching. It was bad enough Lali had gotten a glimpse of Cade last night. Whatever I'd knocked over in the pantry was surely going to creep her out more. Even if she believed my uncle had only been a figment of her imagination, this was something that everyone else could see, too.

You should've grabbed her, you idiot. I winced, shaking the image of Cade's disapproving face from my mind. For Lali's sake, and the sake of helping her learn to control her ability, I couldn't terrify her into submission. I had to do this right.

Pacing the stretch of carpet along the foot of my bed, I ran through my options. If Lali was in the kitchen—undoubtedly distracted by whatever I'd knocked over in the pantry—I could try and snoop through her room. All I needed was one clear photo of her. Then I wouldn't have to wait around for her to leave.

I previewed the upstairs hall outside her bedroom, happy to find it empty. Following through with the projection, I dove into Lali's room and closed the door before anyone could catch me.

A backpack and a coat waited on her bed, and there was no telling when she'd be up to get them. I needed to hurry. Doing a quick scan of the space, I searched for framed photographs. Her desk was a mess of papers, but no pictures. Same story for the dresser. All along her ceiling were prints of paintings that looked like dreams gone wrong.

No help there, either.

I paused when I saw the easel tucked into the corner. A half-finished painting of a river running through snow-capped evergreens covered part of the canvas, all deep blues and bright whites. Behind it, I could see the beginnings of a mountain range in the distance. Even incomplete, the painting made it obvious Lali was a talented artist, just like her mother proved to be when she drew the other members of XODUS.

Remembering my need to move quickly, I tugged open the closet door. Shoeboxes lined the shelf above all the hung-up clothes. Maybe there was something useful in one of them. I pulled the closest box from the shelf, and the lid fell off, sending loose photos fluttering to the ground. I cursed under my breath as I scrambled to pick them up. Why was I suddenly such a klutz?

A horn beeped outside, and a moment later, footsteps sounded on the stairs. Fearing it was Lali, I swept the remaining photos into the closet with my foot, pulling the door closed behind me just as she burst into her bedroom.

I watched her through the slats, my heart thumping so

loud I wondered if she'd hear it. Her dark, blue-streaked hair moved in a wave behind her as she grabbed her bag and coat. She headed back toward the door but stopped short. Peering over her shoulder, she scanned the room until her eyes locked on the closet. My fingers clenched around the shoebox in my hands. Could she see me?

No. I could barely see her now, and I hadn't been able to see anything in the closet before I opened it. So why had she stopped? I wanted to disappear, but I couldn't just leave scattered photos on the floor right after knocking something over in the pantry. She had enough to freak out about already. I didn't need her skipping school to file a police report.

The horn beeped again, and Lali and I both startled. Then she shook her head and raced out the door, closing it behind her.

I exhaled as softly as I could and waited an extra few minutes before moving in case she'd forgotten something. When I was sure the coast was clear, I stepped back out into her room and picked up the dropped photos.

The first one showed Xiomara and Lali—as evidenced by the blue bits in her hair—painting side by side and wearing identical smiles. I couldn't help but notice that Lali was essentially a taller, darker-skinned version of her mother, except with a more prominent nose. The image of the two of them so happy together made my insides squirm. I stashed it in the box and grabbed up one of the entire family holding corn dogs, followed by a picture showing Lali with her mom and what must've been her two sisters all lined up getting pedicures. Why were all these hidden away in a box?

The final picture on the floor showed Lali and Xiomara with intense gazes in what looked like their attempts at model faces. It was cheesy, but at least they weren't smiling. I studied the image of Lali, committing her features to memory. Previewing her just to be sure I could, I saw her riding in a vehicle with a brown-haired guy who seriously needed to discover a comb.

Pulling out of the preview, I shoved the box into place on the top shelf of the closet and projected to my own bedroom before anything else could go wrong. From here, I'd just check on Lali every few minutes until she got to school. In the meantime, I had to figure out how to bump into her and make it seem like a coincidence.

21

SIDETRACKED

W HEN I SHOWED UP IN THE LIVING ROOM AT HOME, THE basement doorknob was jiggling. I groaned. Solstice must have been trying to get out again. Hadn't she learned her lesson last night? Not wanting her to set off my uncle again, I marched over and yanked the door open. Solstice fell into my shins, knocking me back a step.

I frowned down at her. "What are you doing? Trying to pick the lock?"

She stared up at me, eyes crazed. "Take me back to my apartment. Please! I won't run, I swear."

All I could do was stare at her. She was still in the same blue dress from yesterday, but that was the only part of her that resembled the woman I'd met last night. Now her red hair was wild, as if she'd been pulling at it for hours. Her freckled face was so twisted she was almost unrecognizable. Was all this because Cade threatened her last night? I told myself he would never have shot her, but maybe he was starting to lose it because we'd hit so many dead ends.

"I have to get out of here." Solstice used my legs to pull herself upright, and I nearly lost my balance. "He's going to kill me."

"He's not going to kill you."

"You didn't see the way he looked at me." She grabbed my biceps, squeezing them like she was trying to pop a balloon. "You didn't see how close the gun was to me when he fired it. My ears are still ringing! If you have any humanity in you at all, you'll help me get away from—"

"What's going on in here?" Cade stepped out of the stairwell with his hand on his forehead, and Solstice cowered against me. My uncle's eyes were bloodshot and barely open, which only added to my irritation. This was his fault for being a drunk idiot last night.

"You tell me," I snapped, shaking Solstice's grip from my arms. I wanted to shout *you're the one who made her crazy,* but Solstice shoved past me before I could get it out.

"Stop her!" Cade hollered as she tore across the dining room.

Letting out a groan, I appeared behind Solstice just as she made it to the door. I hooked my arms around her waist and pulled her back, feeling like a high school principal breaking up a fight.

"Let me go!" She thrashed wildly. "Don't trap me here! Not with that monster!"

"If she doesn't want to be here, take her to the cage,"

Cade said, his voice flat and unmoved by the scene. "I'm not in the mood for this."

As if this was what I'd been hoping to deal with this morning. This madness was already ruining my plan to catch Lali on her way into school. Reaching out to grasp the bare skin of Solstice's arm, I projected her to the shipping container. She drooped forward, and I had to hold up most of her weight as I eased her onto the mat.

Standing again, I sighed at the pitiful sight. She was all but hyperventilating. Was she going into shock? Did she have some type of post-traumatic stress from thinking she was going to die last night?

"Take me home. Please, I need to go home." Her sobs echoed around me, and I chewed my lip. What would it hurt to take her home? I didn't think she'd run; she wanted to undo the sink, after all. Even if she did try to get away, she admitted that she had no idea how to use crystals, so she couldn't set up a block. I'd be able to get to her again if I needed to.

And it wasn't like we had the others, or any way to find them. I'd already given up on getting all the members of XODUS. Even if we pulled it off, I wanted them sane enough to give my uncle his ability back.

Solstice sobbed again, and I clenched my jaw. "Fine," I conceded. "But Cade can't know about this." Reaching out my hand, I took her to her apartment. She seemed to calm down once we appeared, and I left her to get herself together.

I appeared in my room next. Cade was probably expecting me to come straight home, but I needed to check on Lali. I just hoped my chance of staging a run-in with her before class wasn't already gone.

I shut my eyes and previewed her at the exact moment she walked straight into a stumpy little man who was barely up to her shoulder. The guy was clearly annoyed, but I didn't have time to watch him go off on her. I quickly scanned the locker-filled hall and pulled out of the preview before my body could follow it.

Working with an open hallway was going to make this tricky. I'd been hoping to catch a glimpse of the outside of the school so I could show up unnoticed, but thanks to Solstice, that option was out the window. Even if I managed to preview my way down the hall, I needed to appear somewhere with a closed door. The problem was, I wouldn't be able to see the inside of any space through said closed door.

I sighed. Maybe once the bell rang, I could find a secluded corner or something. I quickly slipped into another preview, just to make sure I could get back before I lost what little I had to go on.

The man was still standing across from Lali, looking like a peeved Oompa-Loompa. "Oh, after you," he sneered. "I don't want to get flattened on my way to the bathroom. *Again.*"

The bathroom!

If he was headed there, I could see the inside and show up when it was empty. Sure, I'd feel like a major creeper for going after a guy while he was taking a leak, but the opportunity was too perfect to pass up.

I studied the man for an extra moment, pulled out of

the preview, and then previewed him again just to be sure I had his pointy face memorized.

Waiting a bit to give him time to get to the restroom, I pictured him in my mind for what I hoped was the last time. Sure enough, he had just stepped through the door. A handful of guys who looked to be about my age rushed out at the sight of him. I had to say, I didn't blame them. He didn't exactly look like a bucket of laughs.

I scanned the blue tile walls as fast as I could, focusing in on the crack running through the one to the right of the urinals. That would have to be my landmark.

After one last preview to make sure it worked, I collapsed onto my bed to catch my breath. My chest was heaving, and I'd started to break a sweat, but it had been worth it. Now I had a way into the school that wouldn't arouse suspicion. I didn't know when class would start, but if that man had time to make a bathroom stop, maybe I still had time to "accidentally" bump into Lali.

I waited another couple minutes to give the man time to finish his business before I checked back. Mercifully, the bathroom was empty. I appeared inside and raced through the door. Not knowing which direction would lead to the hall where I'd just seen Lali, I followed the trickle of students to avoid attracting a ton of attention while I tried to figure it out.

Not five seconds later, a hand came from behind me and landed on my shoulder.

22

ENTROLLMENT

"CAN I HELP YOU?" AN AUTHORITATIVE VOICE ASKED. I turned around slowly to see a gray-haired woman with a sharp widow's peak and shoulder pads that could've doubled as pillows. This must've been a small school if she could spot a stranger so easily. Then again, I did tower over most of the students filing around me.

"Uh…" My mind raced to catch up. "Where's the office?"

She gave me an unconvincing smile. "I was just on my way there." *Of course you were.* "I'm Principal Rockbridge," she said, holding out a veiny hand.

I shook it and muttered, "Kai Awana." Damn. I shouldn't have used my real name. I'd been too frazzled by her catching me to think of a lie.

The bell rang then, and my shoulders sank. There was no way I was going to bump into Lali now.

"Did you just move here?" the principal asked.

I nodded.

"Well, welcome to Browshire."

Browshire? Really? Where were we, trapped in a *Lord of the Rings* movie?

"I assume you're planning to enroll here." She made it a statement instead of a question.

Another nod.

"Excellent." Her tone of voice implied the opposite. Feet still firmly planted, she looked around the now empty hall. "Did you come with your parents?"

My body clenched. "I live with my uncle."

"I'm sorry. I shouldn't have assumed. Is your uncle around?"

I shook my head, reaching for a lie. "He's outside."

"Outside?" She blinked at me, her angular face coming to point as she poked out her thin lips. "It's freezing out there."

"Yeah, well…he's in the car. He's…finishing up a work call."

The line between her brows deepened. "Well, if he's your legal guardian, he'll need to fill out your enrollment papers."

"No problem." I shoved my hands into my pockets, wishing someone would appear to save me from this interrogation. "I, uh, just needed to use the restroom. My uncle's probably already waiting for me in the office."

"Well, let's have a look." She finally started walking, gesturing for me to follow. I slunk behind her at a snail's pace. How was I going to get out of here to pick up Cade? I couldn't just project out of sight with Principal Hawkeyes on the loose.

I struggled to come up with a plan as we passed blocks of blue lockers and posters designating the school as a *Drug Free Zone.* Maybe I could say I had to go out to the car to get my uncle. Provided the principal didn't follow me outside, I could project out of sight when she wasn't looking.

If she *ever* wasn't looking.

I followed her into the office, and an old lady looked up from the main desk.

"Kai, this is Mrs. Moubrey, our head secretary."

The old lady smiled, her eyes twinkling with vitality despite her well-worn face. She looked like the storybook grandma who did nothing but bake cookies all day. "Nice to meet you, Kai," she cooed.

The principal scanned the row of empty chairs across from the desk. "Looks like your uncle isn't here yet." I clamped my teeth together to keep *duh* from flying out of my mouth and did all I could to look surprised that Cade wasn't waiting for us. "You're welcome to have a seat until he's ready."

"Thank you." I cleared my throat. "But I think I'll just go get him. He loses track of time easily."

The two women exchanged skeptical looks.

"Be right back," I said, already halfway out of the office.

"Don't you have a coat?" Mrs. Moubrey asked. "You'll catch cold going out like that."

Oh yeah. I'd forgotten that I showed up in shorts and a t-shirt. I did my best to act nonchalant. "The cold doesn't bother me. We lived in Alaska for a while."

Wow. That had to have been the lamest lie in the history of man. Another skeptical look passed between the two of them, but I booked it out of there before they could stop me.

The arctic air hit me like a brick. The wind blew icy needles against my skin, but I fought the urge to fold into myself and shiver. I was sure the principal was watching me through the window, and I had to live up to my oh-so-brilliant Alaska fib. I raced around the side of the school, but instead of heading into the parking lot a hundred yards away, I remained close to the building to stay out of sight.

Leftover slush that must've been snow at one point crept over the edge of my sandals, chilling my toes as I moved along the side wall. I turned to the back of the school, glad to see there were no windows. Glancing left and right to make sure no one was around, I projected home.

Cade was in the kitchen pouring tomato juice over stalks of celery in the blender. "H-hey, Uncle Cade," I stammered over chattering teeth. "Can you come register me at Lali's school?"

He pressed the button to start the blender, and I scowled at him as we both waited for the loud grinding sound to finish. "I told you, you're putting too much effort into this," he said once the room was silent again. "Just grab her out of that place and be done with it."

"I only need fifteen minutes, tops. Please. I have to get this over with so I can see her at lunch."

"Are you trying to find your sister or catch a girlfriend?" He finally looked at me, but the disgust on his face made me wish he hadn't. How could he ask me something like that? "We should be at Delta's, waiting for her to come home."

"You said she wouldn't be able to get home for a few days."

Lifting the plastic container off the base of the blender, he poured his pinkish mixture into a glass. "You never know."

My fists balled. Why wasn't he taking me seriously? This was the best lead we had.

"Well, you need me to go to Delta's," I reminded him. "The sooner you help me, the sooner I'll take you over there."

Cade slammed his glass on the counter so hard I was surprised it didn't shatter. "That's what this is coming to? You're turning on me now?"

"I'm not turning on you," I huffed. "I'm trying to make sure we don't let an opportunity go to waste."

"And if Lali sees you with me? Won't that ruin your little plan?"

"She's in class. That's why we have to hurry."

He turned his back to me and gripped the edge of the counter. "Have it your way, nephew. But as soon as we're done, we're going to Delta's house."

"Deal." Hurrying to the closet, I pulled out one of his coats and grabbed the sunglasses from the end table near the door. I hoped the glasses would help mask his hungover appearance. I'd tell the office lady he was having a migraine or something.

Without a word, I draped his coat over one of the bar stools and set his sunglasses on the counter next to him. Then I headed to our home office to dig out my birth certificate and social security card. I figured that was enough to get me enrolled.

A few minutes later, I'd projected us to the windowless wall behind the school. Racing down the side of the building, I rushed back through the main doors and into the office with Cade taking his time to catch up.

"Found him," I said too loudly, gesturing to my uncle as he came through the door ten paces behind me.

Principal Rockbridge and Mrs. Moubrey eyed Cade warily, but the secretary made quick work of signing me up. She offered to show me to my classes, but I made up an excuse about needing to pick something up from the store. I promised to come back around lunchtime to tour the school, which I hoped would give me a chance to see Lali in the cafeteria.

Cade and I were barely out the door when Mrs. Moubrey called my name.

"I'll wait here," Cade said, slumping onto the bench just outside the entrance. It was probably better that way, so I didn't argue. I wasn't sure how long classes were, and I wasn't going to risk him catching Lali's attention in the hallway.

I followed Mrs. Moubrey back into the office so she could snap a Polaroid of me. Apparently that was a thing in this town. Maybe the principal studied all the photos during the day so she could spot new kids faster.

"Okay," the old woman said. "You're all set."

"Thanks." I forced a smile. "See you at lunchtime." As I spun around to leave, the door flew open and bounced off my shoe.

"Whoa," I called out.

I heard something hit the floor, followed by a high-pitched, "Sorry!"

I sighed. How many times was I going to get hit with a door today? I poked my head into the hallway, and all my blood drained into my feet. There, standing on the other side of the door with wide eyes, was Lali.

23

DRAWING

Damn it. I wasn't prepared for this.

Lali looked panicked, too, though I wasn't sure why. Did she think I was going to flip out because she hit me with the door?

"Um, hi," she squeaked. "Sorry about that. I didn't see you."

Remembering I'd read somewhere that girls liked it when guys teased them, I decided to make a joke about it. "Don't sweat it," I said, moving toward her and rubbing one side of my face. "I'm sure my jaw will realign eventually."

She stared at me like I'd told her I murdered kittens for fun.

"Kidding." I forced a laugh. "No harm done. I'm Kai, by the way."

It took her an extra beat to shake my hand. Surprisingly, hers was soft and warm. Almost every other girl I'd met had extremities like ice.

"Lali," she said cautiously. Her eyes held mine, the exact same shade of gray as Xiomara's. They were framed with thick lashes and way too much blue eyeliner. Even so, Lali was cute, in a trying-a-little-too-hard-to-be-different kind of way.

I squeezed her fingers. "Pretty name. Suits you." Her cheeks darkened, and I felt a small twinge of victory. Maybe it would be easier to win her over than I thought.

She pulled back her hand and ran it along her arm. "Um, thanks." I caught her scanning me from head to toe, and something fluttered inside me. Was she checking me out?

Then I remembered I was dressed like it was a hundred degrees outside when it was practically a frozen tundra out there. Lali had on a heavy black sweater and jeans like a normal person. She was probably wondering what I was thinking when I got dressed.

Time for a change of subject. I caught a glimpse of a notebook at our feet. That must've been what I'd heard hit the floor.

"I believe this," I said, bending down to grab it, "is yours." My eyes landed on a doodle in the margin, and I almost dropped the notebook onto the tile again. She'd drawn the symbol Solstice and Xiomara had tattooed inside their bottom lips. And it wasn't just the symbol—it was drawn inside a mouth.

Lali snatched the notebook from me before I could register what it meant. "Yeah. Thanks." She clutched the drawing close to her chest and avoided my eyes.

I couldn't speak as my brain sped through possibilities.

Even if she knew her mother had a tattoo like that, what were the odds she would just happen to draw it right after Xiomara and Solstice had shown me their tattoos last night? Did Lali project to her mother while we were trying to come up with plans in the living room? It hadn't quite been midnight, but I doubted her ability was on that specific of a schedule. Instead of the usual Astralii style of projecting that had their astral forms appearing just above them, maybe Lali could track people like I could.

But we would have seen her if she projected into our living room. Cade told me astral forms were transparent and silvery, but they were definitely visible.

Unless Lali was hovering above us without our noticing.

The thought made my heart race. If that were true, it meant Lali could travel. But if I wanted the chance to find out, I had to say something to keep her talking. The expression on her face said she was about to run for the hills.

"Do you draw much?" I blurted out. I cringed internally. That was the best I could come up with?

She blinked twice, and I could have sworn she swayed backward. I read the panic in her eyes, and my stomach plummeted as realization hit. If she projected to her mother last night, then she would have seen me, too. Was that why she looked so startled when I'd stepped around the office door?

A loud fake cough came from behind me. "Good morning, Lali. Were you planning to come in?"

Principal Buzzkill. Great. The tension in her tone told

me any chance of figuring out what Lali had seen was ruined.

"Um, yeah." Lali glanced at me again, still clearly shaken.

"I'll get out of your way," I said, playing my part of the clueless new kid as well as I could. "It was nice to meet you."

Lali moved her head up and down slowly. "You, too."

"See ya." I took a few steps backward to feign light-heartedness before turning to head down the hall. I felt my face fall as soon as my back was to Lali. That drawing had to mean something, and I needed answers. If I came back during lunch, I could find a way to pull her aside. Now that I suspected she knew something, maybe it was better for me to tell her I knew her secret and get past the pretense of getting to know her. That would certainly speed things up.

Thankfully, even if she had seen me with her mother, she would have seen us all working together. She wouldn't have any way to know that I was the one who'd kidnapped her.

And you'd better keep it that way. I wanted to kick myself for not thinking of it sooner. We would have to make Xiomara set up a block before Lali saw anything. Or, anything *else*.

Cade was still sitting on the bench when I stepped outside. "You're never going to believe this," I whispered.

He peered at me over his sunglasses before standing. "What?"

"Lali drew Xiomara and Solstice's weird lip tattoo in her notebook."

He looked over his shoulder toward the school as if he'd be able to see what I was talking about.

"Do you think she traveled in her sleep and saw us last night?" I asked.

"That's a pretty big leap, nephew. We would have seen her."

"What if she was floating above us?"

Cold air whipped past, and we both shivered. "Let's go before you freeze to death," Cade said, starting down the walkway. "We can talk about this at home."

I followed behind him, my brain still firing at full speed to make sense of things. "Whatever the case, I'm coming back later to talk to Lali." We stepped around the side of the building, and I was thankful to have a break from the wind—even though the slush covering the ground tried to make my toes numb as we walked.

Cade scoffed. "Why?"

"Because she might've seen something. And if she really can travel, then she can get to Alea."

"Getting to Alea won't help us if I still can't project," Cade grumbled as we turned around the back of the school. "They won't let me into the lab."

I frowned. Where did that come from? He never mentioned not being able to get into the lab when we were trying to see if I could get to Alea. Why was he just realizing that issue now?

"Maybe her ability can get us inside the lab," I offered. "If Lali didn't project to Xiomara last night, then

Xiomara must have shown Lali her tattoo before. What if Lali knows more about Astralii than we thought? I need to talk to her."

"Come on, nephew. Think about this. You don't even know for sure that she can travel."

"You didn't see that drawing," I argued. "She has to know something. She could be exactly what we need."

"Need?" Cade let out a harsh laugh. "We need her like a hole in the head. She'll only complicate things."

I sighed. I was done arguing with him. I didn't care what he said; I was going to explore every possibility. But first, I had to get Xiomara to set up a block that would stop Lali from projecting to her and ruining my plans.

24

BLOCK

WHEN I APPEARED IN THE IN-LAW SUITE, XIOMARA STARTED so hard she nearly knocked over the easel in front of her. Even though my attempts to project to the others based on her art had failed, apparently she wasn't giving up on that approach. Not that I blamed her—it wasn't like anything else was working. But hopefully that would change soon.

"You know, it might not kill you to give me a heads up before you do that," she scolded, slipping off her stool to retrieve the charcoal pencil she'd dropped from my startling her. She had her short hair pulled back into the tiniest ponytail I'd ever seen, the front held in place by the same ridiculous pink headband she'd been wearing the night I took her from her home. It was hard to believe that was two months ago.

She set the pencil in the tray along the base of the easel and dusted her hands on her jeans. "What'd you do with Solstice?"

"Took her somewhere she can't attack you," I said flatly. "Listen, I need you to set up a block."

Her nose quirked up at the sides. "Why?"

"Because if Lali ends up with an ability like mine, I'm not going to risk her showing up and plucking you out of here." *Or seeing that I'm the one responsible for your absence...if she hasn't figured that out already.*

I couldn't help but cringe at the thought. I told myself Lali hadn't pieced it together. If she had, she would have said something when she saw me. Right?

A range of emotions played out across Xiomara's face. I could tell she was hesitant, but the logic behind keeping Lali away couldn't be argued. Even Cade had agreed, which was why he'd been okay with my coming here instead of staying at Delta's house with him. I'd reluctantly given him back the gun and dropped him off there just in case Delta showed up, but he was as eager to get the block set up as I was, even if it was for different reasons.

"I'm only agreeing to this because I know my daughter," Xiomara finally said. "If she projects to me, she won't rest until she finds me in person."

I shrugged. "That's as good a reason as any." Why she thought I cared about her motivation, I didn't know. Maybe she was trying to justify it to herself. "What do you need to do it?"

"If I remember correctly, a crystal grid, black tourmaline—"

"Let me rephrase that," I interrupted before she gave

me the full rundown of terms I didn't understand. "Where do we go to get what you need?"

She eased back onto the stool behind her. "Any crystal shop should have everything."

"Cool."

"I don't know how to set up a personal block, though." The way she said it made the statement sound like a shameful confession. "Delta only taught me how to block a particular space."

"Okay…" The stressed-out look on her face made me feel like I was missing something.

"I just thought you should know," she murmured. "Since you won't be able to project in and out of the house anymore."

Oh. Well, damn. That was going to be a pain. "Wait, that means you won't be able to leave the house anymore either?" I asked.

"Not if you don't want to risk Lali projecting to me."

Great. More complications. Between Xiomara being grounded here and Cade wanting to make sure someone was always at Delta's, communication was going to be interesting to say the least. And I would have to find a place near the house to come and go unnoticed. Not to mention, I'd have to run back and forth to whatever place I found a million times a day now that I was going to be in and out of Browshire.

I sighed, looking around the in-law. Was this my karmic payback for trapping Xiomara in this bubble for most of the day? And here I thought I was being nice by not making her stay in an old shipping container.

Wait. Could she put the block around that? I struck down the idea as soon as it came to me. I couldn't make her stay in there again. Besides, if she blocked it, I wouldn't be able to get in and out anymore. Cade and I had fused the lock shut to make sure no one could escape.

But maybe...

"Could you set up the block just around the basement?"

She chewed the inside of her cheek as her eyes roamed over the walls. "I can try."

After a quick online search for the nearest crystal shop— which was thankfully in Miami—I drove Xiomara to pick up supplies. We were back in the in-law less than an hour later.

"So, did you have any trouble dropping off the letter?" she asked as she dug the stones and candles out of the shopping bags. She didn't look at me, but I could feel my face flushing. I hadn't given the note a second thought since the previous night. As far as I knew, it was still crammed inside the pocket of yesterday's shorts.

"Well, um, Lali was awake last night," I mumbled.

Xiomara's posture drooped, but she lifted her eyes to meet mine. "Oh. Well, she's at school now. Maybe it's better to leave it today."

I nodded, but I still wasn't sure I wanted to pass the note along to Lali. What if it just opened up old wounds about her mother's disappearance? I was still hoping to keep her as level-headed as possible.

"Who knows?" Xiomara forced a laugh. "If she realizes I didn't run off and forget about her, maybe she'll take it easy on me in her diary."

My head snapped up. "She has a diary?" Would she have written about seeing her mom last night? That would at least give me a definite answer about the symbol she'd drawn in her notebook, and something to use to convince Cade that it was worth pursuing her.

Xiomara frowned at me, and I realized I'd sounded way too excited. I cleared my throat. "I mean, isn't a diary kind of middle school?"

"It's a perfectly legitimate means of expression," she snapped.

I lifted my palms. "Okay, touchy subject."

"I'm sorry," she said quickly. "I'm just worried about her dealing with so much at once." I forced my face to stay neutral. If she was trying to guilt trip me, it wasn't going to work. "And I was thinking…" she went on. "Maybe you could give her some tips on how to control her ability. Perhaps you could be like a guide or something. Just so she knows she's not alone."

I couldn't stop my reaction to that; my eyes bulged and shot to her face. Was she serious? Or did she suspect that I was trying to bring Lali into my mission to Alea?

"Um, why don't we just start with the note?" I hedged. "I can go drop it off now." *Or pretend to so I can check out her diary.*

"No, wait. I need your help with this."

"What? Why? I don't know anything about crystals."

"I'll tell you what to do. Two intentions will make the stones stronger."

I rolled my eyes. "Fine. Let's just get it done." *Then I can see if your daughter's diary mentions seeing you with us last night.*

The two of us moved the coffee table aside, and Xiomara went to work. She spread out a round, white cloth covered with an angular black pattern on the floor and lit a bunch of candles to go around it. I turned off the light as she lined up stones of various colors along the intersecting lines. She seemed to second-guess herself over which rocks went where every ten seconds, but finally, she got everything set up in what she called a sacred space, whatever that meant.

"We have to program each one individually," she said, picking up one of the little black stones from the pile in front of her. "It shouldn't take long. Just repeat after me, and do as I do."

With that, the ritual began. Xiomara held up the shiny chunk of rock and began chanting. "Reject the energy of astral forms. Keep us safe and close the doors." She pricked her finger with the dagger we bought at the shop and held the wound to the stone as she said the chant again. Her blood made a sound like bacon frying in a pan with extra grease.

I fought back a shudder and followed suit, repeating the chant, stabbing my finger, and letting my blood sizzle against the stone, too. We then spoke the chant together, and the crystal lit up as if a floodlight were inside. The glow died down almost as quickly as it began. If it hadn't been bright enough to hurt my eyes, I might have thought I imagined it.

We repeated the chant-and-give-blood process with four more stones, which Xiomara then placed in the corners of the room, with a final one in the light fixture hanging from the center of the ceiling. Once the rocks were in place, we spoke the intention again, and I couldn't help but notice the candles were flickering as if there were a breeze in the room that I couldn't feel. A glow came from all the stones and connected into one final shock wave of light.

Then everything went dark.

"So I guess it worked," I said, standing up to hit the light switch. I wasn't sure how all the candles had gone out, but I assumed it was a good sign.

Xiomara smirked up at me from where she sat with her back against the bottom of the couch. "Only one way to find out."

"What?"

"You have to test it. I can't project, remember?"

Oh. That was why she was fighting laughter—I was going to have to project into a block. I groaned. Hitting Delta's block once was enough for my lifetime.

"It will only take a second," Xiomara insisted, still annoyingly amused. "Just try to project upstairs." She bit her lip. "But you might want to sit down. If it works, you don't want to go flying into a wall or anything."

Glowering, I headed for the armchair, plopped into the seat, and shut my eyes. I tried to project upstairs and felt an invisible kick in the gut. I grunted and doubled over, gasping.

"Looks like it worked," Xiomara chirped, all perky and irritating. "I guess you're going to have to walk down the stairs like a normal person now."

I wanted to glare at her, but I was too busy trying to breathe. As much as hitting the block sucked, I was glad it would keep Lali out if she ended up with an ability that could somehow get her here. I couldn't help but wonder what Cade and I would have done if all of the members of XODUS had set up blocks around themselves. Not that it would've mattered. Just having one around Delta had already screwed up all our plans.

But maybe Lali would be the key to getting around that.

Speaking of…

I pulled my phone out of my pocket and checked the time. There was still about an hour before I needed to go back for her school's lunch period. That gave me just enough time to do a quick search of her room and see about her diary.

25

DIARY

LALI'S ROOM DIDN'T GIVE ANYTHING AWAY. I SCANNED THE space for the second time, racking my brain for typical diary hiding places. I started under her pillows before moving to under the mattress. When neither turned up any results, I tried under the bed itself. The entire space beneath the bed frame was packed with plastic storage containers.

I hauled one out, bending down to pull off the lid. It made a cracking sound, and loud bark rang out, followed by claws clattering across the wood floor. Within seconds, sniffs came from under the door, and the dog howled so loudly I was sure he was going to alert everyone within a five-mile radius.

If I was going to calm the animal down, I knew I had to let it do the sniff-and-approve routine. Letting out a sigh, I stood up and pulled open the door. The dog saw me, and the hair along his spine stood on end in some sort of weird mohawk as he barked like crazy.

"Shh," I urged. "It's okay."

The dog wasn't convinced.

"It's okay," I repeated over another earsplitting howl. "I'm not going to hurt you." Realizing my towering over the dog probably wasn't helping, I slowly lowered myself to the floor and held out my hand as a sniff offering. That at least stopped the barking.

I kept my arm steady, my fingers just shy of the dog's nose. He moved forward to sniff my skin, his tail lowering, and then twitching from side to side.

"See, I'm not so bad, right?" I slowly reached out my other hand to pet him. The next second, he jumped at me, and his tongue connected with my cheek.

A laugh came out before I could stop it. Growing up, I'd always wanted a dog. Grandma Naida only had a cat that rarely came out from under the bed. Hardly counted as a pet if you asked me.

Now that Lali's dog wasn't on a rampage, he was kind of cute, all droopy ears and short legs. "Do you know if Lali saw me with her mom?" I asked, scratching the top of his head. He blinked at me. "You probably do. I wouldn't be surprised if you knew how Lali's power worked, too."

I peeked over the side of the bin I'd pulled out from under her bed. It was filled with clothes—shorts, tank tops, and t-shirts she clearly wouldn't need for a while. With the dog by my side, I snapped the lid back on and tried the second tub. This one held a bunch of papers and yearbooks. Written across the top of each assignment was *Xitlali Marie Yavari*.

Huh. I hadn't realized "Lali" was a nickname for... however her full name was pronounced. Between that crazy moniker and *Lalisaurus,* I was starting to wonder if the girl's parents secretly enjoyed making her suffer.

I shuffled through the papers, all of them marked with perfect scores. I knew Lali probably wouldn't want to keep things she didn't do well on, but damn. There were so many of them. I'd been lucky to pull off a single A in all my years of public school. Yet another reason I was glad Cade decided to homeschool me.

Accepting that there was nothing useful in this bin, I arranged everything into to some semblance of order, put the lid back on, and shoved it into place under the bed.

Next stop, the nightstand. Unfortunately, the lone drawer only housed a couple of books and some ChapStick.

The dog followed me over to Lali's desk. Papers were thrown haphazardly across the top, so I didn't bother trying to memorize how to put them back. Most of them were study guides and half-finished worksheets. Digging through the drawers, I found a few small notebooks.

The first one turned out to be a sketch pad. Not surprising.

I opened the second one and found a date scribbled in the top corner of the page. The first line explaining that the day had been hectic told me what I needed to know: it was a diary. Sucking in an excited breath, I quickly flipped to the back, turning the blank pages until I found the most recent entry. My heart sank as I saw it was dated Christmas Day of last year.

Why was I even surprised? I'd already seen time and time again that I shouldn't expect anything to be easy. Shaking my head, I started to close the notebook, but my eyes caught on the first line. From there, I couldn't help reading.

I hate you, Mom.

I hate you so much for doing this to us. You ruined Christmas this year, on top of everything else. Sal is so upset she's slept in my room every night since you left. Dix looks like he's on the brink of breaking. Lyx hardly ever smiles, and all Oxie does is snap at everyone now.

I hope you're happy. What was so important that you could leave us like this? Didn't we matter to you at all?

A puckered spot blurred the words just after the question mark, and I swallowed hard. Lali's tears must've hit the paper. A quick skim over the page, and I could see the writing increased in size and illegibility with each line, like a meter of her emotions.

You did this to her.

I dropped the notebook. My legs folded beneath me until I was sitting on the floor. No matter how much I could justify holding Xiomara captive, I couldn't justify what it was doing to her kids. If anyone should understand the pain of losing a parent, it was me. Yet, here I was keeping a mother away from her children.

Something cold and wet nudged my hand. The dog

wagged his tail, his eyes looking at me like he understood that I felt like a monster. He nuzzled against my palm, and something heavy settled onto my chest. I wondered how many times he'd tried to comfort Lali and the rest of her family in their moments of sadness.

Moments *I'd* created.

Shoving the thought to a dark corner in my mind, I forced myself to my feet and dropped the diary back into the drawer. I couldn't do this to myself. I had to remember why I'd taken Xiomara, what was really important here. I hadn't done it to hurt Lali, but maybe I could make it up to her.

If anything, she needed me to help her sort out her ability—her mom had even asked me to guide her. I hadn't delivered Xiomara's note, but an in-person trainer was better than a piece of paper any day. At least that would balance out some of what I'd done. And finding Lali during her school's lunch period was the perfect way to start.

…Yeah, sorry about reading your diary. If it's any consolation, I stopped after that one entry. But in truth, that was probably the best thing I could have done at that point. It made it harder for me to ignore how all this was affecting you, and it made me more determined than ever to keep things moral and civil.

I told myself I would approach you peacefully to explain. That day, you weren't there for lunch, but I planned to go back the next morning and fill you in on everything calmly and rationally. But, well, we both know how that went…

26

APPROACH

I took a long breath of briny air and looked out at the ocean. The moon glowed overhead, flooding the beach with enough light that I could see the waves as they broke a few feet from where I sat. The water looked black now, but I knew the gorgeous crystal blue that sparkled when the sun came out. Usually this spot and the smell of the sea soothed me, but not today. Even my favorite beach in Lanai couldn't make me feel better.

My subconscious had spent the night trying to make me crazy again with more dreams of a devastated family. Reading Lali's diary only gave my conscience more ammunition, and it was having a field day tormenting me.

I sighed and leaned back onto the book bag propped up behind me in the sand. Looking up at the night sky, I told myself that no matter how bad I felt, it didn't change that I needed to get to my sister. Even though I was playing the waiting game with Lali, she was the only option I had any faith in right now.

She hadn't been in the cafeteria when I'd gone back for her lunch period yesterday, so I was sitting around waiting for school to start again this morning—well, later morning in Virginia. It was still the wee hours in Hawaii, but I'd set my phone's alarm to go off when it would be time for me to head to the school.

Cade was planning to stay at Delta's all day, but I still thought the odds of her showing up were slim to none. I lied and told my uncle that Solstice and Xiomara were still trying to get the block around the in-law to work. I didn't feel like dealing with Solstice's hysteria if I took her to Delta's house. I hoped she had calmed down, but I didn't have the energy to handle her if she hadn't. Everything felt so hectic; I just needed a minute to clear my head.

Watching the movement of the ocean, I imagined outrunning the waves with my dad like I did when I was a little boy. Whenever I was too slow, he would grab me and pull me into the air before the water could catch me. At least, that's what Grandma Naida told me.

My memories of my life before the raid were hazy and scattered, but my grandmother recognized how much I longed to know my parents. She saved up her money so she could bring me to this island—to this particular secluded beach—for my thirteenth birthday. That day, she told me story after story about how my mom discovered this hidden spot when she was young and came out here when she wanted to think, how my parents used to picnic here, how it was the first place my dad told my mom he loved her, how my parents brought Kala and me the first chance they got.

I'd memorized every detail of this place that day. It felt like my only connection to my parents, and I'd revisited it in my mind every night before going to sleep. I was sure that was why it was the first place I ever projected.

My phone buzzed in my pocket, and I reached to silence it. Time to find Lali at school. I closed my eyes, and a second later I saw her standing outside the office talking to two blonde girls.

Good. I could stroll by the office and pretend I had some new-student stuff to take care of. Getting to my feet, I slipped my backpack over my shoulders to make myself look more legitimate and projected to the boys' bathroom stall from the previous day. Thankfully, there was no one around.

Handfuls of students stood clustered along the hallway, but hardly anyone noticed me as I moved toward the office. Keeping my head low, I let my mind run through how to approach starting up a conversation with Lali.

Hey, good to see a familiar face.

No. That sounded too eager. Girls hated eager guys.

Maybe I could make a comment about her hair and overdone eyeliner. "Why so blue?" I tried aloud as I passed a water fountain. No, that was even worse.

"Good golly, Miss Lali." I cringed as soon as the words were out. I was getting cornier by the minute. Besides, Lali probably wouldn't get the reference. Grandma Naida had played Little Richard songs all the time, but I doubted anyone at this school even knew the name.

Maybe it was better to skip the greeting. A firm *we need to talk* would at least intrigue her enough to come with me. Well, if it didn't terrify her.

I turned the corner just in time to see Lali shove something into her backpack and walk into the office.

Damn. I didn't want Mrs. Moubrey to overhear me demanding to speak to Lali. I stayed back, debating. Should I linger and wait for Lali to come out? I could fall into step with her when she came back this way.

If she came this way. I didn't want to have to chase her if she went in the opposite direction.

Screw it. I was going in. I'd just have to wing it with small talk until I could get her out of earshot of any staff members. Dodging the group of skinny freshman-looking guys, I made my way to the office and slowly turned the door's handle. It barely clicked as I pushed it open.

"I, uh, forgot what he said his last name was," Lali was saying to Mrs. Moubrey. "Writing *Kai and family* just doesn't sound as personal, you know?"

My ears perked up. Why did she want to know my last name? Before I could decide how to play it, Mrs. Moubrey moved a hand in my direction and said, "Why don't you ask him yourself?"

I grabbed the straps of my book bag and forced the corner of my mouth up, doing my best not to look suspicious.

Lali turned around a centimeter at a time, as if she were expecting to find a flesh-eating zombie behind her.

She paled as soon as we made eye contact. She had definitely figured out something to do with me. Had she seen me with her mother before we set up the block yesterday?

"Awana," I said, hoping Lali's reaction to my last name might give me a clue. No luck. She just gaped at me like I was holding a machete.

"My last name is Awana," I clarified.

"Oh." Her eyes shifted.

"Why do you ask?" I tried to sound casual, but I knew I fell short. Then the bell rang, and it looked like Lali had a small heart attack.

"Okay, you two. Get to class," Mrs. Moubrey ordered.

Lali was off like a shot, the blue streaks in her hair like flashes of light as she shoved past me with a shrill, "Bye."

"Hey, Lali." The words were out before I could think. She stopped so abruptly that a skinny girl with frizzy hair bumped into her and threw out some choice words.

Lali turned around slowly. "Yeah?"

I couldn't let her run away. If she knew something, she was only going to keep avoiding me. "Can I walk you to class?" I asked, remembering that the office staff might still overhear us.

Lali's face went blank. "Why?"

"Because I'm a nice guy?" It came out sounding like a question. At this point, it kind of was.

"I—" she stammered. "I mean, didn't you have to do something in the office?"

"Just needed to get a form signed. No big deal. It can

wait." I read panic all over her face. She wasn't buying it for a second.

"Actually, I, um…" Her eyes darted around like she was looking for an excuse to get as far away from me as possible. "I have to pee."

I exhaled a combination between a scoff and a laugh. "Glad you're so open about that." I scanned the hall, noting the sign for the girls' restroom not a hundred yards away. I knew she'd meant it as a way to deter me, but if she insisted on running, the bathroom would make it easier for me to corner her. Everyone was heading off to class, so there wouldn't be anyone around to notice me go in after her. That was, if there was no one else in there.

I'd take my chances. I might not have another opportunity to catch Lali somewhere that would keep her from bolting.

"I just have to hurry, you know?" she breathed. "Don't want to be late. Maybe next time."

"Sure," I said. "Next time."

She spun around and all but sprinted toward the bathroom, her Sharpie-covered book bag wobbling as she moved. I watched her push open the door to the girls' room. Waiting for it to swing shut, I let out a long breath, jogged toward the door, and shoved in after her.

FORCE

LALI LOOKED LIKE SHE MIGHT PEE HER PANTS WHEN SHE saw me. "I-I think you have the wrong bathroom," she spluttered.

I pinned her with a look. "Why are you afraid of me?" No point beating around the bush now that I'd cornered her.

She shook her head, but the movement couldn't negate the terror written all over her features. "I-I'm not."

"Lali, please. Your face reads like a book. You're terrified of me, and I just want to know why." *And why you were trying to figure out my last name.*

"I told you, I'm not." Except her voice quivered, and she was leaning toward her backpack like she was considering using it to attack me. Though I could see she was lying, I didn't understand her reasoning. If she knew I had her mom, why wasn't she saying it? Why didn't she say it yesterday when she first saw me?

Unless it wasn't the first time. My eyebrows lifted as I realized the obvious answer. She'd seen me in her house the other night. Maybe it took her an extra moment to place my face yesterday, but she had to have seen me. Nothing else made sense.

"You saw me too, didn't you?" I asked.

Her eyes bulged. "What?"

"In your hallway. I thought I got us out of there before you noticed me, but I guess not."

"You were there?"

Well, so much for that theory. But if she didn't see me there, then what was her problem?

"That was you in the pantry, wasn't it?" she gasped.

I cringed at the thought of my embarrassing lack of spy skills. Knocking something off the pantry shelf was just the tip of the iceberg, but at least she hadn't stuck around to see I'd spilled her pictures everywhere, too.

"That was an accident," I said. "You startled me."

"But how…?"

I lifted my shoulders, still grasping for answers myself. "Just how my power turned out. I can project my whole body, and I happened to get the bring-a-friend bonus."

Her face stayed motionless, not an ounce of under-standing lifting her features.

"But the more important question," I said, inching toward her, "is what power did *you* get?"

She staggered back, almost falling into the sink behind her. "Stay away. I'll scream."

I raised my palms. "Hey, I just want to know how your power works."

The bell rang again, and she let out a yelp. Damn, I

must've scared her more than I thought. I opened my mouth to explain that I didn't want to hurt her, but she swung her backpack at me before I could get the words out. Her books crashed into my shoulder, sending a shock of pain right to my bones.

She lunged for the door, but I caught it and held it closed with my hand. I reached for a calm voice. "Wait a min—"

"Help!" she shrieked, yanking on the handle like her life depended on it. "Somebody help me!"

I winced. I didn't want to terrorize her, but I couldn't let her get away. If she made it out of here, she would never let me within a hundred feet of her.

Kicking my foot against the bottom of the door to keep it shut, I quickly covered her mouth. "Lali, just *listen.*" She screamed, her hot breath on my palm making my mind flash back to when I'd kidnapped her mother. I hated that I was already resorting to these methods. But what choice did I have?

Lali threw herself back at me and attacked my hand like a wild animal, ripping my skin with her nails.

I swore under my breath. She was making this more difficult than it needed to be. "You want to do it this way?" I grumbled. "Fine. Then brace yourself. And you might want to close your eyes." I added the warning in hopes she wouldn't collapse when we arrived. If she was already this panicked, temporary blindness certainly wasn't going to help.

I decided to take her to Lanai. It was a peaceful spot,

and it wasn't like killers took their victims to beautiful beaches. That should at least show her I wasn't trying to hurt her.

She was still struggling when we arrived, but she froze suddenly. I could see her blinking and squinting, and I knew she'd ignored my warning.

Perfect. Now she was going to be even more freaked out because she couldn't see.

"Told you to close your eyes," I muttered.

Something seemed to snap inside her at my words, and the next thing I knew she was thrashing and screaming, "Let me go!" I lost my hold, and she dropped straight into the sand. She stayed put, gasping for air with her face half buried.

"You'll be okay in a minute," I said, hoping to reassure her. "Projecting with me takes some getting used to." Feeling the weight of my backpack, I dropped it by my feet.

As soon as it thudded to the ground, I realized I'd left Lali's bag on the floor in the school's bathroom. I projected back to get it before someone could find evidence of our scuffle.

When I appeared behind Lali again, she was pushing herself up to a seated position. I dropped her bag next to my own, watching as she tried to get her bearings. Not surprisingly, her eyes bulged as she took in the moonlit beach. I moved over to try and explain, but she crazy crab-walked in the opposite direction and told me to stay away.

I fought to keep my patience intact. "Lali, I'm not trying to hurt you."

Her gray eyes were so wide she looked like she was going to die of fright. I knew she must've been shaken from appearing on a beach and everything, but honestly. How many times did I have to say I wasn't going to hurt her?

"I don't know where she is," she wailed out of nowhere.

What? "You don't know where who is?"

"My mom. She left, and I have no idea where she went."

I tried not to let my relief show. I didn't know why Lali was telling me this, but if she thought her mother left, then she didn't know I was behind Xiomara's disappearance. That good-bye note actually came in handy after all. But if Lali didn't know I had her mother, why was she so terrified back at the school?

"Why would I care where your mom is?" I asked, praying that playing along would lead to some answers.

But Lali wasn't listening. Her eyes darted toward the trees across the beach.

"Hey, take it easy," I pleaded. "Let me help you up." I reached out to her, but she winced as if I'd raised my hand to hit her. It was like dealing with an abused puppy.

I sighed. "Or you could just hang out in the sand."

Finally, the worried creases between her eyebrows faded back into the smooth olive skin of her forehead. She reached for my hand, hesitating just before she touched it. "Why did you bring me here? What do you want?"

Hallelujah. Time to be rational. Leaning to help her up, I started to answer. The second I opened my mouth, she launched a handful of sand at my face and took off running.

28

PROOF

I SHOUTED PROFANITIES AROUND A MOUTHFUL OF SAND.
Lali's cries for help were growing more distant by the
second, but my eyes had already teared up so much I
could barely make out her form racing for the trees in the
darkness. I wiped my face with my hand and spit. This
was what I got for trying to spare her the trauma of
kidnapping her in the middle of the night?

"Lali, wait," I called after her, though I knew she
wouldn't. I'd be lucky if she didn't try to swim home from
here.

Forcing my already swollen lids shut, I projected just
ahead of her. The next second, she crashed into me and
knocked me backward into the sand. All the breath
ejected from my body at once, but somehow Lali
managed to stay balanced and keep going. Frustration
must've fueled me faster, because I rolled onto my hands
and knees and caught her around the waist a moment
later.

She fought me and screamed for me to let go, but I wasn't about to subject myself to another faceful of sand. Instead, I got a headbutt that made my teeth slice into my tongue.

Cursing again, I wrapped my arms around hers in a bear hold, refusing to let her do more damage to my body. "Just stop for a sec!"

She kept screaming, but eventually she would have to run out of energy. Then I could get a word in edgewise.

Seeming to realize I wasn't letting up, Lali finally stopped struggling. "What do you want?" she wailed.

"I want you to calm down so I can explain." The words reflected my impatience more than I'd intended, but I was too exasperated to care.

"*Calm down?* I'm not going to calm down, you psycho! I know you're working for that murderer!"

My arms loosened out of pure shock, and she almost fell to the ground again. "What are you talking about? What murderer?"

She turned on me, rage twisting her features so they cast heavier shadows in the moonlight. "The man with the scar," she snapped. "I saw him shoot that woman."

The man with the scar. That had to mean Cade. She must've seen him when he'd gone on his drunken rampage with Solstice the other night. And if they hadn't noticed her, Lali must have been hovering somewhere above them. Which meant...

I thought my heart might explode out of my chest. "So you *can* travel," I said, willing it to be true.

167

She started to speak, but couldn't get whatever she was trying to say out.

"I knew it," I went on. "That's why you drew that picture in your notebook. You saw my uncle with Solstice, didn't you?" Lali must have heard the gunshot as she came out of her projection. That had to be why she thought Cade killed Solstice.

"Look, you've got it all wrong," I told her, though after her thrashing session, I doubted she'd believe anything I said. I'd just have to take her to Solstice and prove that my uncle wasn't a murderer.

Thank God I left Solstice at her apartment.

I reached out to grab Lali's hand, but she whipped back like a slingshot. "I just want to show you Solstice is okay," I explained. "Cade didn't shoot her."

"I *saw* him."

"You're wrong." I tried to rein in my frustration. This was such a waste of time, but I knew I had to do it if I was going to get Lali to calm down. "Come on, I'll show you."

I reached out again, and she backed up. Her chest rose and fell like she was trying to think of a way to run, but I caught her by the hand before she could go anywhere. If she wasn't going to come willingly, then I was going to have to take her without permission. It was for her own good, anyway—she was only panicked because she had her facts wrong.

Lali collapsed when we appeared at Solstice's place, but I was already on my way to get the woman she thought was dead. "Solstice?" I called, heading for the bedroom. I was halfway there when the sound of running water stopped me. It sounded like Solstice was at the bathroom sink.

I didn't have time to wait; we'd already wasted enough time as it was. I shoved the door open and slammed it shut behind me.

Solstice cried out and almost fell backward into the tub, her light purple robe barely managing to keep her covered. The towel that had been wrapped around her hair slipped over her face and piled onto the floor beside her. The fear in her expression turned to anger when she saw me.

"What do you think you're doing?" she shrieked. "Get out."

"I need your help," I said, undeterred. "Can you come out for a second and show this girl you're still alive?"

"*What?*"

"I'll explain later. You don't even have to say anything. Just come out here."

"No way." She stood up and gestured to her light purple knee-length robe.

"Look, I don't have to let you stay here," I reminded her. "I could have easily made you stay with Cade. Now can you please just come out here for two seconds?" I opened the door and stepped out of the bathroom, gesturing for Solstice to lead the way.

She huffed, grabbing up the towel that had fallen in her scramble and twisting her hair back into it. I followed behind her as she marched down the hallway.

Lali was back on her feet when we walked into the living room, but she froze and turned white as a sheet when she saw Solstice. "You're alive," she gasped.

I rolled my eyes. I'd just told her the woman was alive a few minutes ago. I gestured toward the walking proof. "See? Solstice is fine. She's not dead."

Moving with all the grace of a drunken giraffe, Lali stumbled forward and held out a hand to steady herself on the back of the smaller couch. She stared at Solstice like the woman was part of some freak show.

"Now do you believe me?" I asked.

But Lali didn't take her eyes off Solstice. "Your lip," she breathed.

Solstice glared at her. "I beg your pardon?"

"Your lip," Lali repeated. "Pull it down."

Now what was she doing? Checking to make sure the tattoo was there? Did she think Solstice had an evil twin or something?

Solstice responded with a snort, making it clear she had no intention of following the command. Not that I blamed her. I didn't bring Lali here for show and tell. Just seeing Solstice's face should have been enough.

Without warning, Lali dove at Solstice and pulled down her bottom lip.

"Are you crazy?" I yelled, grabbing Lali's wrist to pull her back. As soon as her fingers released the woman's lip, I projected us out of there. After what had happened with Cade last night, I didn't need anyone else attacking Solstice.

Lali and I appeared in Lanai again, and I released my

hold on her. "What's your problem?" I shouted, pressing my fists into the sides of my forehead. She sank into the sand, and I paced to keep myself from flying off the handle. "Why would you attack Solstice after I just proved she was still alive?"

Her only response was a whimper.

"If you would just *listen,*" I went on ranting, "I could explain everything. Aren't you even a little bit curious why I went to all this trouble just to talk to you?" My whole body clenched, but watching Lali try to push herself up and make it exactly nowhere diffused my anger.

A little.

I blew the air out of my cheeks. "You're going to have to stay put for a while. Projecting is draining, especially when you're not used to it."

"Great...can't...get away."

"Well, hanging out with you hasn't exactly been a bowl of cherries so far, either," I shot back. I regretted it immediately. We were never going to make any progress if we kept going back and forth butting heads.

Taking a deep breath of salty air, I sat down next to her. Maybe the way to get her to act normally was to appeal to her compassion. "But I need your help," I admitted. "If you really can travel, you're the only shot I have of finding my sister."

She blinked at me but stayed quiet. I shoved my hands through my hair, hating how weak I felt. No wonder Cade preferred forcing people to cooperate over asking. But I couldn't keep up this battle of wills with Lali. It was probably my fault she was acting this way, anyway. I'd completely butchered my plan to talk things out with her.

"Please," I forced out.

Still looking shaky, Lali sat up. Her mouth opened, but no sound came out. For once, her face didn't give away what was going on in her head. Based on the struggle it had been to get her to this point, I had to say something to get her on board. Anything.

"Look," I said. "What if I offered you a trade?"

"What?"

I studied her eyes, praying this would work. "Help me find my sister, and I'll take you to your mom."

Her mouth fell open. "You—" She swallowed hard. "You have my mom?"

My stomach dropped as I realized what my offer implied. I'd just screwed up everything.

29

CLASH

"What? No!" I backpedaled. "No, I meant I'll help you find her." I held my breath, waiting for Lali to blow up and accuse me of all the things I was guilty of—kidnapping her mother, keeping the two of them separated for months, destroying her family for the sake of trying to get back part of my own. But her body just slumped like a week-old balloon, making me feel even worse.

I started to explain, but then she scoffed and said, "If you can't even find your own sister, how are you going to find my mom?"

Her words were a slap in the face. Every ounce of guilt in me dried up. Who would say something like that? She had no idea what I'd been through, no idea that I could get her mom back in three seconds while there was no telling how long it would take me to find my sister. Yet, here she was making fun of me for being powerless.

I took a deep breath and shifted my legs to fold them

under me, hoping to let out some of the tension building inside my body. Maybe she didn't mean it to come out so harshly. Even if she did, I still needed her help.

"That's how my power works," I said, somehow managing to keep my tone even. "I can project to anyone I see, even if I only look at a picture. That's why I could appear right in front of you when you were running across the beach, screaming like a banshee. All I have to do is think of someone, and I end up right next to them."

Her face lifted and then fell a second later. "If you can appear next to whoever you want, then why do you need me to get to your sister?"

"Because I can only find people if I know what they look like." I resisted the urge to slam a fist into the sand.

"You don't know what your sister looks like?" Though I was pretty sure Lali hadn't intended to be condescending, her question still stung. The fact that I wouldn't be able to pick Kala out of a crowd killed me. She could walk right past me and I wouldn't even know it. What kind of big brother was I?

"I haven't seen Kala since she was a baby," I admitted, the words burning in my throat.

Lali stayed quiet, and we both watched the water inching toward us. The moon reflected off its surface, creating small sparkles that faded as the ocean's edge pulled back again.

I would have given anything in that moment to have Grandma Naida here to talk me out of my spiraling. She knew how much I hated not knowing my only sister, and she always had a way of making me feel better about it.

But the truth was, everything I knew about Kala was a second-hand memory of her as a baby. My sister was virtually a stranger to me. She probably had no idea I even existed, but I still wished every day that I could trade places with her, that I could take on even a part of the pain she had to endure at the hands of the Eyes and Ears.

"So, how am I supposed to find her?" Lali's voice shoved into my thoughts, lifting part of the heaviness that had settled over me. If she was considering helping me, then all this hadn't been for nothing.

"That depends on how your power works." I shifted to face her. "You can travel, right? That's the only way this can work."

She stared at me, incredulous. "You abducted me before you even knew if I could help?"

"I wouldn't have had to do that if you would've let me explain without screaming bloody murder," I snapped.

I knew I shouldn't have let her comment get under my skin, but it did. Because, in all honesty, I could have held her hostage in the shipping container. I could have kept going along with Cade's failing plan and kept Xiomara captive for the rest of time. But I was trying to move things along faster, for Lali's sake as well as mine. Yes, I wanted my sister back, but getting Kala back sooner meant Lali would get her mom back sooner, too. All Lali had to do was cooperate, but instead—

She scoffed. "Gee, I'm really sorry I made it too hard for you to kidnap me."

Now it was my turn to look incredulous. "You didn't give me a choice," I reminded her. "I tried to do this the easy way. I pretended to sign up at your school just to talk to you, but you bolted in the other direction every time I tried. What was I supposed to do?"

"How about *not* resorting to criminal activity?"

I clenched my jaw. If only she knew the amount of criminal activity I had *not* resorted to for the sake of trying to avoid traumatizing her even more. But she'd made it impossible just to have a conversation.

"You know what?" I growled. "Sometimes morality has to take a back seat. This is my family we're talking about. Imagine not knowing if your little sister was safe, or even alive." My mind jumped back to when I'd almost kidnapped that very little sister. Lali had no idea how close she'd come to facing that reality.

"What would you be willing to do to make sure she was okay?" I challenged. "For just the *chance* to see her again?"

Not surprisingly, Lali stayed quiet.

"Exactly," I said. "You don't know what you'd do in my situation, and for your sake, I hope you never have to find out. So feel free to quit judging me now." Crossing my arms, I stared out at the ocean again. The crashing waves and the smell of the saltwater were the only things keeping me sane, and even they were struggling.

"I never said I was judging you," Lali argued.

"You didn't have to."

"Oh, so you can read minds now? All I'm saying is there are other ways to handle things."

"Not that work." I had already attempted *other ways to handle things*, and it still resulted in Lali freaking out.

"Have you tried?" she pressed.

I glared at her. I so badly wanted to set her straight, to tell her *I have your mother, and I'm not giving her back until you help me*. I knew Lali didn't know how I had tried to be gentler with her than I had been with anyone else, but her verbal attacks made me regret wasting all that energy when I could have just grabbed her like Cade suggested.

"You don't know what I've tried," I snarled.

"Yeah, and based on what I've seen so far, I probably don't want to."

"It doesn't matter!" I exploded, my blood boiling in my veins. "Can you just shut up for five seconds and tell me if you can travel?"

"I can't shut up and tell you at the same time, moron."

Fury stole my response, and I had to take a second to breathe. "For crying out loud, Lali," I finally managed. "Can you travel or not?"

"I don't even know what that means."

I held in a sigh. "Traveling means flying in astral form."

"Well, why can't you do it?"

Still holding my breath, I stared up at the dark sky and prayed for patience. It was going to take a miracle for me to put up with Lali long enough to find out if she could even help.

"I don't have an astral form," I said. "You may have noticed that my whole body projects, along with whatever I'm touching." I lowered my gaze to meet hers. "Now, can

177

you fly in your astral form or not? You do know what an astral form is, don't you?"

She narrowed her eyes. "Shut up. Yes, I know what it is."

Well, thank God for that. I was glad she'd figured it out somehow, even without the letter from her mother.

"But if you don't have an astral form, what makes you so sure I do?" she asked. "How did you even find me to begin with?"

Damn. I hadn't thought through how to answer that last question. I turned to mocking her instead. "I can't shut up and answer questions at the same time," I parroted, mimicking her annoying tone. "*Moron.*"

Her eyes told me she wanted to strangle me. "Let's just get to the point," she huffed. "How do I know if I can fly? And why do I even need to? Where is your sister that I have to fly to get to her?"

"I'll explain everything after you figure out if you can do it."

"How do I do that?"

"You project and try it."

She shifted her weight but didn't say anything.

After a full minute of silence, I blew out my breath. "Or we could build a fire and sing 'Kumbaya' all day. You know, whatever works for you."

Shooting me another death stare, she turned to face the breaking waves. She stayed quiet for a long, uncomfortable moment. When she finally looked at me again, she suddenly seemed nervous.

"The thing is…" she started, and I felt my heart

clench. *Please don't tell me you can't travel. Anything but that.* "I'm still learning how to control it."

My relief released in a heavy exhale. "Of course." I hadn't expected her to have full control of her ability, and I was fine with trying to teach her. I opened my mouth to tell her as much, but her glare caught me off guard.

"Give me a break," she huffed. "I didn't even know I *could* project until yesterday." Her blue-streaked hair blew in the wind, making her look more like a vengeful goddess than a misplaced teenager.

"I didn't mean it like that. I just meant I should have figured you'd still be learning the ropes. But it's not hard once you figure out how to trigger your projecting. After that, it's just a matter of building up your strength."

She blinked. "How long will that take?"

"It's hard to say for sure. I don't have an astral form." I wasn't crazy about the idea of telling her exactly how long it had taken me to get my strength up after I figured out my trigger—the emotion I had to feel in order to project. She was already tightly wound as it was, and I didn't want to give her another reason to flip out. Then again, I didn't want to give her false expectations and have to deal with her losing her cool again later.

"But I got really drained after projecting for the first few weeks or so," I added, my eyes sliding to her face as I waited for her to freak out.

Instead, she asked the one thing that promised to unravel my whole plan: "Then can you take me to my mom first?"

30

AGREEMENT

I COULD ONLY STARE AT HER. HOW HAD I NOT SEEN THAT coming? It was a reasonable request, but I couldn't take Lali to her mother and blow my cover. And there was nothing I could say to turn her down nicely.

Damn it. Why couldn't I even make an agreement without being a jerk? Any response other than *sure, no problem* was going to turn this into another argument, and we'd already wasted enough time bickering.

I had to shut her down quickly. Effectively. Maybe it was time for me to accept that the nice guy approach wasn't going to work after all.

Forcing my face into the harshest expression I could manage, I said, "This ain't my first rodeo, Lali. Helping you now would take away my leverage. Who's to say you'd still go along with this after I took you to your mom?"

"Well, how do I know you'll keep your word?" she bit out.

I shrugged, hating how easily I slipped into the role of the bully. But I couldn't exactly tell Lali I was holding her mom captive. I didn't want this to turn into me using that as leverage.

Even if I did, Lali would be useless. Judging from our interaction so far, I was sure it would turn her into an emotional mess. Well, *more* of an emotional mess. If I had to be a jerk to keep that from happening, then so be it.

"You'll just have to trust me," I told her.

"Oh, but you can't trust me?"

"I'm still deciding."

Her face flushed, and I could practically feel the hatred coming off her body in waves as powerful as the ocean crashing beside us. "In case you forgot," she snarled, *"you're* the bad guy in this equation, not me."

"Maybe so. But we're doing this my way."

She tried staring me down, but I didn't flinch. "You need me," she tried. "You're the one who said you went through so much *trouble* to talk to me."

I let out a sardonic laugh. All the trouble I'd gone to had been my failed effort to do the right thing, and it had only come back to bite me. All Lali had done was prove that Cade was right. *Again.* Trying to do things the nice way wasn't efficient, and it caused me more headaches. Apparently, threats were the only way to get anything done, especially with someone as bullheaded as Lali.

"That's right," I said. "I did. I should've just appeared at your dinner table and abducted you in front of your entire family, but I tried to be human about it. And now you're trying to take advantage of my compassion."

She squinted. "*Right.* I'm the one taking advantage of you."

I could feel this turning into another fight. Time to pull out the big guns and shut her down, Cade-style. "You know, this whole bargaining thing was really just me doing you a favor. I could hold one of your sisters hostage until you help me. Would that be a more effective way of getting you to cooperate?"

"Don't you dare threaten them," she hissed.

"Well, you're not giving me much of a choice."

"I'll call the police."

I wanted to laugh. Was that supposed to be a threat? She had to realize how ridiculous it sounded. "Go ahead. They'd never be able to catch me."

She kept her mouth shut, but the tension in her expression told me she knew I was right. Still, she scrutinized my face, moonlight reflecting in her eyes as they searched for a way to one-up me. I stared right back, keeping my expression smooth. I couldn't let her see how much I was depending on her.

Though the air was hot and thick, she shuddered, and I saw the fire behind her glare die out. "Fine," she conceded. "You win. I'll help you."

...I know how much you hated me in that moment, but ~~I could have kissed you~~ I wanted to jump for joy. After everything else had failed, you were all I had to keep me going, to keep me believing that there was a chance for me to find Kala. I don't know if you can ever understand how much that meant to me.

I admit that I shouldn't have been so quick to snap at you and threaten your family, and I'm sorry for that. It seemed like my only choice then, despite my plans to get you to help me without resorting to threats. I told myself I would have time to make it up to you—I knew it was going to be a long road for us when it came to teaching you how to control your projections.

Even so, I don't think either of us was prepared for where that road would lead us...

31

COVER

I APPEARED IN DELTA'S HOUSE, STILL REELING FROM MY victory with Lali. I'd wanted to get started teaching her to trigger her projections right away, but the bags under her eyes told me she was fading fast. I was sure projecting with me so many times had taken its toll on her, and I didn't need her keeling over—especially since she seemed to be my best shot at getting to Alea. I dropped her off at her house so she could get some rest and promised I would come back later.

In the meantime, I wanted Cade to know we had something else to focus on besides sitting around waiting for Delta.

"Uncle Cade!" I rushed to where he sat in Delta's living room, poring over the photo albums we'd already been through. "I was right," I announced. "Lali has an astral form." I left out the part about her not knowing if she could travel. It shouldn't matter; Cade already explained to me that having an astral form pretty much guaranteed the ability to travel.

He frowned at me from the floral-print chair. "What are you talking about? How could you know that?"

"Because I talked to her." A smile stretched over my face as I sat down on the sofa across from him.

"Oh, really? You just waltzed up to her and asked?"

"More or less. The point is, she could get us to Alea."

He rubbed his eyes with the base of his hand. "Look, I don't want to discourage you, but even if she can travel—even if she can get us to Alea—it won't help us get Kala. You can't get into the lab. There's a block around it that only the most powerful Astralii know how to penetrate. That's why I need my ability. They won't let me into the lab without it."

I huffed. "Well, what were you going to do before? Back when you thought I might be able to travel, you were planning on going to Alea with no ability."

"I hadn't thought things through, nephew. At first, yes, I was disappointed that you don't have an astral form, but now that we've started hunting down XODUS, I see that it was all for a reason. And you know what? Maybe Lali came into it for a reason, too. Can her ability help us find the others? Did you talk to her about that?"

"Not yet," I said, though I had no intention of pulling Lali into that dead end. "But if she can get us to Alea, I can find a way into the lab. I'm sure—"

Cade shut the photo album in his hand so hard I jumped. "That's way too dangerous."

I heaved a sigh. I understood why he was worried—

after all, they did horrible things to semmies in that lab— but one of these days, he was going to have to accept that my going in might be the only way. As much as it scared him, I would do it in a heartbeat if there was a chance I could get Kala out of there. But maybe my uncle didn't need to know that just yet. Maybe he didn't need to know about my plans with Lali at all.

Later that afternoon, after a quick visit to check on Solstice and explain what happened with Lali, I appeared back at Xiomara's house. Lali was on the sofa, staring into space with the dog in her lap. He barked before she noticed me, and she jolted so hard she nearly fell over the side of the couch.

I chuckled, but Lali wasn't amused. "What are you doing in here?" she asked, crossing her arms as the dog rushed over to my feet with his tail wagging. For some reason, his excitement made me nervous, like Lali might somehow figure out that I'd snooped around her room based on her pet's reaction to me.

I pushed aside the irrational concern as I bent down to scratch his ears. With all the things I was hiding, Lali figuring out I'd read part of a diary entry was the least of my worries.

"Just came to see how you were doing," I said. "And to see if you were up for practicing." The dog jumped to try and lick my face, and I couldn't help but laugh.

"Gotty," Lali scolded. "Stop."

I arched a brow. "Gotty?"

"It's short for Gottfried."

I nodded, fighting another laugh. This family managed to come up with the weirdest names.

"My dad got him after my mom left." She shrugged. "He gave the dog the name my mom refused to let him give one of my brothers."

"Oh." A spite name. I didn't know how to respond.

Lali pulled her knees to her chest, and her dark hair spilled around her thighs. "So what kind of practicing?"

"Well, for starters—"

Gottfried took off toward the kitchen howling.

"Crap!" Lali jumped to her feet. "My brothers and sisters are here." Grabbing my arm, she practically dragged me upstairs and into her room, slamming the door behind us.

"Panic much?" I teased.

"You have to go," she whispered, shooing me with her hands. "Do your little disappearing thing."

"What about practicing?"

"Keep your voice down." She pulled me away from the door, and I nearly bumped into her dresser. "If they find you in here, I'll be grounded for life. We'll have to practice after they go to sleep."

I scoffed. "After they go to sleep? It's not even four o'clock."

"Yeah, well I can't go running off whenever I feel like it. And besides, I have to start dinner at some point, too."

Start dinner? Was that normal?

It probably is for her since you hijacked her mom. The thought made me lower my gaze.

"Lali?" a voice called from downstairs.

"Be down in a sec!" Lali gave me an impatient look. "Can you come back around—" She slapped a palm to her head. "Crap."

"What?" I asked, starting to feel tense myself. She was like a walking ball of nerves.

She rushed over to grab her phone from the nightstand. "I meant to cancel my plans with my friends."

"You made plans to go out tonight?"

"Yeah, before I knew about the whole astral projection thing. We were supposed to go bowling."

"Oh, that's perfect," I said, formulating an idea. "Great cover."

She frowned, still holding her phone. "What?"

"You won't have to wait for your family to go to sleep. Let them think you're going bowling. Then while you're out, I can come pick you up." To keep up appearances, I would have to find a place to rent a car—preferably somewhere with an employee I could bribe to let me rent something even though I was way under twenty-five.

"What am I supposed to say to my friends about where I'm going?"

"I don't know. Pretend you're sick or something."

She looked at me like I'd just suggested she slaughter a nun. "You want me to lie to them?"

"Yeah. What's the big deal? You've never lied about where you were going before?" Her silence answered for her, and I laughed out loud. "Really?"

She scowled. "Forgive me for not leading a life of crime."

I swallowed another snicker for fear she might throw her phone at my face. She was so offended by the thought of lying it was almost cute.

"Okay, better idea," I said. "I'll come with you. Tell your friends you invited the new kid along because you felt bad or something. Then run to the bathroom like you need to hurl."

She wrinkled her nose. "Why?"

"So you can call me from the stall. Then I'll say it's my uncle that I have to pick up from dropping his car off at the shop." I grinned. For a plan made on the fly, I was sure it would work.

My soon-to-be partner in crime shook her head. "It was way too easy for you to come up with that whole lie."

"It's a gift."

"Lali, I need help with my math," a high-pitched voice called.

"Coming, Sal!" Lali tossed her phone onto the bed and made another shooing motion. "Okay, seriously, you have to go."

"I'm going," I said. "But you have to admit, my plan is a perfect cover on both ends."

She rolled her eyes. "Just be there at eight."

"Where is there?"

"The only bowling alley within twenty miles. Drop Pins."

"Droppings? Nice." Another naming fail.

"Drop. *Pins,*" she corrected, enunciating each word.

"Name's still horrible."

"Whatever! Just get out of here!"

"Okay. Don't forget to tell your friends you invited me."

She tried to murder me with her eyes.

Giving her a playful wink, I disappeared. The next second, I was back in Lanai. The sun was up now, bathing the crystal clear water in its glow as I collapsed into the warm sand. The scene around me was as beautiful as ever, but even in my favorite place in the world, I knew it was going to feel like forever waiting until eight o'clock.

INVISIBILITY

LALI WAS EASILY THE WORST LIAR OF ALL TIME. AND THE most pathetic. It took us forever to get out of the stupid bowling alley, and she'd nearly had a conniption in the parking lot because she lied to her friends—even though that was the plan going into it. As if we hadn't wasted enough potential practicing time waiting for her to work up the courage to pretend to be sick, she got sidetracked with questions when we finally made it to Lanai.

I didn't have a problem quickly explaining what Astralii were and that astral projection abilities came out differently for semmies, but then she hit me with a question I wasn't prepared for: "How did you even know I was a—a *semmie?*"

My heart stuttered. I wanted to kick myself for not anticipating it. Of course she would want to know that; any normal person would. But I hadn't thought through an explanation that wouldn't give away the truth. Striving for an answer that would buy some time, I shoved a hand through my hair and said, "For one, you don't know how to control your ability." I knew that wasn't what she meant, but I needed a minute to think. What could I say that wouldn't incriminate me?

"But how did you know I had an ability in the first place?" she pressed.

"There are ways to trace astral energy." Another purposefully vague answer, but at least the statement in and of itself was true.

Lali seemed to be satisfied with it at first, but then she frowned. "You were in my hallway before I ever used my power."

I studied the sand as if it might give me the response I needed to get her off my back. "There must've been some kind of residue from when your mom still lived there or something."

As soon as it came out, I cringed, realizing my mistake. I scrambled to think of an answer for how I knew her mother was the Astralis and not her father, but by some miracle, Lali didn't hit me with the question I expected.

Instead, she asked, "After two months?" She looked thoughtful, not suspicious.

"Apparently," I blurted, trying not to let my relief show. "But we haven't found any others to compare notes."

I needed to change the subject. Fast. I was talking out of my ass, and I was sure it was going to catch up to me. I decided to go for the easiest target—her family. Saying something negative about them was surely the fastest way to get Lali ranting and on to another topic. I'd seen enough of her fiery side to be confident that she'd snap if I played my cards right.

"Your parents really should've explained this to you," I mumbled, doing my best to look disgusted.

"Yeah, well, my mom is gone, and my dad doesn't even know about any of this."

Though I already knew about her clueless dad from overhearing Xiomara and Solstice's argument the other night, I pretended to be shocked. "Your mom never told the poor guy he was marrying a freak? That's messed up." It was a low blow, and I knew it, but at least Lali would stop grilling me. I'd have to go over everything on my own later and make up a story so I could have answers ready for her next time she wanted to play Twenty Questions.

Sure enough, Lali was already turning purple. "She tried," she snapped. "My dad just didn't believe her. He's a scientist, and he's logical. And my mom used to tell us stories about a girl named Astralis who could travel the world in her mind, which was obviously her way of leading into it."

That got my attention. Why would Xiomara tell them "stories" instead of the truth? Well, Grandma Naida hadn't exactly been forthcoming with me, either. Cade guessed she wanted me to have a normal childhood. Maybe Xiomara was hoping to do the same thing for Lali.

Too bad it backfired.

"Besides," Lali went on ranting. "You just said this is

new to you, too. Your parents didn't explain it all to you either, so lay off mine."

"My parents were murdered before I could even *pronounce* Astralis. I'd say they get a pass."

Lali blinked at me like a doe in the headlights, the same reaction I'd seen countless times after people found out I was an orphan. It was the expression I hated most. A wave crashed and rolled in close to where we sat before she found her voice. "Kai, I—"

"Spare me the sympathy speech." I'd heard enough of the backpedaling people did after finding out about my parents to last a lifetime. I knew I'd started this whole fight, but now I was more than happy to end it. Hopefully, Lali was done with the third degree.

"No," she protested. "I feel terrible. I didn't mean to—"

I held up my hand. "Look, we didn't sneak you out to sit here and chitchat about family all night. Let's focus on figuring out how your power works."

She looked like she wanted to say something else to apologize, but she settled for leaning back in the sand. "How do we do that?" she asked. "I haven't been able to project when I want to. It just kind of happens on its own, and I show up in random places—usually next to your uncle."

So I'd been right about her ability being similar to mine. "Okay. So you can track people like I can."

"Yeah, except I can't seem to find the only person I want to track."

I knew she meant her mom, and I offered her an understanding smile. "Welcome to my world."

It did seem pretty screwed up that both of us had powers that could find anyone except the people we wanted. That alone should've given us something to bond over so we at least had a common ground to stand on. Maybe we could even be friends. I hadn't had a real friend in years.

We looked at each other for a long moment before she fidgeted in the sand. "What's that about anyway?" she huffed. "Is there some rule that says we can't use our powers to benefit ourselves?"

"Not if I can help it," I said. "We can both get what we want, Lali. We just have to work together."

She nodded, determination bunching her brow. "I can do that."

Finally. "Good. Then let's figure out your trigger."

"My trigger?"

I hurried through the explanation of how she would have to find the feeling that made her project, the way I had discovered that a longing to get away made my power kick in. Then she would be able to manipulate her emotions and create whatever feeling she needed to in order to make her ability work.

Of course, that was easier said than done. At first, she thought her trigger might be the desire to follow someone. But then she couldn't project after me when I disappeared, and it didn't take long for her to get cranky.

I kicked out my feet in front of me and sighed. "It took me a few guesses, too." I hoped that would reassure her, but she was so all over the place it was tough to know what would be helpful and what would set her off. "Try thinking about the last time you did it," I offered. "What was going through your head?"

She paused to think. "I was freaked out. I saw you talking to Cade, and I thought he was a murderer. I was convinced you guys were following me."

Damn. She had picked up on my stalking her. And here I'd thought my new student gig was clever.

"Part of me wanted to run after you both so I could figure out who you were," she went on. "Then, the next thing I knew, I was standing right in front of you."

Wait. What? When was she ever standing in front of us?

"I don't remember seeing you," I said.

"Yeah, no one seems to see me."

No way! I gaped at her. "Are you serious? You're *invisible?*"

"Is that bad?"

I wanted to laugh with relief. "That's awesome!" This was even better than I thought. Astralii—and most semmies from what Cade had told me—were visible in astral form. If Lali wasn't, she'd be able to spy on the Eyes and Ears and figure out all their secrets, like how to get into the lab despite the block.

Lali's face gave away her confusion at my excitement, and I tried to explain. "I just assumed Cade and Solstice were too distracted to notice you," I breathed. "But if no one can see you, you might be more useful than I thought."

"Useful? I'm not a power drill, Kai."

I had to stop myself from rolling my eyes. "That's not what I meant." But even her attitude couldn't bring down my excitement at this discovery. Now I was more determined than ever to get Lali's ability under control, and even more confident that she was the key to finding my sister.

33

FLIGHT

I BLEW OUT MY BREATH, DESPERATE TO SAY SOMETHING that would calm Lali down. *Again.* Clearly, bringing her to the most relaxing place I'd ever seen, on a gorgeous sunny day, had done nothing to help her unwind.

As soon as we figured out her trigger was fear, the first thing she did was try and project to her mother, even after I told her not to do it. Of course, she hit the block and went into full-blown meltdown mode. I projected myself into the same block hoping to get her off my case about taking her to Xiomara myself, but then Lali flipped out because she assumed her mom was dead.

Thinking on my toes again, I'd just made up a story about her mom setting up a block to prevent Lali from coming after her, but that backfired and only made Lali storm down the beach claiming she didn't want to find her mother at all. She still stood with her back to me, and honestly, she was making me reconsider my hope of friendship. I wasn't sure I had the energy to keep up with her roller coaster of emotions.

"Did you ever consider the possibility that she's trying to protect you guys?" I tried, praying that would put out some of the fire raging inside Lali. I couldn't believe I was defending Xiomara, but actually, what I said was kind of true. Xiomara had only agreed to set up the block because she didn't want Lali to become obsessed with trying to find her.

"From *what?*" Lali threw out her arms so hard I thought they might fly out of their sockets. "She didn't protect me from being terrified and thinking I was losing my mind."

She wanted to. My conscience called me a slew of unflattering names. I told myself I didn't owe Xiomara anything, but letting her daughter blindly hate her based on my actions and lies still gnawed at me.

"Yeah, but there's a lot you don't understand about what it means to be a semmie," I said. "There are people who will kill you for it."

"What are you talking about?"

A breeze blew across my face, the air a cool contrast to the heat rising in my cheeks. I hated the thought of discussing the Astralii responsible for taking my family from me, but I had to get Lali back on track.

"I'm talking about the Eyes and Ears," I told her.

It felt like another round of forever as I explained Alea, how the Alean government banned Astralii from having kids with non-Astralii to prevent the creation of more semmies, and how the Eyes and Ears were nothing but glorified spies who kidnapped illegal semmies and killed their parents. I saw the pieces connect in Lali's head, and I knew she'd just realized why I was an orphan in search of his semmie sister.

I nodded. "They have Kala. They'd have gotten me, too, but I wasn't there when the raid happened. My grandma took me to the store while Kala was napping so my parents could rest, and when we got back—"

I run through the front door, clutching the plastic toy frog in my palm. Mommy and Daddy will think it's so funny, the way he jumps when you push on the tab coming out of his bum. "Mommy!" I call out over the swishing of my shorts. "Daddy!" They don't answer. I turn into the living room, and one of the chairs is flipped over. When I look to the left, I see Mommy and Daddy. Why are they sleeping on the floor? No, they're not sleeping. Their eyes are open. Wide open like they are scared. Their faces make me scared, too.

I cleared my throat. "I should've been there."

"Kai." Lali's voice sounded like it was on the brink of breaking. "You couldn't have known."

That was what everyone said. But there was no excuse. "I still should've been there for her," I insisted. "I could've gotten her out. Even if they had us both in the lab, as soon as I figured out my power, I could've gotten us out. But she's trapped there because I was a bratty little three-year-old and wouldn't stop whining until someone took me to the store to get some stupid quarter-machine toy." The familiar stab of regret made me wince. If I had just been more patient...

"I'm so sorry," Lali whispered.

I kicked a shell into the ocean. I hated that she felt

bad for me when she should have loathed me for what I'd done. She *would* have loathed me if she knew the truth.

But I couldn't dwell on that. Not right now. I turned to face her. "I'm not looking for your sympathy. Just some assistance."

"Of course." She looked at me like she'd just noticed the color of my eyes or something. "I want to help. Really, I do."

For now. As long as you don't know the truth. "Thank you," I said anyway. "I want to help you, too." That was mostly true. I wanted to give her back her mother, because that would mean I finally had my sister. "But I can't do that if you freak out when I tell you things. There's still a lot you don't understand, and you can't go jumping to conclusions before you know the whole story."

She straightened up, and I hoped that meant I'd finally gotten through to her. "I'm sorry. I'm just so lost. Everything is coming at me at once."

I sighed. I could understand that. Maybe I was being too hard on her, throwing too much at her in a short time. I was so eager to get her to help me, I'd forgotten she was a scared sixteen-year-old girl who hadn't had the luxury of being prepared for any of this like I had. Even with Cade there to guide me, it had been a lot to deal with.

"I know the feeling," I admitted, remembering the number it had done on me when I realized that what I'd believed for most of my life wasn't true. "For years, I thought they'd killed Kala, too. Right after I developed my ability, Cade told me there was still a good chance she was alive, and that my projecting might help us find her. Talk about overwhelming."

"Kai?" Lali's voice came out too high, and her sympathetic expression had morphed into fear. "Could they…is there a chance they know about my family?"

Oh. I hadn't considered that. From the way Cade talked about the Eyes and Ears, it seemed they mostly went off tips. I couldn't imagine anyone would know about Lali's family, especially in a small town like Browshire.

Unless it's already on their radar like South Creek.

That seemed unlikely, though, and I didn't need Lali panicking again. I'd just gotten her calmed down.

"I doubt it," I said with as much conviction as I could muster. "I lived with my mom, my grandma, and Kala in a kind of underground community. It was full of Astralii spouses and their semmie children. My dad was an Astralis, so he lived in Alea most of the time and had to visit us in secret." Not that I remembered many of those visits.

I kept going before the heaviness of that thought pulled me down any further. "All the semmies' Astralii parents had to sneak away from Alea to visit. Our whole group was supposed to be a secret, but someone must've leaked our location to the Eyes and Ears." Saying the words out loud made my blood boil. If I ever found the person responsible, I'd kill him myself.

Lali's eyes darted out toward the water, and I wondered if she could read the murderous thoughts on my face.

I shook my head to clear it. "We shouldn't have lived together in one spot. It was too easy for them to get to all of us at once. We should've lived our lives apart like your family instead of clustering in San Francisco."

"San Francisco?" she squeaked.

"Yeah. What's wrong?"

"My parents used to live there. *I* used to live there." She swallowed. "Is there a chance we lived in that community, too?"

I felt my brow furrow. Was *that* how Xiomara knew me? How Delta knew me?

"Maybe," I replied, running through the possibilities myself. Not that it mattered. Even if Xiomara and the rest of the group had been my neighbors, it didn't change anything. We weren't suddenly going to be friends. They had destroyed my uncle's life.

"But I thought you said your dad doesn't know anything about Astralii," I said, remembering Lali's earlier rant.

"He doesn't. But how old are you?"

Her question caught me off guard. "Seventeen. Why?"

"Well, if you were only three when the raid happened, then it was around the time my family moved to Browshire. That seems like a big coincidence."

She was right. That had to be it. Maybe Xiomara only lived there before she met her husband, and then left. Apparently, she'd kept Lali's dad in the dark. But even if they hadn't lived in the community itself at the time of the raid, they had to be near enough and in contact with the people there for Xiomara to hear about it and flee to the opposite side of the country.

I shifted my weight, feeling the sand mold beneath my feet. We couldn't afford to get hung up on our potential shared history. I knew Lali deserved to know the truth, but we were going to waste all the time we had talking instead of practicing.

"Well, we can only get answers from one person," I said, doing my best to pull us back to the task at hand.

"Yeah." The corners of her mouth drooped. "One person who's impossible to find."

"Not impossible." I reached for a story that would keep Lali focused and motivated to get to Alea without sending her into another series of questions. One came to me easily, and my mind jumped to when she had scolded me for coming up with my plan to lie to her friends so quickly before we'd gone bowling. With everything she'd asked me already, I was surprised she hadn't just flat out asked if I was making this up as I went. Honestly, it seemed like I was. I just had to remind myself that it was for a reason.

"I have a pretty good idea of where to start," I told her.

"What? How?"

The hope in her gray eyes gutted me, but I couldn't stop. I needed Lali as invested in getting to Alea as I was, and I could only think of one way to make that happen.

"Well, the crystal that blocks astral energy can only be found in Alea," I lied.

She stared at me with her mouth hanging open. "You think my mom is in Alea?"

"She has to be. That's the only place to get the crystal." I half-expected my nose to start growing as I spoke. "And even if she's not, there's a way to get through energy blocks." There. Maybe if I threw in at least some truth, my fibs would be less obvious. "Cade told me it's possible, but only the most powerful Astralii know about it. We just have to find out what that is, which should be easy with your invisible spy skills."

Her face lit up. "So once I get to Alea…"

"I'll project to you," I finished for her. "Then when I've seen the area, I'll be able to get there whenever I want, and I'll be able to get us around quickly."

"You can project to places, too?"

"Yeah. I just visualize landmarks instead of people."

"And you know where to find Kala once we get there?"

I explained that Cade would know what to do, but I could tell from Lali's reaction that she didn't trust him after what she saw happen between him and Solstice. I still defended him. He was my uncle after all. And I was sure he would help us figure out what to do once we made it to Alea—once Lali figured out how to get into the lab.

Next, I ran through some quick instructions on how to figure out if she could fly in astral form, and a determined look passed over her face. She bit her lip and closed her eyes. I could hear her forcing herself to breathe faster to mimic the body's response to fear, just like we'd talked about earlier.

She started sounding like she was about to hyperventilate, but then her breath moved into a peaceful rhythm. Her face relaxed, as if she were sleeping on her feet. I scrutinized her serene expression, looking for any flicker or hint of what she was doing in her astral form, but her features gave nothing away.

As I studied her, I couldn't help but notice that she really was pretty—when she wasn't ranting. Her olive skin was smooth and even, and her thick lashes curled up where they pressed against her cheeks. A light gust of air shifted her hair along her shoulders, and I had to fight the urge to reach out and touch it.

I wasn't sure how long I watched her like that, lost in examining her face and imagining what we could accomplish once she mastered her ability, but without warning her breathing became choppy again. The next second, she was falling.

I lunged to catch her, my arms looping around hers just in time. "Easy," I said, easing her to the sand. "I think you pushed yourself a little too far."

"I did it," she whispered, her eyelids struggling to stay open. "I flew."

34

PEACE

"I THINK THAT'S ENOUGH PRACTICE FOR TODAY. YOU'RE looking a little queasy." I eyed Lali, surprised she hadn't passed out yet. She'd spent the last few hours on the beach projecting, and even with the darkening evening sky, I could see how her eyes drooped.

"Yeah, I'm starting to get dizzy," she admitted, wiping her forehead. The temperature had dropped since Lali shed her sweater in favor of the tank top beneath it, but the strain of projecting still made her sweat.

"Don't worry, you'll get stronger the more you practice," I promised. "It's kind of like working a muscle."

She inhaled deeply, studying the water as it ebbed and flowed. She looked the most relaxed I'd seen her, and I realized I felt lighter somehow, too. It was nice to have confidence in an approach after so many recent failures.

Lali was getting pretty good at triggering her projections—at least, from what she'd told me. It wasn't like I could see anything with her invisible astral self. If it weren't for the fact that I knew she was borderline inca-pable of lying, I might not have believed how quickly she was picking it up.

I let myself get carried away with the possibilities. Now that Lali had figured out how to project, we could spend tomorrow focusing on permeating—or moving through objects in astral form. She would have to be able to permeate in order to get to the transposer that switched astral forms to physical bodies in Alea. Unfortu-nately, I couldn't project to Lali's astral form—I'd tried while she was practicing—so I needed her to switch to her physical body before I could project after her to get to the other realm.

But before she went there at all, I wanted to make sure the transposer would work for her. As far as I'd heard, transposers hadn't been tested on semmies. Full-blooded Astralii used them to switch into their physical bodies when they traveled between realms, but I didn't want to have Lali work up her strength and go all the way to Alea if I couldn't follow her.

I'd figured the best way to make sure the transposer would work on Lali was to have her try out the one in this realm. She would still have to be able to permeate to reach it—it was hidden in a closed tunnel under the San Francisco Bay—so basically, if she could successfully get to it and switch to her physical body, all systems were go for the transposer in Alea.

"You never told me the name of this place," Lali said, pulling me out of my thoughts.

My smile was weak at best. "Lanai." Just saying the

name filled me with peace, but it was always tinged with sadness.

Lali made an agreeable sound. "Cool."

I could tell she had never heard the name. "Hawaii," I informed her. "This is one of my favorite beaches. My mom and dad brought Kala and me when we were little." I left out the fact that I didn't really remember it.

"It's beautiful."

"We can come back to practice again tomorrow if you want. But right now, you should get some sleep." I clambered to my feet, deciding not to overwhelm her with details of our next steps until the following day. I knew permeating would be hard to learn—Cade told me how much work it took to master it back when he thought I might be able to do it. I couldn't, of course, which we'd concluded was because I didn't have an astral form. But Lali at least had a chance, so long as I could help her maintain her composure.

"Come on," I said. "I'll take you to the hotel." I already had one in mind; I figured out where I'd book a room for her while I was sitting around watching her practice projecting.

"Hotel?" Lali asked, looking scandalized.

I tried not to laugh. "Yeah. It would kind of blow our cover if you show up at your house again." I reminded her that she'd told her family she would be spending the night at her friend Paisley's house.

"I can't just sleep on the couch at your place?"

"Eh." What was the best way to word this? I had already told her in the parking lot of the bowling alley that my uncle wasn't happy about my working with her, but she was so flustered about lying to her friends that she hadn't asked me why. "I'd rather Cade not know we're working together until after we've made it to Alea."

"Oh. Right." She squirmed. "So what exactly is his problem with me again?"

More questions I hadn't thought through how to answer. I couldn't tell her he thought it was too dangerous when I'd finally gotten her to agree to help. I made up an excuse about how Cade didn't want to waste time explaining stuff to a semmie when a full-blooded Astralis would already know everything. Before she could suggest I go with a full-blooded Astralis instead of her, I told her we hadn't found one yet because they all kept their true natures hidden to be safe.

"I thought you said Cade can trace astral energy," she said, making me cringe. It was like she was poking for holes in my story. If I didn't know any better, I would have thought she'd figured out that I was full of crap.

"He can," I lied, straining to keep up with her. Technically, I never said he could trace astral energy—I only said there were ways to do it—but making that distinction would only lead to more questions. "And he's trying. I don't fully understand how it works, but there are limitations." She yawned, and I pounced on the opportunity to change the subject. "We can talk about all this later. You need rest."

She paused, and her face fell. "Um, can you take me home first? I left all my stuff in Nelson's truck."

Nelson. I fought the urge to scowl at his name. He was

the guy I'd seen bringing Lali to school the previous day, and the guy I'd almost come to blows with at the bowling alley because he didn't want me driving her home. He was way too protective of her, and just as big a goody-two-shoes. They were like a little morally-superior match made in heaven. Something about the thought made my stomach turn.

"Sure," I said anyway. I took Lali's hand, fighting off disturbing images of her and Nelson in nun and monk gear.

I projected us to her room, and she started digging out clothes. I caught a glimpse of her bra, and I couldn't stop my mind from running with the image of her in it. I looked around her room to distract myself and spotted the half-finished painting on her easel.

Lali announced that she was ready to go, but I didn't take my eyes off her art. I tilted my head toward the canvas. "You're really good."

"Er, thanks." Even without looking, I could tell she'd shifted her weight. Apparently, she didn't take compliments well.

"Why don't you hang up any of your stuff?" I asked, glancing around at her prints of other people's paintings.

"Dalí intimidates me."

"Why?"

"Are you kidding? He's incredible. Just look at this." She pointed to a boxy image among the cluster on her ceiling. "*Gala Contemplating the Mediterranean Sea which at Twenty Meters becomes a Portrait of Abraham Lincoln.*"

I failed to hide a snort. "That's quite a title."

"Yeah, I know. But it's amazing," she gushed, more animated than I'd seen her all day. "Up close, it's a woman looking out a window, but from far away, it looks like Lincoln."

"Ah." I felt the corner of my mouth twitch. It was cute when she fangirled.

"Don't act like that's not awesome." She gazed longingly at the painting, which did sort of look like Lincoln now that she mentioned it. "I'd give anything to see it in person."

I studied the print and decided I'd project Lali to the real painting one day. Maybe that would be my way of thanking her for her help once we got to Alea.

"Forget it," she muttered, her cheeks flushing. "I'm easily amused. Ready to go?"

"Only if you're done drooling."

She grabbed my hand, half smiling and half scowling. "Shut up and take me to the hotel."

"Lucky for you, I actually *can* do both of those things at the same time." I gave her a playful nudge.

She fought it, but I could tell she wanted to laugh. "You're still a moron."

A fluttering feeling took over the top half of my body. Was I flirting with her?

Was she flirting with me?

I pushed away the thoughts. The last thing I needed was to get emotions involved. Still, I knew it would be much easier to work with Lali if she liked me. Now that we seemed to have made peace, I wanted to keep it that way.

With that in mind, I took her to the nicest hotel I knew. For some reason, it made me feel good to put her in their best suite, as if it somehow made up for what I'd done to her and her family. Thankfully, the concierge working third shift was happy to take a little extra cash to let me book the suite despite my young age.

Lali made a fuss about the cost, and I had to work to keep myself from laughing in her face. If only she knew how little of an issue money was for me. But there was no way I was going to tell her that I ripped off various stores when Cade and I were low on cash. She had just stopped looking at me like I was pond scum, and I knew she'd never understand that I had to steal so my uncle could stay home with me. She couldn't even handle a little fib to her friends.

After reassuring her that the cost wasn't an issue, I led Lali up to her accommodations for the night. The awe in her eyes as she took in the lavish suite was the last thing I saw before I projected to Solstice's apartment.

It was late, but thankfully Solstice was still awake and staring into the flames crackling in her fireplace. She jumped when she saw me. "What do you think you're doing? You can't just show up in my home whenever you want."

I shot her a look. "Considering that I don't have to let you stay in your home, I say I can." She glowered in response, but I kept going. "Listen, do you know how to permeate? Or, did you—you know—before you lost your ability?"

She crossed her arms over her maroon sweatshirt. "Why does that matter?"

"Because I can't do it, so Lali will need your input. Obviously, I can't have Xiomara explain, and I've already told Lali that Cade wouldn't be involved."

"So I get the pleasure by default?"

"You're also the only one who gets to stay at your own place," I reminded her. "I'm sure Xiomara would love to be home, too. So if you want to *keep* staying here, I'm going to need your help."

Solstice sucked her teeth. "Fine. Let's go."

"Well, she's going to sleep now. I'll come get you tomorrow after she wakes up."

"Can't wait."

I was too excited to let her sarcasm get to me. If Lali picked up permeating as quickly as she'd picked up triggering her projections, we could be in Alea even sooner than I thought.

COACH

LALI SAT BOLT UPRIGHT ON THE HOTEL SOFA. "I ALMOST had it."

My heart skipped as I pushed off the wall to face her. "Really?"

She nodded, her ponytail wobbling so the hints of blue wove in and out of the dark locks. She almost looked like a different person with her hair pulled back and without all that crazy eyeliner. From what I could tell, she didn't have any makeup on, and she looked radiant—if a little out of place with her long-sleeved shirt and jeans in a Hawaiian resort.

"Don't get your hopes up." Solstice slunk back into the white leather chair she'd claimed. "I'm sure it will be a while."

I shot her a glare, and not for the first time since I brought her here. Though she'd explained the basics of permeating to Lali, she'd been discouraging the poor girl at every turn. As a result, the two of them had been bickering all morning.

"Thanks." Lali gave Solstice a dirty look of her own. "That's really encouraging."

I shook my head. With all Solstice's discouragement, it was a miracle that Lali had managed to make progress with permeating at all. She'd been trying to get through the glass coffee table in her astral form for the last twenty minutes, and from the sound of it, she was getting closer to pulling it off.

No thanks to the worst coach of all time.

Solstice at least went along with the story we made up about the Eyes and Ears stealing her ability—it was the best I could come up with to avoid explaining why a bunch of women trapped Cade's astral energy—but she'd done everything else to make this experience as painful as possible. Lali held her own, though, for once making me glad she had a fiery side. Even so, it was all I could do not to tear my hair out listening to them argue.

I wondered if Solstice was being spiteful because I forced her to help us or if she made a point to argue with whoever was around. There was no reason she should still be angry with Lali after the whole lip incident. I'd already explained what happened, and Lali had apologized as soon as she saw the woman again.

"Look, I have to get going," Solstice said suddenly. "I've done all I can do."

Hardly. I shot her a questioning look. Why was she so eager to leave? Then again, it didn't matter. I was happy to get rid of her. I walked over, holding in the less-than-friendly words I wanted to shout at her.

"Back home?" I asked, hoping my falsely pleasant tone would remind her that my letting her stay in her apartment was still a privilege I didn't have to allow.

"Yes." She scowled as I took her hand, and I knew she'd caught on to my message.

"Thank you for coming over to help," Lali piped up. Her words took me by surprise. Why was she being nice after Solstice had done little more than shoot her down all morning? I had to admit, even though she could be a little Mother Teresa at times, I admired Lali's determination to be a good person.

But I wasn't that nice. Just for spite, I decided I'd take Solstice to Delta's house, where Cade was still camped out waiting in vain. Somehow it felt like irritating Solstice could be my way of standing up for Lali. Besides, the deal had been that I let Solstice stay at her apartment in exchange for her help, not her negativity. She'd brought it on herself.

She didn't bother responding to Lali with more than a nod, which only annoyed me more. *Delta's house it is.*

We appeared in one of the floral print covered bedrooms, and Solstice frowned. "Where are we?"

"Delta's house," I said. "Since you made every effort to discourage the one person who can help us, I thought you should hang out with Cade today. Maybe you two can swap stories of how you can't go along with anything *I* want."

I didn't even feel bad when Solstice's face twisted. "You can't leave me here with him," she hissed.

"Oh, but I can."

"Nephew?" Cade called.

Solstice reached out, but I disappeared before she could grab me. I needed to show her that I was in charge, that I wasn't going to let her take advantage of me. And it wasn't like my uncle was actually going to hurt her. The night he threatened to, he was just drunk and upset. He wasn't drinking now, and as far as he was concerned, they were both on the same team. Solstice needed to get over her fear of him.

I found Lali back at the hotel, looking lost in thought. "Want to practice some more?" I asked.

"I'd like to, but I should get home. It's already almost three o'clock in Virginia." Before I could ask what difference that made, she added, "I'm usually back by now when I spend the night at Paisley's."

"Oh." I realized I hadn't needed to be home by a certain time in years, and a dull ache spread through my chest. "Okay. Where should I drop you off?"

"I guess just far enough from my house that no one can see. I'll tell my dad I stopped at Nelson's for a bit."

Ugh. Nelson again.

Still, I agreed to go along with Lali's plan. I'd spent enough time creeping around the area when I was spying on her family to know a good place to drop her off.

She rushed to get her stuff, and I took her to a small patch of evergreen trees near her house in Browshire.

Thankfully, she didn't ask how I knew what her street looked like.

The second we appeared, Lali pushed her hands into her coat pockets, and I fought the urge to shiver. I'd forgotten how cold it was in this town. It didn't help that I was in a t-shirt and shorts.

"Maybe I can find an excuse to leave the house later tonight," she said. "So we can practice some more."

My mouth twitched. "You want me around even though you don't technically need me to practice?" I put my hand over my heart. "Why Lali, if I didn't know any better, I might think you actually enjoyed my company."

I hoped my teasing her would mask the fact that saying it made my insides squirm. No one had *wanted* to hang out with me in years. Cade didn't have much of a choice—he got stuck with me, just like Grandma Naida did.

Lali blushed. "Or all this projecting is affecting my brain."

"Nah, I'm just awesome. Call me later."

She opened her mouth, but I vanished before she could mention how much she didn't like me. As much as I hated to admit it, I really wanted her to.

COMPROMISE

I FINALLY HAD A WINDOW OF TIME TO SQUEEZE IN A MUCH-needed few hours of sleep. All the bouncing around with Lali and the constant need to stay on guard so I wouldn't accidentally out myself had taken its toll on me, especially after back to back nights with limited sleep. It was hard to believe only two and a half days had passed since Cade and I got busted sneaking around in Lali's hallway. So much had happened since then, I was sure I would need at least a week to recover.

When I woke, I immediately checked my phone. No calls from Lali, or anyone for that matter. Still, I couldn't help but wonder how things were going with Lali's permeating practice. If she hadn't called me, I figured that meant she hadn't been able to think of a good excuse to leave her house. That didn't exactly surprise me—dishonesty clearly wasn't her strong suit.

Maybe I could drop in to touch base. She'd bitten my head off for appearing in her room to get her phone number just before we'd met at the bowling alley, but that was before we had come to the understanding we seemed to have now. Not to mention, she said she wanted me around while she practiced. Just remembering that brought a smile to my face.

I previewed her and saw that she was sitting on her bed, glaring at her phone. No one else was around, and she was decent, so I showed up in her room.

"Hey," I said. "How's practicing going?"

She pressed a finger to her lips and turned on her radio. "Kai," she hissed, careful to keep her voice just under the volume of the bad music blaring around us. "I need your help." In ten seconds, she flew through an explanation of how Nelson had come to her house to drop off her backpack last night after she left it in his truck. Now her dad had grounded her because he knew she lied about where she was, and her friends were upset because of her lying, too.

I shook my head. Of course Nelson screwed everything up. I knew I didn't like that guy.

"And everyone hates me because I can't explain what's going on," Lali continued without taking a breath. "I can't prove anything with my stupid invisible astral form. I need you to help me show them the truth. If you disappear in front of everyone once, they'll have to believe me."

Oh, great. Now she wanted to blow my cover, too? No way. I didn't want to upset her, but what she was suggesting was dangerous, even if they were her friends.

I adjusted my stance, bracing myself for her rage. "That's not a good idea, Lali."

"Why not?"

"It's just—" How could I put this to make her understand? I felt like an idiot for not making it clear immediately while we were on the beach. "The fewer people who know about us, the better," I told her. "If word got back to the Eyes and Ears, we'd be in danger. You, me, your brothers and sisters." Maybe I was being paranoid, but that was better than being stupid and getting caught.

"They wouldn't tell anyone," she insisted. "Especially not if we explained that it would be dangerous."

Yeah, right. Whoever opened up to the scumbag that leaked the underground community's location to the Eyes and Ears probably thought the same thing.

"People slip up," I said. "And I'm sorry, but that's not a risk I'm willing to take. Besides, even if the Eyes and Ears weren't a threat, it's still dangerous to out ourselves."

"But—"

I shook my head, and she stopped before she got out her thought. Not that anything she said would have made a difference. I wasn't budging on this.

"Think about it," I pleaded. "People feel threatened by what they don't understand. And they do crazy things when they feel threatened. I'm not trying to be killed or hunted down by some crazy scientist."

"What do you care?" The line between her full eyebrows was becoming all too familiar. "No one would ever be able to catch you."

"But they can catch *you*. They can catch your whole

family." Her eyes widened, and I hoped that meant she would at least consider keeping things under wraps for the sake of the people she loved most. "And a well-timed bullet will kill me all the same," I added, jabbing a finger toward my heart. "Don't forget, I'm still human underneath this freak show."

She slumped onto her bed and huffed. "Why do you get to make the decision here? What happened to being a team?"

"I'm just trying to do what I think is best."

"Well, what about what I think is best? Don't I get a vote?"

"Not with this." Even if she was mad at me, I couldn't do what she was asking—not for the sake of appeasing her friends and helping her avoid being grounded. Both were such small problems in the grand scheme of things.

"Kai!" she whined.

"I'm sorry. It's too risky."

"But—"

"I'm not going to argue about this." I put up my hands in surrender and projected to my room before she could lunge for me. I could see in her eyes that she wanted to claw my face off. *And we just started getting along.*

I paced beside my bed, frustrated questions swirling through my mind. How could she be mad at me for trying to keep both of us safe? Why was it that every time I tried to do something good, she bit my head off for it? And what was the big deal about being grounded, anyway? Had she never been in trouble before?

Actually, knowing her, probably not.

Still, it wasn't like being grounded would really mean anything. It was just a technicality—I could take her out of her house whenever she wanted. That was, if she could tolerate my company now that she was upset with me again.

I let out a sigh. Maybe I'd jumped the gun with Lali. Could I put all my hopes of getting my sister back on a girl who was so up and down all the time?

Well, it's better than chasing dead ends with Cade.

Speaking of my uncle, I wondered if I should have gone back for Solstice by now. Admittedly, I felt a little guilty for leaving her with him. I figured if she started hyperventilating or something, Cade would have called me to get her out of there. I hadn't heard anything from him, which I hoped meant they had gotten over their little drama. But there was only one way to find out.

When I appeared, the two of them were sitting side by side on the rose-print sofa. They jumped apart as soon as they saw me, like two teenagers who'd been caught making out.

I arched a brow. "Glad to see you two made up."

"Some of us didn't have a choice," Solstice grumbled, getting to her feet.

Cade shifted, resting an ankle on his opposite thigh to form a wide triangle with his legs. "Solstice and I have been talking," he said. *Obviously.* "And she tells me things are a bit of a struggle with Lali."

I set my jaw. Solstice *would* tell him about my working with Lali. I was sure she was trying to get back at me for leaving her with Cade. I should have realized she'd find a way to make me pay for it.

"Things aren't a struggle," I lied. *Except for the fact that she's mad at me right now.* "She's just learning to permeate, and she already made more progress than I expected."

"Listen, nephew, I get that you think she's our best chance at getting to Alea, but we can't give up on our other plan."

I rolled my eyes. "It's not hard to give up when your 'plan' consists of sitting around here twiddling your thumbs and waiting for Delta to show up."

"Easy now." Cade exchanged a look with Solstice, who had moved to one of the chairs at the kitchen table. An understanding seemed to pass between them before my uncle went on. "We've come up with a couple leads to follow."

I huffed. "The following the leads game got old a long time ago."

"Just hear me out," Cade countered. "Spend this weekend trying things our way, and if nothing pans out, then I'll support your teaching Lali what she needs to know. Solstice says she'll explain everything about how to get to the transposer, where to find the portal —everything."

I eyed him cautiously. "Seriously?"

They both nodded, though I didn't like the sneaky look in Solstice's eyes. Not to mention, after this morning, I wasn't sure I wanted her explaining anything else. But it wasn't like Lali would listen to Cade—she still had issues trusting him.

"I can compromise." My uncle offered a smile so tight his scar barely shifted. I knew this had to be killing him; he was so used to being in control of everything. Up until recently, I'd never questioned him. Deep down, I might have been afraid he'd get tired of me and decide it was a mistake to take me in. But mostly, I felt I owed it to him to make every effort not to be difficult after he had upended his life for me.

Even now, the gnawing feeling returned. If he wanted to compromise, the least I could do was cooperate—especially if that meant he was finally willing to explore the possibility of going to Alea with Lali's help.

"Fine," I said. "I'll give you this weekend."

Cade shifted his leg to the floor and leaned forward, his eyes fixed on my face. "Well, it's not just this weekend." Before I could ask what he meant, he held up a hand to stop me. "We figure it's only fair to alternate. If this weekend doesn't pan out, we'll focus on Lali for a week. Then, if we haven't made any progress, you'll give me another week of doing things my way."

I let my head drop to the side. "Isn't that a bit much?"

"Not at all. I'm trying to be fair here, and to take your wishes into consideration, too."

I couldn't deny that his heart was in the right place. And if he was willing to help me navigate Alea when the time came, what did I have to lose?

"Okay," I said.

Cade steepled his hands in front of him. "Does that mean we have a deal?"

I nodded, glancing at Solstice again. Why was she so quiet?

"Good," my uncle said. "Then let me tell you what we have in mind for this weekend."

FRIENDS

THE WEEKEND WAS A WASTE. CADE AND SOLSTICE HAD gotten their hopes up about an address book they found tucked under Delta's mattress. Solstice recognized one of the names listed in the book as Ori's fake name, but the phone number listed beneath it was disconnected and the address was no help. After we spent the better part of a day searching for a landmark and renting a car to drive to the house from that landmark, the family living there told us they had no idea who Ori was. Using her fake name didn't work, either.

We then tried tracking down the other people listed in the book to ask about Delta in case she'd resorted to staying with a friend, but none of them had any guesses as to why she wouldn't be home. Not that it was surprising—after all, it was our fault she was too scared to return to her own house.

By the time Monday rolled around, I had made up my

mind that I was done stalking XODUS. Even the members of the group that we'd already found were more trouble than they were worth. Knowing Xiomara was stuck in the basement in-law all day because of the block wore on me, and for my own peace of mind, I'd let her go for walks at night—after previewing Lali to make sure she was sleeping, of course. I just unlocked the basement door, told Xiomara to be back within twenty minutes, and waited in my room to make sure Lali wouldn't see me with her mom on the off chance she projected to Xiomara in her sleep.

Other than those quick previews, I didn't have any contact with Lali all weekend. As much as I hated to admit it, I did kind of miss her company. At the very least, she kept me on my toes.

But she hadn't called or texted me, and I assumed that meant she was still upset. I'd hoped giving her a little space and time to think would make her more likely to reflect and realize that I was right about keeping our secret, but clearly that hadn't happened. Maybe it was a good thing—I wouldn't have been able to see her even if she did call. I had every intention of sticking to the compromise I made with Cade and Solstice so my uncle wouldn't have an excuse to back out of his promise to help Lali and me. When the time came, I would hold him to it.

After two wasted days of doing things my uncle's way, I was chomping at the bit to see if Lali had made any progress with permeating. I tried waiting until the end of her school day, but by the afternoon, I was ready to explode. I figured there was no reason I couldn't pay her a lunchtime visit just to see how things were going.

Using my usual bathroom stall, I projected to the school and took the back way to the cafeteria to avoid passing by the office. The last thing I needed was for the nosy principal to stop me en route. I was sure she knew by now that I hadn't gone to any of my scheduled classes, and I didn't want to deal with her interrogating me about it.

The cafeteria was flooded with people when I walked in, but I quickly spotted Lali by the vending machines. She was talking to Nelson.

Of course.

I scowled, studying him from a distance. What was so great about this guy? His ridiculous hair made him look like the poster child for cowlicks, and he was actually wearing tie-dye.

I didn't get it.

He had his gangly arms crossed over his chest, and I thought I heard him shout about something being illegal.

He would, with his preachy self.

Even from the side, I could see that Lali looked like she was about to cry. The sight made my fists clench. I started toward them, ready to shut Nelson down.

A table of girls broke into giggles as I passed, announcing my presence before I did. Lali turned around, her heavily lined eyes rounding when she saw me.

"Hey, Lali," I said. Since she was probably still mad at me, I forced myself to greet Nelson, too. His lack of intelligible response told me he disliked me just as much as I disliked him. Or he sensed that I wanted to punch him for putting that look on Lali's face.

"Kai, we have to tell him," Lali begged. "Please."

I frowned at her. There was no way I was going to tell this schmuck anything about our abilities.

An idea popped into my head, and I felt my face perk up at the thought of making Nelson squirm. "You want to tell him we're an item?" I asked, putting on my best acting skills. "I thought you wanted to keep that under wraps."

Lali hit me, her cheeks turning fifty shades of red. "I'm serious!"

"Clearly," I said, unable to stop smiling. "I heard some girls talking about you and me this morning." That wasn't true, but the look on Nelson's face made the lie worth it. "Word travels *fast* in this town." I let my gaze bore into hers, waiting for her to grasp my double meaning. Just to piss off her annoying friend even further, I slid my arm around her waist.

It worked. His whole body went rigid.

"You know what, Lali?" he seethed. "You do what you want. I'm done trying to talk sense into you." He thundered past us without another word, nearly running over some poor chubby kid who got in his way.

My smirk lingered until Lali shoved my arm off of her. "Are you *trying* to ruin my life?" she yelled.

I rolled my eyes. Getting rid of her lecture-happy friend was hardly ruining her life. I would go so far as to call it an improvement. All that guy had done since I met him was stress her out.

"I'm trying to make sure you *have* a life to ruin," I said. "I told you it's dangerous to go blabbing to people."

She held her head like she was on the verge of a panic attack, and I did feel kind of bad. Not for making Nelson angry—that was one of my finer moments, actually—but for giving Lali something else to be upset about. She already had enough on her plate as it was.

"Your friends will get over it," I insisted, even though I kind of hoped Nelson wouldn't. "I'm trying to keep us safe. They don't need to know every detail of your life. If they can't give you a little privacy, forget 'em."

"Says the person who has no friends to speak of."

I flinched, knowing she was right. I'd lost touch with the few friends I had back in Hawaii, and homeschooling wasn't exactly conducive to making new ones. The sad truth was, Lali was the closest thing I had to a friend. Too bad every time I turned around, she was angry with me. And even if she was right, she didn't have to throw it in my face.

"Well, that was unnecessary," I muttered. "I'm going to let that one go because I know you're upset. But you don't have to be. You'd be amazed at how little you actually need the people you think you need."

Trust me. I've survived without people this long.

"I don't want to not need them. I *like* needing people."

"Fine." I glanced up at the crowded lunchroom, thankful for the roar of voices to drown out this conversation. "Then I'll be your substitute."

Her responding scoff stung more than I wanted to

admit. Just because I was out of practice didn't mean I couldn't be a good friend. Well, not counting the secrets I *had* to keep from her and the lies I had to tell to cover them up.

"I mean it," I said, suddenly eager to prove myself. "You need a ride to school? I'm your guy. I'm much more efficient than a car anyway." I'd hoped that would get a laugh, but her frown didn't budge.

"And I can give you a cutesy nickname," I added. "Lollipop is the obvious play." I tried not to roll my eyes thinking about Nelson's stupid pet name for her. I'd had to endure it the night I sat through bowling with her friends. "I'm going to go with something more creative. Something like Lali Green Giant."

"Great." Still no smile.

"No? How about Lali Lali Oxen Free?"

"Wow." Her tone stayed flat as a pancake.

"Lali Want A Cracker?" That at least got a hint of a chuckle. I snapped my fingers. "I've got it! Laliwood!"

Her mouth stayed turned up at the corners. "You're such a loser."

"I got you to smile," I countered. "That makes me a winner." She shook her head, but I could tell she wanted to laugh. "We'll get through this without them," I promised. "Just wait, you'll be permeating like a champ in no time. You've been practicing, right?"

"I got half of my arm through my window." She swirled a finger in the air with as much enthusiasm as a pet rock. "Whoop dee doo."

"Hey, that's a start. You'll get it faster than you think."

I saw her eyes drift over to where Nelson sat at the far end of the room. He saw it, too, but he turned away and Lali's face fell back into despair.

Man, I hated that guy.

"You will," I assured her. "And I'll help you. That is, if you let me."

She sighed and looked up at me with a vulnerability I hadn't seen from her. "Thanks," was all she said.

But then, that was all she needed to say.

...As I got to know you over the next few weeks, it became harder and harder to keep things from you. I honestly wanted to be a friend to you, and I had no plans to lie about anything other than the obvious stuff involving your mom. You made great progress with permeating, and I had more faith in you than I could even express. I was sure that as soon as you were ready to test the transposer under the bay, it would switch you back to your physical body, and we'd be on our way to Alea.

From there, I knew I would be able to figure out a way to get to Kala and give you back your mom so you and I could both live our lives—hopefully remaining in each other's lives. But, of course, something else threw another monkey wrench in all my plans...

38

CALLER

THE DAYS FELL INTO AN EXHAUSTING ROUTINE FOR THE next few weeks. I had already given up on the weak leads Cade was coming up with, and I only spent the afternoons pretending to follow them. Really, I was just fitting in sleep whenever I could, but I wanted my uncle to think I was honoring our deal so he would still be willing to instruct Lali and me if we got to Alea. No, *when* we got to Alea. More than ever, I believed we would.

The nights—and very early mornings—were saved for teaching Lali the art of sneaking out. Of course, it was much easier with my ability to take her out of her house without using the door. Even so, once her family turned in for the night, we stuffed her bed with pillows the good old-fashioned way. I even played recorded "sleep breathing" on my phone and left it hidden near her bed in case her dad came by to check on her.

From there, I took her to construction sites—per

Solstice's suggestion—so she could practice permeating different materials of varying difficulty until she worked her way up to steel. She'd already mastered glass, wood, brick, and cement. I wasn't sure what value I brought other than moral support while she practiced, but she always seemed to want me there, and I couldn't deny how much that meant to me.

Tonight, I sat next to her on a half-built brick wall as she stared down her challenge for the evening. This time it was the collection of steel beams above us. They would be the deciding factor on whether she was ready to try and find the transposer under the bay. If she could consistently permeate the beams, then we would know her astral form could get through the steel wall blocking the tunnel under the San Francisco Bay—and the steel dome surrounding the transposer in Alea.

The cloudless night sky offered a peaceful enough backdrop, with a smattering of stars that seemed to offer encouragement. At least, that was how I saw them. Then again, I wasn't the one with all the pressure on me.

Lali sighed loudly, wringing her hands as she stared at the beams above us. Her hair was pulled back into a half-hearted bun, revealing the worried expression that would otherwise hide behind it.

"You can do it," I said in the best encouraging voice I could manage. "Just don't think about it so much."

She pursed her lips and gave me a sideways glance. "I thought the key was focus."

"You know what I mean. Just try." I nudged her with

my shoulder. "If you don't get this show on the road, I'll have to take back your favorite nickname. I don't call you Laliwood for nothing."

She breathed a laugh in spite of herself. "Maybe losing that nickname is my sole motivation for not projecting right now."

"Oh, please. We both know you love it."

"I thought I hid it so well." The ghost of a smile lifted her cheeks as she took a deep breath and closed her eyes. A second later, her breathing deepened into the rhythmic sound of sleep, and I knew she had projected.

As always, my mind wandered while I sat there waiting. When we teased each other, and when her face was relaxed this way, it was almost as if I hadn't completely upended her life. Somehow, it made it easier to ignore the guilt. I couldn't help but wonder what would happen once all this was over. I was really starting to look forward to spending time with Lali—probably too much—and I didn't want to give that up.

Lately, I'd been toying with the idea of returning her mother to her without telling her the truth of why she had been gone. I could say Cade and I had managed to trace her and found her on the run from the Eyes and Ears or something. But that meant Xiomara would have to go along with whatever story I made up, and that presented its own set of problems. I would have to trust that she would never slip up and tell Lali the truth, and I knew that was a tall order.

Still, it was a possibility—one that I wanted to make a reality.

Lali's breathing started to sound labored, snapping me out of my pondering. I didn't know exactly how much time had passed, but she'd built up her strength so she could stay in her astral form for nearly twenty minutes at a time, and I was sure it hadn't been that long.

Before I could shake her out of her projection, her eyes flew open and she leapt to her feet. "I did it!" she squealed. "I moved through the beam three times in a row!"

I shot to a stance, barely resisting the urge to throw my arms around her. I clapped my hands instead. "I knew you could do it." I grinned, and she beamed back at me.

"Does this mean Solstice will finally tell me where to find the tunnel to the transposer?" she asked.

"Definitely," I said, though I couldn't be sure. Technically, this week was supposed to be dedicated to Cade's plan, and Solstice had remained tight-lipped about where to find the tunnel this whole time. She said she didn't want to throw off Lali's focus. At the time, I agreed because I knew how overwhelmed Lali was already, but now I kind of regretted it. I hoped Solstice wouldn't make a big deal about the whole alternating weeks thing. Even if she did, I could find a way to make her cooperate.

I reached for Lali's hand. "Come on. I'll take you home so I can go see if Solstice is still awake."

It was getting late, but it had only been a couple hours since I dropped Solstice off at her apartment. She'd spent the day brainstorming with Cade and going through Delta's house for what must have been the hundredth time. She should have been willing to help Lali find the

transposer if for no other reason than to give her something to focus on besides digging through boxes of junk.

I took Lali to her room and showed up in Solstice's
apartment. Solstice was at her kitchen table sipping tea in
her pinstriped pajamas, her red hair knotted on top of
her head.

"Lali did it," I told her, a proud smile taking over my
face. "She got through steel."

Solstice's eyebrows shot up. "She did?"

"Yeah. I told you, she's going to be the one who gets
us to Alea. I know it. I can feel it." I really could. Lali was
my little light of hope, and it was only growing from here.

"At this rate, it seems like she's our only shot," Solstice
admitted, setting down her mug. "Cade and I have pretty
much exhausted the list of Delta's friends and every
friend I can remember coming to visit Ori and Ursula."

I nodded, hoping my face didn't give away that I
hadn't actually followed up with most of those friends.
But it wasn't like it would matter anyway, not when Delta
was still MIA. "Well, Lali just needs your directions to get
to the transposer, and we'll get her ramped up," I said.

Solstice sighed. "Okay. Bring her here."

Lali was squirming next to me on the blue and white
sofa a minute later. She must've been exhausted, but I
knew how the anticipation of success could replace sleep.
That was the only thing getting me through my own
exhaustion lately.

"So, the transposer," Lali said, bouncing her knees.

"Yes." Solstice gave her a dirty look until she stopped

moving. "The entrance is hidden inside the arch of the upside-down U-shaped rock just below Point Bonita." She looked up at me. "You remember where that is, right?"

"Um, yeah." I frowned. Did Cade tell her that he had me project there after I got my ability under control? He'd hoped I would be able to get to the transposer, but, as usual, my lack of astral form ruined his plan. But why would he feel the need to share that with her?

"Under the arch," Solstice went on, "inside the curve that extends out toward the water, is the tunnel entrance. It's circular, not much wider than a manhole cover, and it's covered with a decal to match the rock. Just search for where the uneven rock becomes smooth and circular. Once you find that, you can move through it and into the tunnel."

I heard Lali swallow, and I reached over to squeeze her hand.

"Follow the tunnel," Solstice said. "It's about nine miles, and it will be dark, but you can feel your way through using the walls. Note that it dips up toward the end rather steeply. You can't miss the transposer; it's a big glowing ring. Just make sure you don't go diving through it if you see anyone else in there. I don't know how long it's been since the Eyes and Ears used it, but there's still a risk that they'll be there. Traveling Astralii will not take kindly to intruders."

Wow. She sounded like she cared. That was new.

"Also," she added. "There's a one-way exit, a trap door at the end of the tunnel that leads up to a house. Do *not* go in there, under any circumstances. Do you understand?"

Lali nodded.

"Repeat the instructions," Solstice insisted. She wasn't satisfied until Lali had parroted her words back to her three times.

"Okay." I checked the time on my phone. "It's already after one in the morning. Lali, you should try to get some sleep. We won't be able to see a thing out there until sunrise, anyway. I'll come get you tomorrow morning."

Solstice stood up. "Do you know how much is riding on this?" Her gaze was focused on Lali, as if challenging her.

Lali shifted uncomfortably. "Yes. Believe me, I know."

"She knows, and she doesn't need any more pressure on her," I said, giving Solstice a challenging look of my own. She must have given up on Cade's plan, too, if she was this desperate now. "Let the girl rest. We'll be back tomorrow." Instinctively, my arm twitched to reach for Lali before I remembered I was already holding her hand.

She's letting me hold her hand! My stomach fluttered, but I forced my wayward thoughts away. Now wasn't the time.

I dropped Lali off at home, and we agreed that she would call me as soon as her dad left for work in the morning. Then I would take her to San Francisco to find the tunnel.

By the time I projected back to my room, I was ready to collapse. Just as I started stripping off my shirt, my phone buzzed in my pocket. Thinking it was Lali calling to clarify something about our plans for the morning, I went to answer it. My jaw dropped when I saw the number flashing across the screen.

It was Delta.

39

SECRETS

I NEARLY DROPPED THE PHONE. MY MIND SWAM AS I stared at the screen with my mouth hanging open. I couldn't answer it—Delta might remember my voice. Plus, she thought this was Solstice's phone number.

Solstice!

I projected to her just as she was folding herself into bed. She jumped when she saw me, but her annoyance quickly turned to confusion as I forced my phone into her hand.

"Delta!" I managed. "Answer it!"

She tossed back her blanket and sat up, studying the screen. Her blue eyes looked like they might fall out of her head.

"Answer it!" I repeated.

Fumbling her fingers over the touch screen, she hit the button to accept the call. "H-hello?"

The voice came out muffled on the other end, and despite my straining to listen, I couldn't make out what

Delta was saying.

"No, no, that's okay," Solstice breathed. "Where are you now?...That's actually not too far from me. Can I come pick you up?...Yes...Perfect. Then I'll bring you back to my apartment so we can set up a block here."

She moved toward the closet and started pulling out clothes as she spoke. "Okay. I can be there in about two hours...Good. Thank you for calling me back. I'll see you soon, Del."

Solstice hit the end button and looked at me like she'd just won the lottery. "Delta's still here in California. She couldn't fly back home because she lost her ID, and she just switched her phone over and got my message. I can't believe that worked!"

I shook my head, still in shock myself. "Thank God she didn't ask how you got her number."

"She probably will," she said, handing my phone back to me. "But we have time to come up with that story on the ride over. I need you to navigate."

Damn. I wasn't looking forward to spending two hours in a car with Solstice, but I couldn't project to Delta when she was wearing her stupid block.

"Listen to me." Solstice's expression was suddenly tense. "I can get Delta to tell me anything she knows about where to find the others, but she can't know I'm working with you and Cade—at least not yet."

"Okay."

"And Cade can't know anything either. Let him stay put at Delta's thinking she might still come home. I don't want him interfering before I get an idea of what she knows."

I huffed. I was already lying to my uncle too much for my liking, especially when he had always been brutally honest with me. But his way of doing things wasn't working, and if he found out about Delta, he would demand to come along. He would just have to stay in the dark until we got what we needed. Then I'd fill him in. If we got Delta to tell us something useful, he would be grateful.

Or so I hoped.

"I won't say a word," I promised.

Solstice smirked. "Good. We're going to do this the right way this time. I'm not going to let anything screw it up."

Solstice drove like a bat out of hell. There were hardly any other cars on the road, which wasn't surprising considering we were driving in the wee hours. Using the GPS on my phone, I helped navigate until we got to the parking lot of the motel where Delta was staying.

Apparently, she had a backup credit card that she'd used to book the room. It was like she was the queen of contingency plans. Then again, if I'd been abducted and taken to another realm as a teenager, I'd probably be the same way.

"Okay," Solstice said once we pulled into a parking space. "Take a look at whatever you need to see to come back here, but then you have to go. She can't know you're with me."

We had already agreed on the way over that I would scan the motel's exterior so I knew I could come back to the area and go inside in person if I needed to. I hated how dependent I was on Solstice telling the truth, but she had proven more than once that she was as invested in getting back to Alea as Cade and I were. Besides, it wasn't like our plan to round up the other members of XODUS would go anywhere if Solstice couldn't get Delta to talk. Delta had already proven she wasn't going to tell Cade or me anything.

"I'll call you when I get something useful from her," Solstice said, already opening her door. She hopped out of the car and slammed it shut behind her.

I watched as she raced up to the dimly lit building and took the cement steps two at a time. Maybe it would have been smarter for me to burst in and threaten Delta at gunpoint until she took off her block. It wouldn't take more than a quick second to flash over to Cade and take the gun. But with the block in place, I was virtually a regular person. The gun would be my only advantage, and I wouldn't have been surprised if Delta had armed herself with one of her own by now—especially after Solstice fed her that story about Cade and me coming after her.

Letting out a long breath, I told myself I was doing the right thing by letting Solstice try and get Delta to talk without threatening her. Delta was already messed up enough as it was. Not to mention, it meant one less person I'd have to lock in my basement.

Speaking of…

I hadn't let Xiomara out of the in-law all day. Previewing Lali to make sure she was sleeping first, I showed up at home and opened the door to the basement.

Xiomara poked her head into the stairwell a moment later. "Time for my walk?" she asked, not quite managing to sound enthusiastic.

I nodded, swallowing another bout of guilt. I couldn't wait until all this was over and I didn't have to hold her hostage anymore—not just for my conscience, but also for Lali's peace of mind. I could only imagine how much more relaxed she would be when she had her mother back.

Telling myself I'd make sure that happened as soon as possible, I projected to my room. I opened my door and waited for the sound of Xiomara coming back into the house so I could make sure she locked the basement door before I went to sleep.

When she was finally back inside, I checked the door, hurried up to my room, and took a shower. Then I fell into bed, dreaming of the moment Lali would find the transposer and get us one step closer to Alea.

DETERMINATION

THE TEXT FROM LALI CAME JUST BEFORE NINE THE NEXT morning. I projected straight to her room, where she sat waiting on her bed. She was already dressed in her white puffy coat, blue hat, and blue scarf. I'd finally gotten my own coat and scarf earlier that morning, so I was ready to face the cold air of San Francisco, too.

As soon as she saw me, Lali jumped up and grabbed my hand. I squeezed it twice, and she mimicked the gesture. It was our unspoken way of saying everything was good to go. We'd come up with plenty of ways to communicate silently during the last few weeks of sneaking out together. I had to admit, it was nice having that connection with someone. I'd almost forgotten what it was like.

We showed up on the ledge overlooking the San Francisco Bay, the same one Cade and I had come to after I'd gotten my ability under control. It was just before sunrise, and everything was touched with gray. The usual coat of fog had settled over the bridge and the water. Wind whipped past us, sending Lali's hair splaying up into a blue-streaked fan. Shivering, I shoved my face as far inside my coat as I could.

Lali tiptoed forward to peek over the edge of the cliff and let out a soft gasp.

"You got this, Laliwood," I said through my coat's zipper.

Her nod wasn't convincing.

"You got this," I repeated, making my voice sound more authoritative. If this was going to work, she needed to believe it as much as I did. The key to permeating was confidence, and at this point, she didn't seem to have any.

"You're sure this is the right spot?" she whimpered, looking over the edge of the rock again.

"I'm sure. Cade walked me to this very spot back when we thought I might be able to reach the transposer. I marked the lighthouse and everything." I dipped a shoulder in the direction of the tall white building behind us, pushing away the memory of my uncle's disappointed face that day when I hadn't been able to get into the tunnel. "You remember what Solstice said about the entrance, right?"

I'd meant it as a joke after Solstice made Lali say it so many times last night, but Lali sighed and recited, "Circular, hardly wider than a manhole cover, and buried inside the curve that extends out toward the rest of the bay."

I decided to let it go. Maybe jokes weren't a good idea right now. "See, you'll be fine," I said. "You know exactly what to look for."

She took a deep breath in response.

"Come on, Lali. I can tell by your face you're psyching yourself out. Just go."

She didn't move.

Lifting my head out of my coat, I smiled in hopes she would, too. Grandma Naida always told me *fake it 'til you make it,* and right now, Lali at least needed to act confident.

"You can do it," I insisted. "I know you can."

"Thanks." Her face softened for a second before hardening again in determination. "Here goes nothing."

She closed her eyes, and I bounced up and down in an effort to stay warm. I didn't need my attempt at moral support to give me pneumonia. I studied Lali's bundled up form and wondered how the cold would affect her while she was traveling. The way she'd described projecting to me, it sounded like she couldn't feel anything in her physical body. If I weren't afraid I'd snap her out of her projection, I'd run my hands up and down her arms to keep her warm.

I settled for stepping as close to her as I could, careful not to touch her. My eyes landed on her mouth. Her lips were full and smooth, just barely parted. The thought of kissing her appeared uninvited, and I felt my heart stutter.

No. That was the last thing I should be thinking about.

Taking a step back, I wrapped my arms around myself and reverted to hopping up and down. I closed my eyes and visualized Lali finding the transposer as best I could without knowing exactly what it looked like. I'd read about the power of visualization, and though I didn't know if it was supposed to work with another person doing it for you, I had nothing better to do at the moment.

Wait. Actually, I did.

I'd almost forgotten I had promised Lali I would check on her brothers and sisters every so often while we were out here. I knew they'd be fine, but Lali worried about them, and it was sweet that they meant so much to her. In truth, I couldn't help but envy that she had a family to worry about in the first place.

Previewing each of her siblings, I saw—unsurprisingly—that they were all still sleeping. I even previewed the dog and found him lying on the sofa. If he wasn't alarmed, I figured I didn't need to be either.

As I pulled out of my preview, a strong burst of wind made my eyes fly open. Part of me worried it would jar Lali out of her projection, but she still stood with her eyes closed, her features relaxed. I wondered if she had found the tunnel opening yet, if she was inside it now on her way to the transposer.

The thought set butterflies loose in my stomach. Whatever Lali was going through didn't show on her face, though. She stayed perfectly expressionless, breathing like she was in a trance.

Then, just like that, she vanished.

I jumped backward, too stunned to process what it meant at first. My mind raced to catch up, and my heart almost beat itself out of my chest as the realization hit. She had switched into her physical body at the transposer.

It worked!

RECKLESS

SHE DID IT! SHE REALLY DID IT! THE THUNDERING IN MY ears was so loud I could barely picture Lali's face to project to her. Finally, I felt the pull, but instead of appearing the way I usually did, it felt like I hit a wall. I dropped to the ground and toppled backward, but I was too pumped to care. Sitting up, I let my gaze dart around the narrow tunnel until I found Lali's grinning face.

She and I beamed at each other in the golden light from the glowing ring above us. The next thing I knew, she dove at me. Her arms found their way around my neck, and we fell backward together. "I did it!" she squealed.

"I knew you could," I said with a laugh. "That was awesome!"

Lali pulled back, still smiling, and it was like something shifted inside me. I'd never seen her smile so openly. Even lying on my back, I was grinning like an idiot.

"Sorry," she gasped. "I didn't mean to tackle you. I

just got excited." She scooted back to let me get up, and I hoped the disappointment didn't show on my face. Even though I hadn't hugged anyone in years, holding her felt almost natural.

Stop it! Now is not the time to get caught up.

I pushed onto my elbows, determined to keep my voice from betraying me. "As well you should have. That was the coolest thing I've ever seen. One second you were standing there with your eyes closed, and the next, you were gone. Just like that." I snapped my fingers.

She giggled, a light, jovial sound that made my mouth pull up at the ends. "Kai, you do that all the time," she reminded me.

"Yeah, well. What can I say? I'm a bad Ast."

We both cracked up, and she got lost in a fit of laughter. Seeing her so carefree was like watching a stranger. I committed the sight and sound to memory.

"Now, all you have to do is find the portal," I said. "We could be in Alea *today*."

She nodded excitedly. "Then let's get going."

Knowing there was a good chance Solstice was still with Delta, I didn't want to attempt projecting to her and risk hitting the block—or worse, scaring off Delta. After taking a moment to memorize the space around the transposer, I projected Lali back to her room. While she sat on her bed, I moved to the corner near her easel and called Solstice.

As soon as the ringing stopped, I blurted out, "Lali did it! She found the transposer, and it worked!"

"I'm kind of busy here," Solstice hissed. I could

picture her scowl just from hearing her tone, but I didn't care.

"You can take five seconds to talk to us," I said. In the back of my mind, I couldn't help but wonder how things were going with Delta, but that would have to wait. If Lali could get us to Alea today, we needed to focus on her. "I'm coming over there." I hung up, and, not wanting Lali to hear, I sent a quick text that said, *If you're not in your car in five minutes, I'm coming into the room to get you.*

I met the eager gray eyes across the room. "Solstice isn't home. I'm going to go pick her up and bring her to her apartment, and then I'll come back for you, okay?"

"Okay," Lali said breathlessly.

I previewed the parking lot where I'd last seen Solstice to make sure it was okay to appear in the car. Now that the sun was out, there were a handful of people around. Thankfully, none of them seemed to be looking in the direction of her green Honda. I projected to the passenger seat, angling my body to keep as much of myself out of view as possible, just in case someone happened to glance toward me.

Scanning the rooms along the motel corridor, I saw Solstice make her way out of the one at the end of the second floor. She hurried down the cement steps, climbed into the driver's side, and slammed the door so hard the car shook.

"You're going to ruin everything," she scolded under her breath.

"Hardly. You just have to tell Lali how to get to the portal, and then you can go back to grilling Delta."

"It better not take long." Solstice shoved her purse between the seats and jammed the key into the ignition. "I told Delta I had to run to the store for emergency feminine supplies."

I shuddered at the thought.

Solstice started the car and sped out of the parking lot. I didn't know where we were going, but I assumed she was driving so Delta wouldn't ask questions later.

"Your uncle was right, you know," Solstice said, keeping her narrowed eyes on the road.

I frowned. "About what?"

"About going back to Alea without our abilities. It's crazy."

Where did that come from? Now that Delta was in the picture again, Solstice was suddenly changing her mind? "Well, this isn't about you guys going back," I countered. "This is about getting my sister out."

"What's wrong with accomplishing both?"

"Nothing. But I'm not going to put off finding Kala if I don't have to."

"So, what, if you find Kala, then you're not going to try and help Cade get his ability back?"

I sighed as we turned onto an uphill road that led to a Wal-Mart we'd passed on the way to Delta's motel. I did want to help my uncle get back to Alea if that was what he wanted. I owed him that much.

"I'll try," I replied. "But my sister is always going to be my first priority. If things don't work out with restoring

Cade's ability, I don't want to hold people hostage for the rest of time."

"You're not the only one who has something riding on this, you know." Solstice pulled into a parking space at the far end of the lot and cut the engine. Before I could ask what she was trying to say, she grumbled, "Let's just go."

Fine by me. I projected us to her apartment, and then went to get Lali from her room.

"Good morning," she said to Solstice when we appeared, ever the master of manners. "Thanks for—"

"Sit down," Solstice snapped, plopping onto the sofa. I shot her a look. Why did she have to be rude? I knew she was mad that I interrupted her time with Delta, but good grief. We only needed ten minutes.

Lali didn't say anything, though, and we both sat down next to Solstice.

"You made it to the transposer?" Solstice sounded more annoyed than relieved as she scooted to put more space between her and Lali. "And it changed you into your physical form?"

"Yes." Lali looked at me as if she needed me to confirm it really happened. I hardly believed it myself.

"That's actually quite impressive," Solstice admitted, though she sounded like someone had forced her to say it.

Lali thanked her anyway, and said she couldn't have done it without Solstice's help. She turned to meet my eyes, as if to say the same went for me, and I couldn't stop myself from smiling.

"Have you told Cade yet?" Solstice asked, patting her braided hair as she looked at me.

I shook my head. "Nah, I'm keeping him out of it until we make it to Alea. I'm over his lectures about wasting time."

Thankfully, Solstice didn't ask what I meant. I needed to stick to the story I'd given Lali, and I didn't have the energy to come up with more lies on the fly.

"So what's the next step?" Lali asked, unable to sit still. "I'm getting a little antsy here."

"Well, keep your pants on," Solstice grumbled. "You can't do anything until nightfall. You have to wait until the stars are visible."

"What?" Lali looked between us, horrified. "Why?"

"Because you need the stars to find the portal," Solstice replied.

Wait. What? Had I missed something? Cade never talked about needing to see the stars to reach the portal. Then again, he had no reason to; he'd given up on my chances of getting to Alea shortly after discovering how my ability worked.

The disappointment in Lali's face sucked the animation out of my own. This was my fault. I should've gone over all this with Solstice last night. Then I could have mentally prepared Lali instead of getting her hopes up about getting to Alea today.

"But we can go over what to do now, right?" I asked. "Then we can get started as soon as it's dark."

Solstice let out a breath and got to her feet. "I guess. I'll get the star map." She walked down the hall and came back with a rolled-up poster. Moving into the dining room, she gestured for us to follow her. Lali and I went over to where Solstice was spreading the paper across the table and taping down the corners.

"What's this?" Lali asked.

"Directions." Solstice pulled a gold marker from her pocket, bit off the cap, and circled a group of white dots among the plethora that covered the black paper. "This is Cassiopeia," she mumbled around the cap.

Lali stared at her. "You want me to find the portal based on star positions?"

"Last time I checked, that was the only way to find it," Solstice snapped. "So pay attention." She started drawing lines to connect a group of stars, and I took that moment to check on Lali's brothers and sisters. Again, I knew they would be fine, but I had every intention of honoring my promise to keep an eye on them. At least that was something I could contribute.

I previewed each of them within seconds. When I'd finished, I opened my eyes just as Solstice stabbed the marker toward a star that she'd circled. "See this one at the tip of the sharpest angle?" she asked Lali, both of them seeming oblivious to my astral intermission. "You want to aim for that."

Aim for a specific star? I hadn't realized how complicated it was to get to the portal. Cade never mentioned any of this before. *Probably because he knew there was no way I'd be able to make it.* After all, that was the reason we were in this situation in the first place.

"How am I supposed to project to a star?" Lali asked, her face falling.

Solstice ripped the plastic cap from between her lips

and shoved it back into place on the marker like she wished it was Lali's head. "It's not like you're going to *outer space*. You just have to move toward it until you see the portal."

Lali gulped as she eyed the map.

"All you have to do is travel to the center of the Golden Gate Bridge and go straight up from there until you're past all the fog and city lights so you can see the stars," Solstice explained, speaking as if it were child's play. "From directly above the bridge, aim for this point." She used the marker to point at the star she had circled. "Try to travel at a forty-five degree angle from just above the fog."

Lali blinked at her, clearly as dumbfounded by the instructions as I was.

"Look, if you're not up for this—"

"I am," Lali interrupted before Solstice could get the sentence out. "I'm just trying to wrap my brain around this whole thing."

"Don't be intimidated." I took Lali's hand and squeezed, determined to keep her positive. She couldn't give up now. We were way too close. "This'll be a cake-walk compared to finding a hidden tunnel under a rock."

"Yeah." Her lack of enthusiasm told me she wasn't buying it.

"Well, now you know why I didn't want to tell you how to get there until now," Solstice muttered. "You get far too dramatic." I glared at her over Lali's shoulder, but she avoided looking at me.

"When you're in the right place, you'll know it,"

Solstice went on. "There will be a pulsating circle of green light about the size of an inner tube. It's activated by astral energy, so you should see it once you're within a few yards of the right area. When you touch it, it'll pull you into Alea. Right away you'll see a steel dome, which houses the realm's main transposer. It works the same as the one here. Understand?"

"Yes." Lali sounded like a squirrel facing down a growling wolf.

"It's light out now, so you'll have to wait until later," Solstice said. I knew she was just trying to rush us out of here so she could get back to Delta, but she was right. There was nothing we could do now but wait. "I suggest you save up your strength. You're going to need it to stay in your astral form while you're looking for the portal."

"Okay." Lali ran a palm over her face. "Kai, can you take me home? It's been a while since you checked on my family."

"I previewed them while Solstice was playing connect-the-dots with the star map," I informed her. "They're still sleeping." Scanning Lali from head to toe, I realized how exhausted she looked and added, "You should probably do the same. You've hardly slept at all for the last three weeks."

"Well, not all of us have the luxury of blowing off school." She raised a brow at me, and I knew she was trying to call me out for never showing up to class.

"High school is overrated." I shrugged. "Besides, I only enrolled so I could recruit you to help. Mission accomplished."

She just shook her head.

I looked back at Solstice, who was scowling for some reason. "We'll get out of your hair for now," I said. "I'll bring Lali back as soon as it gets dark."

"Sounds like a plan," Solstice replied, not an ounce of eagerness in her expression.

Not that I cared. Whether she liked it or not, Lali was going to get us to Alea. I wasn't going to let anything get in the way of that.

I squeezed Lali's hand again, but she hardly reacted. It was obvious she was still frazzled, and I silently vowed I'd find a way back to the giddy girl I'd hugged in the transposer tunnel. I wished there was a way I could help take some of the burden, but she knew as well as I did that I couldn't do any of this on my own. I needed her.

I left Lali in her room with some encouraging words and took Solstice back to her car. She ran into Wal-Mart to pick up the feminine supplies that would help her stick to the story she'd fed Delta back at the motel.

Deciding I didn't need to stick around for that, I went back to my house with the hope of getting some sleep myself. I had a feeling it was going to be a late night.

I had just started to doze off when my phone buzzed. I accepted the call, and Solstice's voice came through before I could speak.

"Thanks a lot," she spat. "Delta knows."

42

EXPLANATIONS

MY STOMACH DROPPED. HOW COULD DELTA POSSIBLY know? She couldn't have seen Solstice and me disappear —we'd vanished from the empty end of a parking lot. "What are you talking about?" I asked, kicking off my blanket and climbing out of bed. "What does she know?"

"She looked out the window after I ducked out on her, and she saw you in the car." The profanities that played through my head were nothing compared to the ones I could tell Solstice wanted to shout into the phone. "I had to be honest with her about trying to help you undo the sink without Cade. She knows we're trying to go to Alea without risking him getting his ability back."

Her words threw me off until I realized Delta must've been within earshot.

"Now," Solstice continued. "Meet me back in the car, and I'll bring you to the room so you can talk to Delta yourself."

A minute later, I was in the passenger seat of Solstice's

car. Scooting up to look out the window, I saw her come outside. Thankfully, no one else was in the parking lot. I pushed open the door and climbed out as Solstice stormed over.

"You're going to have to lay on the pitiful act, and thick," she hissed. "Apologize to Delta for tricking her, and I know she'll forgive you. She's always had a soft spot for you and Kala, so play up how desperate you are to find your sister."

I nodded, following Solstice through the lot and up the staircase. "That won't be hard. It's true."

"It's still your fault we're in this mess. I have a feeling Delta knows more than she's letting on. I would've had a much easier time getting information out of her if she didn't know you were involved, especially since she already knows you were working with your uncle."

The guilt for keeping another secret from Cade bubbled in my gut, hot and unsettling. I told myself it was for the better, but believing it was another story.

We reached the last door along the upper corridor, and Solstice swiped a card into the electronic reader.

Delta looked up from where she sat on the bed as soon as we stepped into the room. "Hello, Kai," she whispered.

Solstice jabbed me with her elbow, and I cleared my throat. "I'm sorry," I said, taking a tentative step forward on the cheap, patterned carpet. "About all this sneaking around and everything." As the words came out, I couldn't help but think that I should be saying them to

Cade and Lali, too. They were the ones on the receiving end of all my lies lately.

Delta waved her hand, as if dismissing my statement and my unwelcome thought. "Sol already explained. I know how badly you want to find your sister. And if anyone can understand what Kala must be going through, it's me, right?" She offered a weak smile, and my heart constricted. Delta had been kidnapped by the same Astralii, subjected to the same experiments they were probably running on Kala.

I dropped my head, suddenly filled with remorse for adding additional stress to this poor woman's life. She'd already gone through more than her share of struggles.

"Sit down." Delta gestured to the small table with matching chairs, and Solstice and I moved to claim the seats. Solstice's face was tight as she sat across from me, but she didn't speak.

"Kai, I would love to help you," Delta claimed, though the horrified look on her face made it hard to believe her. "Really, I would. But it's not safe. If Cade's not around when we undo the sink, we risk his astral energy finding a home in someone who can't handle it. I've seen what happens to people when they're forced to accept astral energy their bodies aren't equipped to handle. I could never do that to someone."

Her face darkened. "We also risk being tracked by the Eyes and Ears," she went on. "Who do you think taught me how to trace astral energy?"

Oh. I hadn't thought about that. It wouldn't make a difference for me, though—if I had astral energy, I was already traceable. And Delta had no reason to be worried about them finding her again.

"You have a block," I reminded her. "You'll be safe no matter what."

She shook her head. "It's not foolproof. Some of the higher Astralii have stones that can penetrate blocks."

I heaved a sigh. I understood why Delta was paranoid, but if she claimed to care about Kala, why didn't she want to make saving her a priority?

"But Kai," Delta said, "you can still get to your sister." At that, my ears perked up. "And, Sol, you can still get your ability back."

Solstice sat up a little straighter, too. "How?"

"It sounds like Lali has mastered permeating, right Kai?"

"Yeah," I replied, not sure where Delta was going with this.

"So all she has to do is find the portal. Then you'll have access to Alea, and you can drop off Solstice at the transposer." She turned to her old friend. "Sol, if you explain who you are, they'll take you to the lab. By now, I'm sure they've figured out how to restore abilities. If not, they can inject you with something similar to what they used on me. You won't react badly because you were born ready to deal with astral energy."

Solstice wrinkled her nose. "I don't want to be turned into a *semmie*."

I couldn't help but bristle at her tone. What was wrong with being a semmie?

"And there's no telling what they'll do to me if I come

back without being able to project," she continued with a huff. "I'll be worse than just a regular human in their eyes. Then if they know I played a part in losing my ability…" She shuddered. "It will be bad enough trying to explain why I left. You know they have no tolerance for leaving without clearance. I'd have to come up with a lie about that, too, and we both know there's a very good chance they'll see through it."

Her words hit me like a bus. I hadn't realized how serious the repercussions could be for her going back when she couldn't project. No wonder she was so desperate to get answers from Delta. Would Cade run into those same problems?

No. He had a legitimate story. The members of XODUS *stole* his ability and stranded him here. Surely the other Astralii would sympathize with him. And Solstice, well, she had brought it on herself, whether she meant to or not. I couldn't let myself feel bad for her.

"So how am I supposed to find Kala once Solstice is back in the lab?" I asked.

Delta shrugged. "You'd just coordinate with Solstice." It wasn't a bad idea—except the part that involved my depending on Solstice. But I could simply substitute Cade in and go from there.

Solstice shook her head. "That's a horrible plan, and it puts me at risk."

"You won't be at risk if you explain that someone trapped your astral energy," Delta insisted. "That much is true."

"Well, why don't we make sure Lali can even get to

the portal before we start coming up with plans for after she does?" Solstice grumbled, tossing her braid over one shoulder. "Then we can figure out our next steps from there."

Delta sighed, her eyes flicking to me before settling on the carpet. "Okay. Before we try anything else, let's see what Lali can do."

43

DISCOURAGEMENT

SOLSTICE SCOWLED AT ME FROM THE LOVESEAT IN HER living room. "This is a waste of time. She's never going to find it."

"Well, she doesn't need you discouraging her at every turn," I shot back, glancing at Lali. She sat next to me on Solstice's couch, breathing like she was in a deep slumber while she attempted to find the portal. It was almost eight-thirty in the evening—on the West Coast, anyway— and Lali had barely been here for fifteen minutes. In that short time, Solstice had already found multiple ways to imply that we should reconsider our plan.

"What?" Solstice sneered. "She can't hear us."

"Yeah, well she heard everything else you said to try and bring down her spirits before she went up there." I was sure Solstice was acting this way because she knew Delta was listening from the opposite side of the wall. Delta was so eager to see how things progressed that she finally took off her block and agreed to wait in the bedroom. Lali didn't know about her involvement, and I was still convinced it was better that way.

"I swear, you Orian men are all the same," Solstice muttered.

I scoffed. "My last name is Awana."

"Just because your father didn't want to mark you for the Eyes and Ears doesn't mean you don't have the same blood. And apparently, you have the same weakness for Vauhn women, too."

"What are you talking about?"

"I'm talking about how Cade was pathetically in love with Xiomara, just like you're pathetically in love with Lali."

Whoa. What? She must have been making that up. My uncle wasn't in love with Xiomara. He hated her. And I wasn't in love with Lali, either. Sure, I enjoyed her company, and I respected that she was strong and kind and tried to do the right thing, but I'd been lying to her since we met. That wasn't exactly a solid foundation for that type of feeling.

"I'm not in love with anyone," I grumbled.

Solstice preened her hair. "Right."

"What do you care, anyway?"

Her eyes practically rolled behind her brain. "We're never going to get anywhere if you're too busy drooling over Lali to see that this isn't going to work."

"Give me a break. We weren't getting anywhere before, either."

"We were until you screwed everything up with Delta.

I swear, sometimes I think you *like* holding Xiomara hostage."

Lali gasped as she sat up, and I could have sworn my heart stopped. Had she heard us? I didn't know which was more horrifying: her hearing that I had her mother, or her hearing Solstice's accusations of me of being in love with her. Because I wasn't. I was way too damaged to love anyone.

"It's not there." Lali leaned forward on the sofa, struggling to breathe.

I held in the relieved sigh that tried to burst out of me. If that was all she said, she must not have heard us. *Thank God.*

"You probably just didn't get the angle right," Solstice replied, shaking her head. "Semmies."

"So far, this *semmie* is the best shot you've got at getting back to Alea," Lali retorted. "So I suggest you try working *with* me for a change."

I felt myself nod in approval. I didn't have the feelings for Lali that Solstice claimed, but I liked that she was strong enough to stand her ground.

The two of them stared each other down for a long moment before Lali said she wanted to go again.

"Don't you want to rest?" I asked. Solstice gave me a look, and I knew my concern had just made her think I'd confirmed her accusation. "I mean, it seems like it's going to take some serious energy to get up there again. I don't want you passing out and having to wait hours before you can recover."

"I'm fine," Lali said. Without another word, she projected again.

Solstice and I sat watching her, neither of us speaking as Lali projected and came back frustrated and out of breath four more times. My hope started to wither when she opened her eyes another time with failure written all over her face.

"Do we need to go over it *again?*" Solstice grumbled.

Lali huffed. "I did exactly what you said. I'm telling you, something's wrong. The portal isn't there."

"What are you saying?" Solstice's tone was mocking. "It just disappeared?"

"Or I need better directions."

They started arguing again, and I heaved a sigh. "Can we give it a rest with the arguing?" I begged. "This is ridiculous."

"This is a waste of time." Solstice fell back against the sofa. "Cade was right. We should be focusing on—"

"On what?" I interrupted, praying Delta hadn't overheard that. Did Solstice forget she was in the other room? "Sitting around hoping to trace energy? *That's* the waste of time."

I eyed Lali, hoping she didn't pick up on the lie. Cade was much more concerned with stalking Delta than tracing astral energy, but Lali was still in the dark about the whole XODUS thing. I planned to keep it that way.

Solstice's features scrunched. "Well, listening to Lali throw a fit about bad directions isn't exactly efficient. I knew she wouldn't be able to handle this."

"Excuse me?" Lali leapt off the couch, and I had to

hold her back. I wouldn't have put it past her to kick Solstice's ass right there. It was tempting to let it happen, but we still needed Solstice to help us figure out why Lali couldn't find the portal.

Instead of blowing up as I expected, Lali shoved my arm away, stormed down the hall, and slammed the door to the bathroom so hard I was sure the whole apartment shook.

Solstice let out a harsh laugh. "Your girlfriend is having another fit. Might want to go reel her in."

"Stop egging her on!" I shouted. "Why are you making this difficult?"

"I'm not. It's not my fault she can't handle failure."

I bunched my hands around the fabric of my shirt. Now I was sure Solstice was putting on a show for Delta's ears. "She's going to find the portal." I made sure my voice was loud enough for Delta to hear, too. Two could play at that game.

Turning on my heel, I headed toward the bathroom calling Lali's name.

"Go away," she called back.

I opened the door anyway and found her glaring at me. "Hey," I said softly.

"You don't take direction well," she grumbled, lowering herself onto the edge of the tub.

"You don't take encouragement well. Guess we're even." I knelt in front of her, placing my hands on either side of where she sat on the cold porcelain tub. "Forget Solstice, okay? If you want, we can go to the beach and you can figure this out in peace."

"There's nothing to figure out." Her eyes grew moist like she was fighting not to cry. "I'm doing exactly what she told me, but it's not working."

"It's just going to take a little time."

"*Time?*" She gave me an incredulous look. "It already took three weeks just to permeate. How much longer will it take to find the portal? I can't handle all these setbacks and disappointments. I just want my family back. Is that so much to ask?"

Tell me about it.

One of her eyes spilled over, and without thinking, I caught the tear with my thumb. She shut her eyes and leaned into my hand, making my stomach do a little dance.

I do not have feelings for her. I don't.

"I know it's frustrating," I said, fighting to keep it together myself. "And I feel terrible sitting around while you do all the work." I looked into her eyes, hoping she could see the honesty in what I was saying. If I could trade places with her, I would do it without hesitation. Just sitting there helpless while demanding everything from her was excruciating.

"I just wish you could see how much hope you've given me," I continued. "When you made it to that transposer today—" The thought alone made me have to stop and catch my breath. If only she could understand how much that meant to me, how much I'd needed that resurgence of faith. "This is the most confident I've ever felt that I'll see Kala again. Please, don't give up. I need you."

She blew out her breath. "I'm not giving up." My

chest lifted at her words. That was all I needed to hear. "I'm just frustrated."

"That's understandable," I said, standing up again and holding out my hand. "Can I make you some tea while you recover a bit?"

"No, thanks. I want to try again now."

I sighed. "Lali, you need to rest. You were up there for a long time."

"I'm fine," she insisted.

"You're going to—" I stopped when I realized she'd projected again.

Typical. Her breathing became labored within seconds, and I jiggled her shoulders to snap her out of the projection. I didn't need her passing out like she had on the beach when she'd first traveled.

"Why did you do that?" she choked out, her voice barely surviving the sentence.

"Because I didn't feel like carrying you out of here. You were wheezing like your lungs were going to explode."

"I'm told you, I'm fine."

"No, you're crazy. And stubborn. And too pretty to be the first girl to die from projecting too much." I felt my mouth twitch, and hers followed suit. That time, my heart did the dancing.

Stop it! What was my problem?

Before I could say anything else humiliating, I pulled her up from the side of the tub, ignoring the roller coaster sensation I got from her being so close.

"Kai, I—" She started to fall, but she caught herself on the side of the tub.

I gave her a look. "See? You're drained. I'm taking you home so you can rest."

Thankfully, she didn't argue. The only protest came from a little voice in my head that yelled at me for worrying about Lali. Her being drained shouldn't have mattered so much to me. *She* shouldn't have mattered so much to me.

But she did.

...Shortly after that moment, I realized Solstice was right. No matter how I tried to deny it, I cared about you, Lali. Despite all the stress hanging over us and putting both of us on edge, I could see your heart and the goodness there. With so many people in my life encouraging me to lie and manipulate, you were the one person who just wanted to be honest with everyone and do the right thing. You were the kind of person I told myself I would have been if the circumstances had been different.

Though I didn't want to admit it, I took you home because I was worried about your health. Even if it meant delaying getting to Alea, I wanted you to be okay. That was when I truly started to grasp what you meant to me, and it was terrifying. I fought it as best I could, but it wasn't enough...

44

SUSPICION

LALI SLOUCHED AND FROWNED AT ME FROM HER BED. HER face was flushed, her skin dewy from the effort of projecting, and I knew I'd made the right call stopping her. "How long am I out, coach?" she grumbled.

"Until you can project without sounding like a pig having an asthma attack," I replied, unable to contain my laugh at the hateful look she gave me. I sat down next to her. "Just trying to make sure you don't push yourself too hard trying to find the portal. And you *will* find it."

She avoided my eyes, and I could tell she wasn't buying it.

"Hey." I pulled her face up so she would look at me. "You will. I'm sure of it. I've never had as much faith in anyone as I have in you." I felt the truth in my words even more as I said them. Lali had stayed strong for so long, and she'd been my only reason to believe I could find my sister after months of dead ends had chipped away at my hope. I owed her so much.

Gratitude swelled in my chest as I moved my hand up to her cheek, and before I knew what I was doing, I pressed my mouth to hers. Her soft lips parted in surprise, but she transformed in an instant. Suddenly, she was kissing me back, hard.

My pulse hammered as her hands tangled in my hair. Warmth spread through my body, the sensation unlike any I'd known before. I couldn't deny anymore that I did have feelings for Lali. And from the urgency in how she held me to her, she had feelings for me, too.

Too bad she can't trust you. The voice in my head jarred me into reality, and I pulled away. I couldn't do this. Not when I couldn't be honest with her. Not when she was going to hate me as soon as she realized I was the one who had her mom. She'd think I played her just to get my sister back.

Had I played her?

I watched her face fall, and it was like someone had stabbed me. "What's wrong?" I asked. Stupid question. *I* was wrong. Everything about me was wrong.

"Nothing." But I could tell she was lying. I could always tell when she was lying. That was one of the most endearing things about her.

"I just—" She cut herself off, as if she couldn't think of how to let me down gently. But she didn't have to.

"Too much going on right now?" I gave her an out before she could tell me that she didn't feel anything for me, that she wasn't thinking clearly because of the emotional strain on her. Staring at the narrow wooden planks of her floor, I told myself I didn't care if she

279

didn't want me. It could never happen, anyway. Not after everything I'd done, everything I'd lied about. She would never be able to accept me once she knew the truth.

She sighed and nodded without looking at me. "It's not that I don't...*you know*."

"I get it," I said, grasping for what shred of dignity I had left.

"Rain check?"

I forced a smile. Stood up. Put my hands in my pockets so she couldn't see that they were shaking. "Get some rest, okay?" Thankfully, my voice didn't waver. "I'll come by bright and early tomorrow."

I left before she could respond—before I could give myself away. I dropped onto my own bed and ran my hands through my hair. It was better this way. I didn't need to be getting involved with someone who had no idea who I truly was. Besides, if lines got blurred between us, we wouldn't be able to focus on what we were doing, and it would be even harder for Lali to get to Alea with Solstice's confusing directions.

Solstice. I remembered that I'd left her alone with Delta. She was probably convincing Delta to give up on Lali as I sat here wallowing like a loser. I had to get my head right. I couldn't have Solstice derailing our efforts because I let myself get caught up in a moment.

Steeling myself, I showed up in Solstice's kitchen to find her and Delta sitting at the table talking. They both looked tense.

"What's going on?" I asked.

Delta glanced at me and pursed her lips. "It's obvious Lali is struggling…" she began.

Damn it! Solstice had already gotten to her.

I shook my head. "She just needs some time to figure it out. She's overwhelmed." *Especially now that I went and kissed her.*

"Or she can't activate the portal because she's a semmie," Solstice said. "If that's the case, we're beating a dead horse."

I started to argue, but Delta jumped in first. "I've been thinking, and I might be able to undo the sink without affecting Cade's astral energy."

Solstice and I both stared at her. Where did that come from?

"You can do that?" Solstice gasped. "Why didn't you tell me that in the first place?"

Delta's eyes darted between us. "Well, I'm not sure if it will work. I want to try, though."

"You said you couldn't undo intentions if you have fewer people than when the crystals are programmed," Solstice said.

"Well, it's worth a shot, isn't it?" Delta blinked again. "If it doesn't work, then I'll try to help you find the others. I may have a way to find Ori."

At that, Solstice lit up.

"But I insist we try it this way first," Delta added, turning to me. "You have access to a crystal shop, right?"

I nodded slowly. I got the feeling something weird was up, especially after Delta made such a big deal about the dangers of undoing the sink before. But given that Lali probably didn't want to look at me after that awkward post-kiss exchange, maybe it was worth seeing what this was all about.

"Good," Delta said. "They should have everything I need there. Then I'll have to dig up the buried stone with all our astral energy inside. Solstice and I will take it from there."

"Okay." I held out my hand. "Let's go."

The crystal store was dark when we appeared, save for a glowing red *EXIT* sign above us. I started to reach for my phone to use as a flashlight, but Delta grabbed my arm.

"Kai," she whispered. "Solstice is lying about where to find the portal."

I jerked back. "What are you talking about?" Solstice had been more discouraging than ever, but I thought it was to convince Delta that our only option was to undo the sink. I didn't think she'd stoop so low as to lie about how to get to Alea.

"She admitted it after you took Lali home," Delta breathed. "She says she's trying to keep Lali safe, but I know she just doesn't want to return to Alea without her ability."

"Then why are we looking for crystals? We should be getting answers from her."

"She won't tell me the real location, and I know she won't tell you, either. I don't know where the portal is because I've only been carried between the realms, and everything is a blur up there. So I'm letting Solstice think she talked me into undoing the sink."

"Okay…" I couldn't keep up with all the deceit anymore. "What are you really doing?"

"Something that gives you a better chance of getting to Alea. But you're going to have to trust me. And you'll have to lie to Solstice."

I snorted. Lying seemed to be all I did these days. What was one more fib now? "Fine," I sighed. "I'm in. What do you have in mind?"

45

BACKUP

"No way." I crossed my arms over my chest. "Things are crazy enough as it is. I can't bring Lali's brothers and sisters into this, too." My mind was still reeling from Delta's suggestion to use the guise of trying to undo the energy sink as a way to trick Solstice into helping her awaken the astral energy in Lali's siblings. I didn't even know that type of thing was possible, but I was sure I didn't want to do it.

"Do you want to get your sister back or not?" Delta stared me down, her face half illuminated by the red glow of the *EXIT* sign above us. "You'll have a much better shot with four more semmies on your side."

"You just said you wouldn't force astral energy on people."

"I said I wouldn't do it to people who weren't equipped to handle it," Delta corrected. "Lali's brothers and sisters are—they just haven't developed their abilities yet."

I raked my fingers through my hair. Even if they were physically prepared, it still felt wrong. After all the time I'd spent with Lali, I knew how much her siblings meant to her.

"And you think this will work just because they have the same initials as your little group?" I asked. Xiomara had named her kids with the same first initials as the members of XODUS: Lali's full name was Xitlali, and her brothers and sisters were Oxanna, Dixon, Ulyxses, and Salaxia. I wasn't sure how Delta knew that, but that was the least of my worries.

"I can word the intention to make it work. I know it will. I've seen—" Delta cut herself off suddenly.

I frowned. "You've seen what?"

"Just trust me. I can connect them to the group and awaken their powers."

"But there's no guarantee they can help us."

"There's a chance." She glanced around the darkened store as if she expected to find someone eavesdropping. "The Eyes and Ears forced me to awaken plenty of abilities in semmies, and I've seen the ways their powers can turn out. Some can project their thoughts to look like reality, some can project through time, some can project into people's minds and control them. If one of Lali's siblings can get into Solstice's head, they'd be able to make her tell us exactly where to find the portal."

"And what if none of them can do that?" I challenged. "What if none of them can help us at all?"

"Then we'll be in the same position we're in now."

My stomach twisted. I hated this. But if Solstice was

lying to us, we weren't going to make progress anyway. And Lali's siblings were going to get their abilities eventually. Would it be that bad if they got them early? Maybe if they did, it would take some of the strain off Lali. She was doing everything by herself, and it had to be taking a toll on her.

I shifted my weight. "You're sure it won't hurt them?"

"Of course. It will just awaken the abilities that are already lying dormant. After Solstice and I go through the ritual, you'll take the programmed quartz and hold it near Lali's brothers and sisters until it glows. They won't feel a thing."

I sighed heavily. "If you really think this will help—"

"It will." Delta spun around to face the rows of plastic bins, little more than darkened outlines in the limited light. "I'll get everything I need from here. I told Solstice I'd dig up the original quartz we used for the sink, but I can get a similar enough stone that she won't realize the switch."

Grabbing a leather pouch off one of the racks, she moved around the store collecting supplies. I turned on my phone's flashlight and aimed it just ahead of her so she could see what she was doing. Soon, she had at least two dozen stones, a dagger, a bunch of white candles, and a circular cloth like the one Xiomara used to set up the block around the in-law.

We made a detour so she could dig up a bit of dirt in the woods. She said that part was to make it look like she had really found the original quartz they'd used to trap

Cade's astral energy. I didn't argue. I just wanted to get the whole thing over with.

Once we'd gone over what I was to say after the ritual, we appeared in Solstice's apartment again.

"We got everything," Delta announced. She had the leather pouch strung across her torso, and her arms could barely hold all the candles she'd wrapped in the cloth.

Solstice came around the corner from the kitchen and eyed Delta with a skeptical expression. "Del, I don't—"

"Just trust me," Delta said firmly. With that, she scurried into the bedroom.

Solstice stared after her for a long moment before turning to me. "Did she explain it to you? Something doesn't add up."

I shrugged. "I don't understand anything about crystals or energy manipulation. But whatever her plan is, she seems confident in it." I hoped that sounded neutral enough.

"I don't know why she thinks this will work. Two can't undo the intention of five."

"Well, she's the expert, right?" I hedged.

"Okay," Delta called from the hallway. She came into the living room and nodded. "The sacred space is ready."

Solstice charged forward, and I followed her into the bedroom. The white candles were lit and flickering around the cloth on the floor. Each marked the five ends of an asterisk-looking shape made of colorful stones.

Solstice scowled. "Delta, are you sure this will work?"

"It should. I'm using the same intention they made

me use to awaken the semmies' powers. Our astral energy is dormant, just like theirs."

I did my best not to cringe. Delta basically just admitted what we were hoping to make happen with Lali's siblings. I snuck a glance at Solstice. She looked unconvinced but not suspicious. I was probably being paranoid. Delta's words were only questionable to me because I was in on the plan.

Solstice moved to sit in front of the fabric circle, and Delta sat down across from her. I stood off to the side, unable to shake the feeling that I was betraying Lali. This time, it was even worse because I knew her. At least when I took her mom, I had no connection to anyone in the family.

"Awaken the energy that rests," Delta chanted, snapping me out of my thoughts. She put her hand on the clear, fist-sized stone that Solstice held over the middle of the circle and closed her eyes. "Just for X, O, D, U, and S."

The stone flashed, and Delta pulled the dagger from the pouch. Pressing her index finger against the tip of the blade, she squeezed a drop of blood onto the stone. It sizzled, and she repeated the chant.

Solstice went through the same steps, and soon the candles flickered like they were caught in the wind. Delta shut her eyes again and put both hands on the stone. This time, the light that came from inside it washed out everything in the room. The next second, it dimmed into nothing.

I blinked, trying to readjust my eyes. "Did it work?"

"It must've," Delta said. "You saw the light."

"Well, let's try projecting and find out." Solstice squeezed her eyes shut. After a minute, she cursed and shouted, "I can't do it!"

"I can't, either." Delta scratched her head, trying and failing to look distraught. "I was sure that would work." She gave Solstice a long, hard look, but all Solstice did was snap about how Delta's tweaks had failed.

I pushed off the wall. "Hey, we had to try. But if you don't mind, I'm going to head home. I'm exhausted."

"Wait," Delta called, following the script she'd come up with earlier. She took the quartz from Solstice and hurried over to me. "Keep this somewhere safe until we can find the others."

"Okay." I tried to look caught off guard as I took the stone from her. "See you both tomorrow."

Projecting to my room, I stared at the crystal in my hand. I still wasn't sure this was a great idea, but there was no point in turning back now. I checked my phone. It was already two in the morning, so Lali's family would surely be asleep. Knowing I'd probably need a flashlight to get around the house, I switched my phone to airplane mode. With my luck, Cade would call while I was in one of the kids' rooms.

I previewed the upstairs hallway of Lali's house. It was dark and empty. Perfect.

Appearing in front of the door to her littlest sister's room, I slowly turned the knob. Mercifully, it opened without creaking. The girl I'd since learned was named Salaxia lay konked out, her arm draped over the side of the bed the way it had been when I grabbed her stuffed elephant months ago. Just like Delta had instructed, I brought the stone close to Salaxia and waited for it to light up. I kept it toward the back of her head so it wouldn't wake her, but the flash was quick enough that she probably wouldn't have noticed anyway.

I repeated the process with Lali's other sister and two brothers, surprised that the whole thing went so smoothly. One of the twins stirred but didn't wake. Thankfully, her family members all seemed to sleep soundly.

When I was done, I stepped back into the hallway and looked toward Lali's room. I couldn't help but wonder if she was still awake. I kind of felt like I should apologize for kissing her. Things were already complicated enough, and she didn't need more to deal with right now. The least I could do was acknowledge that.

Tiptoeing toward her door, I eased it open and poked my head inside. It was dark, but I could make out the unmade bed. Lali wasn't in it.

I stepped into the room and closed the door behind me. "Lali?" I whispered, though a quick glance around the space told me she wasn't there. Where would she have gone? I'd just passed the bathroom, and I knew she wasn't in there.

Closing my eyes, I tried to preview her. The next second, it felt like a bus hit me. My back cracked against the dresser, and I slumped to the floor before I'd realized what happened.

What the—

How did she have a block around her? Had she found her mom?

No. It wasn't possible. Even if Lali had somehow projected to Xiomara, she wouldn't have been able to switch into her physical body without a transposer. The only one she knew about was in San Francisco, and there was no way she could get from there to Miami that quickly.

Pushing myself to sit up, I pulled out my phone to call her. As soon as I switched it out of airplane mode, it beeped with a voicemail from Lali. I pressed the button to play the message.

"Kai!" Lali's recorded voice gasped. "Call me back as soon as you get this!" She sounded hysterical, and obviously eager to tell me something. There was only one thing that would have made her sound like that. The realization made my body go numb. She'd found the portal.

Lali was in Alea.

RESCUE

I CURSED AND SCRAMBLED TO MY FEET. WHAT WAS LALI thinking? How could she go to Alea alone? I told her not to go without me. Now I had no way to get to her, and she could be in danger.

Swallowing hard, I fought to calm my racing thoughts. Maybe I was overreacting. There might've been somewhere in this realm that was blocked. But where? The only place I could think of with any Astralii link was the house above the transposer. That would make the most sense, and it would have been easy for Lali to get there. I had to check.

Squeezing my eyes shut, I projected to the glowing ring I'd seen under the bay not twenty-four hours prior. It didn't take long to find the steps leading to the trap door Solstice had described. Shoving open the hinged wooden square, I found myself looking around the common area of an enormous house.

"Lali?" I called out, not even caring if there were any Astralii around to hear.

No response.

"*Lali!*" I clambered out of the rectangular hole in the floor and ran through the massive home. I barely noticed any of the details as I raced past the living room, down the halls, up the stairs. I checked each of seven bedrooms and four bathrooms, calling Lali's name the whole way.

The place was empty.

Tearing back down the steps, I took the deepest breath I could manage. *Okay, think. Where else could she have gone?* Even though it was unlikely, I had to check the in-law, just to be certain. It was the only place I knew for sure was blocked.

I projected to my house and sprinted toward the basement. "Lali?" I shouted over the pounding of my feet on the stairs.

Xiomara appeared at the bottom of the steps just as I reached the last one. "What's going on?" she asked. "Why are you calling my daughter's name?"

"Is she down here?" I panted, scanning the small apartment.

"Of course not. How could she be?"

"I can't project to her." I nearly choked on the sentence.

"What? Why are you—"

"She's somewhere with a block! Where could she be if she's not here?"

"I don't know, Kai." Xiomara was suddenly breathing as hard as I was. "What's going on?"

I ran my hands over my face. "She must've found the portal. Somehow, she found it and she went to Alea without me."

"*What?* How is that even possible?" I met Xiomara's gaze, and she seemed to read everything on my face. "Are you insane?" she shrieked. "How could you send her there by herself? Do you know what they'll do to her if they find her?"

"I know! I never told her to go alone. I *specifically* told her to wait for me." I pulled the ends of my hair, hoping the pain would ground me so I could think. "Are there blocks around the transposer in Alea?"

"No. The only blocks are around houses and—" Xiomara made a sharp, shrill sound, as if she'd been stabbed.

"What?" I demanded. "Houses and what?" The terror in her eyes answered my question. *The lab.*

Xiomara grabbed her stomach. "My baby. My *baby!*"

I shook my head, refusing to believe it. Lali couldn't be in the lab. I couldn't lose someone else to that place.

"Delta," I gasped. "She can trace her."

"What?" Xiomara gaped at me. "She—"

I spun around and started up the stairs before she could finish. I heard her footsteps behind me, and she caught my elbow as I stepped onto the main floor.

I projected us to Solstice's apartment without explanation. Solstice and Delta were settled at the table, but both jumped to their feet when they saw us.

"Lali's in Alea," I breathed before they could say anything.

Solstice's jaw dropped open.

"Del?" Xiomara sounded relieved to see her even though Delta looked like she'd seen a ghost. "Can you trace her? Please."

"How could she have gotten to Alea?" Solstice asked. "The—"

"We can figure out how later," I shouted. "We have to find her before…" My voice refused to finish the thought.

"I'll get the stones." Delta booked it to the bedroom with Xiomara right behind her.

I couldn't just stand around and do nothing. I had to try going after Lali again. Maybe there was a chance she had moved out of range of the block.

Heading for the living room, I dropped onto the sofa to minimize the block's effect if I hit it again. Sure enough, I felt my body thrown back into the cushions, the air ejecting from my lungs. Gasping, I tried again. And again.

The kick back felt stronger every time, or maybe I was getting weaker with each hit. But I couldn't give up.

"Stop that," Delta scolded as she and Xiomara came back into the living room, their hands filled with the supplies Delta and I had stolen earlier. "You'll knock yourself unconscious."

"Have to…find her," I choked out, closing my eyes to try another time. The hit made me grunt, and I felt sweat slide down my forehead.

"Not like that," Delta said, frantically setting up the stuff for the ritual with Xiomara scrambling alongside her.

Despite her scolding, I couldn't keep myself from trying to go after Lali. Twice more, I took the block's beating, and every inhale became a wheeze.

"I said stop that, Kai!" Delta shouted. "You'll hurt yourself."

But I couldn't stop. Not until I knew Lali was safe.

"We don't know for sure she's in trouble," Solstice mumbled, kneeling next to the cloth now covered in crystals.

"She's behind a block!" Xiomara exploded. "Where could she be that isn't dangerous?"

Her words seared through me. This was my fault. I should've been honest with Lali from the beginning. All my lying had put my only friend in danger.

I wouldn't rest until I got her out. Closing my eyes, I braced myself for the kick in the gut as I tried to project to her. But this time, the images came together in my mind.

Yes! I followed the preview without thinking. The white-haired man behind Lali didn't have time to react. I tackled him, and metal flashed in my peripheral vision as something in his hand fell to the ground. I jumped to my feet, my brain focused on Lali. Everything else blurred as I dove at her. I didn't care that I knocked her off balance, or that we landed hard in the sand as I projected us back to Lanai.

Gulping the salty air, I lifted my head and took in Lali's bewildered expression below me. I felt my heart stammer. *She's safe. She's safe.* My brain ran on a loop, repeating the thought until it finally convinced me I hadn't been too late.

But my relief quickly gave way to anger. We warned Lali not to go off on her own, and she'd risked her life because she was too stubborn to listen.

"Are you *crazy?*" I yelled, stumbling to a standing position. "What were you thinking going off by yourself? Do you have any idea how dangerous that was? You could've been killed!"

"Kai, we have to go back," she cried.

I opened my mouth to argue, but she cut me off with the only two words that could stop me dead in my tracks: "Kala's there."

47

BACKSTABBER

The world froze. At first, I was sure I'd misheard her. "What?" I managed to get out despite the spinning in my head.

"I saw her in the lab," Lali gasped. I blinked, my brain a million miles away as I stared at where she lay in the sand. Lali had been inside the lab. If she'd seen Kala there, that meant...

I nearly collapsed. I'd just been right outside that place—the closest to Kala I'd ever been since she was kidnapped—and I projected out of there without a second look. I wanted to tear my hair out. I was so stupid! I let myself get so distracted with saving Lali that I didn't even think about bookmarking the location so I could go back.

"She was in a classroom." Lali's voice broke into my thoughts, and I did a double take.

"A *classroom?*" I repeated. No, that couldn't be right. There was no way Kala was going to school in Alea.

Cade would have told me if that were even a remote possibility. Wouldn't he?

"Are you sure it was her?" I asked.

"Positive." Lali clambered to her feet, sand spilling from her clothes as she moved. "I swear. We have to go back and get one of those stones."

"What stones?"

"The guards," she said, still breathless. "They have these purple stones around their necks. They can move through blocks. I saw them do it."

Some of the higher Astralii have stones that can penetrate blocks. Delta had told me that while we were talking in her motel room. That must've been what Lali was talking about.

"There's a block around the lab," Lali continued. "But if we can sneak up on one of them, we can steal a necklace and break through it."

That was all I needed to know. Whatever it took, I was going to get back to that lab. "Okay," I said. "How do we sneak up on them? Where are they?"

"There were some right outside the transposer. Maybe you can peek out the door and get a glimpse of the area before they can catch you."

"I'll have to," I admitted, the whole beach seeming to come into sharper focus. "I didn't get much of a look at Alea when I went after you. I just wanted to get you out of there, and…" I inhaled slowly, studying Lali again. Her hair was matted and tangled, her face was streaked with sweat, and her bottom lip was swollen. What happened to her over there? I wasn't even sure she could make it to Alea again.

"Can you go back?" I asked. "You look—"

"I'm fine." She snapped her eyes shut, and I tried to catch my breath. I waited for her to disappear, preparing for the moment I'd have to project after her. This time, I would go *right* after her. No more mishaps.

But she didn't disappear. At least, not as quickly I expected. I waited, bouncing on my toes impatiently. What was taking so long? She'd already seen the place, so she wouldn't need to go after the portal anymore. All she had to do was picture it and show up next to it in her astral form.

Her breathing went ragged, and I knew something wasn't right.

"Lali?" I jiggled her shoulder. "Lali, you're panting like you're going to faint. What's wrong?"

"I messed everything up," she sobbed.

"What?"

"They're watching the transposer. Their weapons are pointed right at it." She grabbed her head. "I ruined everything."

No. That couldn't be true. After everything we'd been through, I refused to give up now.

"There has to be another way," I insisted, mentally racing through everything I'd learned from Cade about Astralii and their realm. He'd mentioned once that there were more transposers than the main one. That could be our way in. If he knew where they were, he could help us. He *had* to help us, whether it was the week to pursue his agenda or not.

"Cade told me there are more transposers in Alea," I

said. "It's not just the main one. Maybe we can try one of the others. Come on."

I grabbed her hand, not caring anymore about the issues Cade would have with involving her. He couldn't argue now that she'd made it.

I took us to Delta's bedroom, not wanting to startle Cade by appearing right in front of him with Lali. "Uncle Cade!" I yelled, pulling open the door to the hallway. I gestured for Lali to come after me as I walked toward the living room.

"What?" he called back.

"Where are we?" Lali whispered as we moved down the hall.

"This house belongs to a friend of Solstice's," I told her. "Cade has been ransacking it looking for clues about other Astralii and sending me off to follow up on the leads he finds." That was mostly true. I just didn't have time to explain the rest.

Lali and I stepped into the living room, and Cade looked up from where he sat in the middle of a mess of papers and boxes. I didn't even care what he was looking for now. Nothing he found could trump what Lali had done.

His eyes narrowed as soon as they landed on her. "What's she doing here?" he barked. "We agreed to leave her out of this." Of course, he was going to make a big deal about the stupid week rotation.

"Yeah," I started. "But—"

"But you're still running around with her behind my back?" He lumbered to his feet. "Is this why you haven't found anything with any of our leads? Because you've been too busy chasing a crush?"

"She found Kala!" I hadn't meant to shout, but at least it got Cade's attention.

"That's not possible." He glared between us. "You'd never get anywhere close to her without clearance to the lab."

"Well, she did," I said. "She made it to Alea, and they caught her, and now they're guarding the transposer." I watched his face for any type of softening that might suggest he would help us. All I saw was anger. "But you told me there are other transposers," I went on. "If you direct us to one of them, we can get a guard's necklace, and—"

Cade let out a harsh laugh. "You think you can steal a guard's necklace? You'll never even come close. You're *kids*, semmies no less. They'll kill you before you can blink."

"Then come with us," I urged. "Tell them you want your old position back like we talked about. We can go right now."

"And how will I explain how I got there?" He gave me a hard look. "If they find out I'm working with semmies, they'll kill me, too."

"So tell them you met a full-blooded Astralis," Lali suggested.

Cade didn't even look at her. "Don't you think they'll ask who helped me? Even if they let me in, they'd never give me my old position without my ability. You'd know that, nephew, if you listened to me in the first place."

I couldn't back down. I'd spent the last few years doing everything I could to make myself as little of a burden as possible, but this was different. We were too close to give up now.

"Well, we're going," I insisted, trying to match the intensity in Cade's eyes. "One way or another. I'm not giving up when we're this close to getting Kala back. Now, are you going to help us or not?"

"Think about what you're saying." His arms flew out to grab me. "This is a suicide mission."

"Let go of him!" Lali yelled as I pulled away from my uncle. For the first time, I didn't feel guilty for standing up to him

Cade moved his enraged stare to Lali, and I tensed. "*You*," he spat. "You don't even know who you're helping."

"I know exactly who I'm helping." She said it with so much more confidence than I deserved. The thought was like a hot poker to the gut.

"Oh, you don't have a clue, little girl." Cade gave her a condescending smile that made the scar along his cheek ripple. "But since you haven't figured it out yet, let me give you a hint: my nephew has been lying to you this whole time."

"Uncle Cade!" My heart threatened to explode. How could he just call me out like that?

Lali gaped at me, her face as white as it had been the day I'd followed her into the bathroom.

I tried to plead with my eyes. "Lali. I can explain."

"Explain *what?*" Her head whipped between my uncle and me. "What's going on?"

"*Now* you want to come clean, nephew?" Cade laughed, a challenge in his eyes as he looked at me. "Don't you think she'd have wanted to know the truth earlier?"

No. He was going to out me all the way. He was going to tell Lali we had her mom, that I was the reason for all of her suffering the past few months. His sneer only confirmed it. "After all, you—"

I dove for Lali's hand and projected straight to Lanai before he could finish. My fingers tightened around Lali's as she blinked wildly. She must not have had time to close her eyes after I flashed out of there so fast.

Rage burned in my throat. I couldn't believe Cade would do something like that. I knew he was angry, but he was straight up sabotaging me. I swallowed hard, watching Lali try to get her bearings. What was I going to tell her now? What could I admit to lying about without ruining my chance at getting her to finish what we started?

48

HONESTY

"You manipulative jerk!" Lali's voice rang out over the sound of the ocean, killing my hope that bringing her to Lanai would remind her of the bond we now shared. After all the times I'd brought her here just to relax and catch her breath after she practiced permeating, she was looking at me like she was seeing me for who I really was for the first time. Maybe she was.

I'd told her as much of the truth as I could—how a group of Astralii trapped Cade's astral energy, how my uncle and I had been trying to find them so we could undo the sink. Lali jumped to the conclusion that I'd kept it from her because I was secretly threatening people to get them to help. Even with the disgust in her eyes right now, I knew that was a better assumption than the truth.

I sighed, desperate to get her to understand. "Lali, didn't you hear Cade? I haven't been helping him follow up on any of the leads he's found. I haven't gone after anyone else since I got you on my side."

"Then where did Delta come from?" she challenged.

I frowned. How did she— "You were spying on me?"

"Oh, you're offended? How long did you spend spying on me?"

All I could do was grind my teeth.

"You have no right to be angry," she went on ranting. "I'm not the one leading a double life. I'm not the one lying to the person risking her life to help me."

"I never asked you to risk your life. That was your crazy scheme. All I asked you to do was get to a transposer and stay put so I could come after you."

"Then maybe you should've answered your phone."

"Maybe you should learn to take accountability for your actions. Then you can think about thanking me for saving your impulsive butt."

She rolled her eyes. "As if you did that for me. You were just worried you were going to lose your ticket to Alea."

"*What?*" She couldn't be serious. "Are you *blind?*"

"Apparently, since I've been trusting you this whole time. I'm surprised you even have a sister."

Wow. That was a low blow, and she knew it. "You're unbelievable," I muttered.

"Well, that's ironic, coming from you."

That time, I couldn't respond at all. I listened to the sound of the water, wishing it could soothe me now and fix this mess. But I was beyond soothing, and things were beyond fixing. I'd be lucky if Lali ever talked to me again once this was all over.

At least she still thinks she has to help you. As much as I hated to admit it, in that moment, I was glad she still thought her mom was in Alea. That meant she had as much invested in getting a guard's necklace as I did.

And speaking of the necklaces...

I blew out my breath. Even though it was obvious she wanted to strangle me right now, we had work to do. "Lali." I kept my tone as peaceful as I could. "Listen to me."

"I tried that, remember? And now I know it was a mistake. It's bad enough Solstice lied about where the stupid portal is. I need *someone* I can trust."

I squinted. How did she know about that? Had she seen the conversation I had with Delta? Was that how she knew about Delta in the first place? "What are you talking about?" I asked.

"Huh. Look who doesn't like being out of the loop. No fun, is it?"

"I'm telling you the truth now!" *As much as I can, anyway.*

"Because Cade outed you," she shot back. "We both know you wouldn't have said a word otherwise."

"Yes, I would've. Once everything settled down, I planned on telling you everything." *Almost.* The more I tried to defend myself, the more I realized that Lali had more reasons to hate me than she'd ever be able to find to love me. My kidnapping her mother was just the tip of the iceberg.

"Ha!" Her gray eyes burned into me. "You expect me to believe that?"

"It's true, Lali. I hate keeping things from you."

"Then why did you?"

"Because I care about you! Haven't you figured that out yet?" She stared at me, her moonlit face looking just as stunned as I felt at the words that had flown out of my mouth.

"Look," I said, desperate to regain control of myself. "I'm sorry. I should've told you everything before. In my screwed up mind, I thought I was protecting you from getting pulled into this whole convoluted mess. You had enough to deal with, and I was trying to keep you away from all the drama."

"Please. You were trying to make sure you didn't look bad so you could sucker me into helping you."

"Okay," I conceded. "Fine. I wanted you to see that there's good in me, too. I'm not this monster you're trying to make me into." *At least, I'm not trying to be.* "I swear, all I want is to find Kala and reunite you with your mom."

She avoided my eyes, but I grabbed her hands and put them over my heart, praying she'd at least feel the sincerity of that last statement. "Please," I begged. "Don't lose sight of the bigger picture here. We're both so close to getting our family members back. Even if you hate me right now, we still need each other."

She pulled her hands back, still avoiding my eyes. "Fine. Let's figure out how to get one of those necklaces and get it over with."

I inhaled my relief. "Th—"

"Don't you *dare* thank me," she growled. "Just help me figure this out. The sooner we get this over with, the better."

I tried not to read into what she meant by that. I was sure she was implying that she wanted me out of her life as soon as possible, but I had to find a way to change her mind. After everything I'd lost in my lifetime, I wasn't losing Lali, too.

…Things only got more complicated after that. I didn't want to lie to you anymore, but I at least had to cover up the lies I'd already told. Once you said you'd seen Solstice and Delta arguing after the ritual, it was impossible to be sure what you already knew. I decided I would have to be as vague as possible until everything was over, but I swore to myself I'd be honest with you about everything in the future.

I just wanted to spare you the pain of knowing what had really happened with your mom. Okay, maybe it was partially motivated by my selfish desire to keep you in my life, too. The thought of not being able to see you or talk to you anymore wasn't one I had the strength to entertain. But then everything got screwed up again, and I realized it was a reality I would probably have to accept anyway…

49

REQUEST

WHEN I WENT BACK TO SOLSTICE'S APARTMENT, SHE AND Delta stood in the hallway whispering in harsh tones. Xiomara sat curled up on one of the blue and white sofas with her face pressed into her knees. She was rocking back and forth, and even from where I stood, I could hear her whimpering. I hadn't meant to leave her out of the loop, but in all the mayhem, I'd forgotten that I left her, Delta, and Solstice scrambling to trace Lali. Apparently, they'd given up.

"Kai!" Delta called out from the hall.

Xiomara's head popped up, and she shoved off the couch. The two of them nearly tackled me as they bombarded me with questions.

"Did you find Lali?"

"What happened?"

"Where is she?"

"Is she okay?"

"She's safe," I said. "I got to her just in time."

A smile broke out across Delta's face, and Xiomara grabbed the back of the loveseat, looking like she might faint. Her eyes were practically swollen shut, as if she'd been crying the whole time I was gone.

Solstice slowly made her way toward us, and just looking at her unaffected expression made red tinge the corners of my vision. It was her fault Lali had gone rogue and nearly ended up another victim of the Eyes and Ears. If she hadn't lied about the portal's location, I would've been right there when Lali found it. Lali wouldn't have risked her life, and Cade wouldn't have given her a reason to lose faith in me.

"You almost got Lali killed." I advanced on Solstice until her back bumped into the wall just before the hallway entrance. "Why would you lie about the portal? What's wrong with you?"

"What's wrong with *me*?" Solstice's icy blue eyes cut into mine. "I told you it's not safe for us to go back without our abilities, but you wanted to send Lali into the lion's den anyway. I had to lie to protect her."

I laughed in her face. That was how she wanted to spin this? "The only person you want to *protect* is yourself. You've made it very clear you don't give a crap about Lali."

"And you do?"

I could only stare at her. Just last night, she'd accused me of being in love with Lali, and now she was claiming I didn't care at all?

"Of course he does." Delta stepped between us and pressed a palm to my chest to move me away from

Solstice. "He nearly killed himself hitting blocks trying to get to her."

A shudder moved through me at the memory. I couldn't let myself think about what would have happened if I hadn't kept trying, if I hadn't found that window of time Lali wasn't behind a block.

"He only did that because he thinks he needs her to get his sister back." Solstice pushed off the wall, purposely bumping my shoulder as she moved into the living room. "But I can pretty much guarantee she won't be helping with anything once she projects over here and sees you have her mother."

My head snapped in Xiomara's direction, and a new wave of dread washed over me. I'd forgotten she was out of range of the block. Lali could project to her at any minute.

"We have to go." I rushed to where Xiomara was still putting her weight on the arm of the loveseat. She blinked at me, unmoving, as if her brain couldn't process anything else. "Now!" I shouted. Lali was already questioning everything about me thanks to my blabbermouth uncle; I couldn't risk her seeing me with her mother. It was already going to take a miracle to get her to trust me again.

Wrapping my fingers around Xiomara's arm, I projected her to my house and pulled her toward the stairs. She nearly tripped over her own feet, but I managed to get her to the basement without having her fall down the steps.

Still staggering, she dropped onto the bed and gripped

the side of the mattress. She looked like she'd aged ten years in the last hour, and her bottom lip trembled as she stared blankly at the floor. I knew I'd just put her through the ringer, and dragging her back to her prison had probably pushed her over the edge.

"I'm sorry," I said, shoving my hands into my pockets. "I didn't mean to blow up at you. I just don't want Lali to see us together."

Xiomara let out a weak laugh. "I can't believe you just apologized to me."

My face twisted. I supposed of all the things I'd put her through, this warranted an apology the least. But I meant it.

"Listen." I took a moment to steady my voice. "I need you to promise me something." She lifted her head slightly, as if to acknowledge my request. "I need you to promise you won't tell Lali what really happened. With you, with this..." I gestured around the in-law.

"What?"

"I don't want to hurt your daughter any more than I already have. And I'm sure you don't want that either, right?"

She exhaled slowly. "Kai, what are you saying?"

"Pretend you left because of the Eyes and Ears."

Her mouth opened but closed again without a sound.

"We can't tell her the truth," I went on. "She's been through enough already. Do you want her to find out that the one person she's been trusting for the last three weeks —the person who saved her life tonight—has been lying to her this whole time? Do you know what that will do to her?" *How about what it already has done to her?*

I shook my head. I couldn't add another blow to the list. "We can tell her the Eyes and Ears came after you, and you had to run," I suggested. "Maybe I can drop you off near your house and you can pretend you just made your way back home."

Even as I said it, I knew it was a crazy idea. But it was all I had. If Xiomara went along with this, Lali would surely believe it, no matter how far-fetched it seemed. It couldn't possibly sound as crazy as the idea of me keeping her mother locked away in what was basically a studio apartment for months.

Xiomara twitched her head from side to side, but I wasn't giving up.

"We can come up with something," I pressed. "Just tell me you'll think about it. Please." I sounded so pathetic I barely recognized my own voice. Thank God Cade wasn't around to hear me.

"Why?" Xiomara leveled me with her stare. "It doesn't matter what Lali thinks after you find Kala. Once you get what you want—"

"I'll still want Lali." My words took both of us by surprise.

Xiomara leaned forward until she was barely sitting on the bed anymore. "Are you trying to tell me you have feelings for my daughter?"

"No," I said too quickly. I cleared my throat. "I mean —she's my friend. She's the only friend I have, and I don't want to lose her. Please, just go along with this so she doesn't hate me for the rest of her life."

"She won't hate you. Just tell her the truth. She'll understand you were trying to do what you thought you had to in order to find your sister."

I gaped at her. Was she joking? Lali was the most black-and-white person I'd ever met. "I'll tell her the truth about everything else moving forward," I promised. "But I can't tell her the truth about the past."

Xiomara sighed heavily and rubbed her puffy eyes. "I can't discuss this right now, Kai. I'm beyond exhausted. I need to sleep before I can try to think straight."

Glancing at the clock on the kitchenette's microwave, I saw it was nearly eight in the morning. None of us had slept yet. When I looked back at Xiomara, she was already breathing heavily.

I pressed my knuckles into the space between my brows. Somehow, I would find a way to get her to agree to keep my secret. And somehow, I had to find a way to convince Cade to tell me where to find the other transposers. But for now, I had to get some sleep, too.

"Okay," I huffed. "We'll talk tomorrow." Spinning around, I trudged up the steps, praying my dreams would give me some inspiration about how to get both Xiomara and my uncle to agree to my demands. Otherwise, I had no clue how I was going to do it.

50

SUCCESS

I woke to the sound of my phone shrieking. Using my hand to feel for it, I hit the button to silence the piercing noise and forced my eyes open.

It was Cade calling.

I let out a groan and tossed the phone onto my comforter beside me. I still hadn't figured out how I was going to convince him to help, and I was still mad about him throwing me under the bus in front of Lali. I dropped my arm over my face, blocking out the sunlight that snuck in through the crack in my curtains. I needed a minute to wake up before I could deal with him.

The phone dinged again, this time with a text. With a sigh, I peeled my eyes open and read the message on the screen.

Are you going to leave me at Delta's forever?

My brow bunched. He was the one who insisted on staying at that house all day, every day. Now he was complaining about it?

I kneaded my forehead. It was probably his way of forcing me to talk to him. I was sure he'd try to convince me that what he'd done yesterday was for my benefit, but there was nothing he could say to justify his attempt to scare away the only friend I had. I wanted to say as much to his face, but I still needed him to tell me where the alternate trans-posers were. For now, I would have to seethe in silence.

Tossing aside my blanket, I forced myself out of bed to throw on a shirt and shorts. I projected to Delta's house and found Cade pacing the flower-smothered living room. He stopped short when he saw me.

"Nephew," he said, throwing me with his pleading expression. "Listen to me."

Seeing his face only increased my urge to shout at him. I inhaled slowly before speaking. "Listen to what?"

"I only did what I did because I want you to stay focused. I told you from the beginning that girl would be a distraction, and now you want to run off on a dangerous mission with her and get yourself killed. I couldn't let that happen."

"Then why can't you come with us? Or tell us where to find another transposer so—"

"Will you just try trusting me for once?" He threw his arms out behind him, nearly knocking the lamp off one of the end tables. "We both know I can't trust you."

I blinked twice. "What's that supposed to mean?"

"It means I know about Delta." The room seemed to shrink. How long had he known? "Solstice told me everything. Apparently, *she* is the only one I can count on to be honest."

Well, that was rich. After she'd lied to Lali and me about the portal, now she had my uncle convinced she was the trustworthy one. Was that why Cade outed me? Because he was angry I'd lied to him?

"All I'm asking is that you let me keep you safe," he said. "I didn't spend years trying to find you just to lose you." His statement took me back to my first week living with him.

"I didn't spend years trying to find you just to lose you." My uncle's hand is heavy on my shoulder as he whispers to me. But he isn't looking at me. His eyes are on the old lady at the gas pump across from us. "If you don't do this, I can't afford to keep you."

My legs are fidgety, ready to carry me in the opposite direction. "But what if I get caught?" I ask.

"You won't." His voice is stern. "I told you, you're not doing anything wrong. You just have to run to the other side of that gas pump and pretend to hurt yourself. But not until I say go. *We have to wait until just before she puts her credit card in the machine."*

I feel like I'm at the top of a roller coaster about to go pummeling toward the ground far below. I don't want to steal, but I don't want to go to a foster home, either. Cade says everything will be okay if we can just get this lady's credit card. He says he'll always do whatever he has to do to take care of me, and I know he means it. He doesn't really want to steal, either, but it's the only way he can keep taking care of me. So when he says go, *I run as fast as I can toward the gas pump.*

"Will you just take me back home?" Cade asked, jarring me back to the present. "I'm exhausted, and I want to be in my own house. All these flowers have given me a constant migraine."

I studied him, upset with myself for letting this whole screwed up situation hurt our relationship. Even if we didn't agree about the best approach to get to Alea, I knew he was only trying to protect me. He was always trying to protect me. Maybe if I let him know that I understood that, we could come up with a safer approach together.

Wiping my palms on my shorts, I nodded and took his wrist. When we appeared back at the house, he started toward the kitchen.

"Uncle Cade." He stopped walking and turned to face me again. "I get that you don't want me to get hurt," I said, leaning on the glass table between us. "And I appreciate that. Really. But Lali said the guards asked her for her name and took her straight to the lab, so we know they won't just open fire on you. And your name would still be in their database, right? You can tell them what happened. They can't hold it against you."

He pinched the bridge of his nose. "I'm not discussing this anymore. I told you, it's too dangerous."

"Not if you come with me. Just give them your name and start talking. I can grab one of their necklaces while they're distracted. It'll only take a second."

"Think about what you're saying. How would they recognize me? I've been in this realm for two decades. I've aged. They probably won't even believe I'm an Astralis, and I'd have no way to prove it."

"Then I'll get you out of there if it goes badly," I promised.

"I'm not going to risk our lives when I know the odds of us both making it are terrible."

"So what then?" I huffed. "You want to waste more time trying to find Ori and Ursula? How long's it going to take for you to realize we're never going to find them?"

"That's where you're wrong." Cade pointed his index finger at me. "Last night Solstice told me Delta admitted she knows where to find Ori."

I had to fight to keep from losing my temper. "And you believe her? After she lied to Lali about where to find the portal?" Since he seemed to know about everything else, I assumed he knew about that, too.

Cade snorted. "She only did that because she's the only one who seems to understand that going back to Alea without our powers is senseless."

Of course. Now that my uncle was Team Solstice, he was going to justify everything she did. But even if Solstice was telling the truth and we found Ori today, I didn't want to spend another round of forever going on more wild goose chases to try and find Ursula, too. Especially not when we had a much faster option right at our fingertips.

I took a deep breath. "But Uncle Cade, even if we find Ori, we're still short one. And we have another way to get to Kala." Why didn't he want to admit that my approach was the fastest way to get my sister back? I couldn't stop the suspicion from creeping in that all he'd truly wanted was to restore his ability. I tried to force it away, but it lingered like hot oil in my stomach.

"Please, just try it this way," I urged. The blank look in his eyes told me I wasn't making any headway. I had to say something to get him to consider it at least. Since he was so big on alternating our efforts between his way and my way, I decided to offer another compromise. "If I can't get one of the necklaces, I'll go back to doing things your way."

His face didn't even twitch. "I'm not going to agree to something I know could very well get us both killed."

Fire ripped through me. Why was he the only one who was allowed to suggest switching between approaches? I was begging here, and he wasn't even trying to work with me.

"Fine," I snapped. "We'll do it on our own then." I closed my eyes and pictured Lali.

"Would you listen—"

I projected away before he could finish his sentence. If he wasn't going to cooperate, I wasn't going to waste my time.

I appeared in Lali's room, telling myself she'd have positive news even though she hadn't called. With any luck, her siblings had developed their abilities and would be able to help us.

"Have you checked the transposer?" I asked by way of greeting.

She crossed her arms and leaned back against the headboard of her bed. "Yes. It's surrounded."

I cursed under my breath. How could we have been

so close just to have it ripped away? Was there no justice? "Cade still won't help us," I grumbled. "He won't tell me where the other transposers are, and he won't agree to come with me to Alea."

I briefly considered dragging him along against his will, but it wouldn't work if he refused to go along with the plan. If he didn't tell them his name, he'd really get us killed.

"So what now?" Lali asked.

We hope your siblings can help us somehow. I knew Lali would have mentioned it if she had found out about their powers manifesting. They must not have said anything to her yet. Then again, I doubted Lali would be okay with bringing them into this. Maybe if I told her I was considering going along with Cade's plan, she'd be more willing to lean on her brothers and sisters for help.

"You're not going to like it," I said, watching her closely. "But we might be able to find the other two we need to undo the energy sink." Sure enough, Lali went rigid. "I don't want to do it that way," I added quickly. "But it might be our only chance."

"No, it's *your* only chance. If Cade gets his power back, he'll help you find Kala, but what about my mom? Do you really think he's going to help me find her?"

I frowned. I hadn't expected that objection. "I told you, *I'm* going to help you find her."

"Yeah, well you told me a lot of things."

Ouch. And Xiomara thought Lali would forgive me if I told her the truth about kidnapping her mom? Please.

I started to apologize again, but a high voice called

Lali's name through the door. A second later, the knob was turning.

Of course. I disappeared before anyone else could see me. Instead of going home, I showed up in Lanai. I didn't feel like arguing with Cade—at least not yet. He would need time to cool off before we could have a rational conversation.

Collapsing into the sand, I ran through my limited options in my head. I could see about going after Ori. If by some miracle she was still in touch with Ursula, then we really could go through with Cade's plan. But after the rest of the members of XODUS had cut off contact with each other, it seemed like the odds of Ori leading us to Ursula were worse than my chances of getting Lali to forgive me if she ever found out the truth. Maybe I'd just wait it out to see how Lali's brothers' and sisters' abilities turned out.

Unless the crystal didn't work. No. It had to work. Delta was an expert, after all. Granted, she didn't have her ability to project her intention into crystals anymore, but she'd said it should work with the intentions from both her and Solstice.

I gazed up at the sky, searching for answers in the orange haze of sunrise. I had so many doors open, but none of them would lead me to Kala yet. I should have paid closer attention when I'd rescued Lali. Then I could have gotten to Alea by myself.

Closing my eyes, I tried to remember any detail of what I'd seen in the few seconds it took for me to tackle the white-haired guy in a lab coat behind her. I'd hardly glimpsed him or anything else, but I still tried to project to what little I could picture in my mind.

And tried and tried.

When my phone rang, I had no idea how much time had passed. Seeing it was Lali, I accepted the call, praying she would tell me the guards had finally left the transposer. Before I could say hello, her voice came through the phone. "I need you to come over. Now."

I showed up in her room the next second. "Is the transposer clear?" I asked.

"No." She tossed her phone on the bed and turned back to look at me with panic all over her face. "My brothers and sisters got their powers early."

51

BACKFIRE

"What?" My voice came out unnaturally high in my effort play dumb. "How?"

"I don't know." Lali glanced at the dresser behind me like it might pipe up and explain. "But they can do things —projecting things."

"Are you sure?" I kept my eyes wide, faking surprise.

"Yes! Right after you left, Oxanna disappeared out of my room. She just vanished, the same way you do." *Oxanna.* That was the older of Lali's two younger sisters. For both of our sakes, I hoped her ability wasn't just like mine. It seemed unlikely that our projecting styles would turn out to be exactly the same; Cade said there were countless ways semmies' projection abilities could develop. Then again, it would be just my luck if all Delta's little ceremony did was duplicate the powers we were already working with.

"I think they all got their abilities early because of that crystal ritual Solstice and Delta did," Lali went on, talking a mile a minute. "Because they used our initials. Why were they using our initials?"

Damn, she saw that, too? How often did she spy on me? "Whoa," I said. "Calm down. What initials?"

She grumbled under her breath. "Never mind. I need you to show them what you can do. They don't believe me, and we have to make sure they understand that they can't tell anyone."

As much as I wanted to make sure her brothers and sisters didn't draw attention to themselves, I wasn't sure it was a great idea to freak them out by tossing me into the mix so soon. They were probably overwhelmed enough, and they needed to keep level heads to figure out how to control their abilities. "Lali—"

"Don't Lali me. You owe me. Besides, they might be able to help us get one of those necklaces."

My heart skipped. So she *was* willing to let them help us if they could. Before I could react, she yanked me by the arm and tugged me down the hall.

We turned into the girliest bedroom I'd ever seen. It was practically swimming in pink and posters of baby animals. Lali's four younger siblings were perched around the room, two girls and twin boys. They all had gray eyes and dark hair, just like Lali, and all of them were looking at me like I had an extra head.

"Who's that?" Salaxia asked from a giant circular chair in the corner. She had a haircut like Mowgli from *The Jungle Book*, and though Lali had told me she was nine, to me the girl barely looked old enough to be in second grade.

"This is Kai." Lali made a quick gesture in my direction. After I'd helped awaken Salaxia's ability and nearly kidnapped her, it felt ridiculous going through an introduction. Still, I forced a smile. "He's the one who explained all of this to me," Lali told the group. "He's going to prove to you that everything I said is true."

Still standing in the doorway, I felt my face grow hot from all of their gazes on me. For some reason, I felt pressure to make a good impression on them, like maybe it would help their big sister think better of me after our fight. I knew it was stupid, but I couldn't help it.

I shifted my weight. "Lali, I don't want to freak them out."

"They're already freaked out," she insisted. "Please, just show them."

I looked around at their expectant faces, the resemblance between all of them making my throat tighten. I wondered if Kala looked like me at all, if we made any of the same facial expressions the way these kids did.

You'll never know if you don't find a way to Alea. Swallowing hard, I focused on what I needed to do to get the ball rolling with my new potential helpers. If a quick projection show was the way to find out what Lali's brothers and sisters could do, then so be it.

"Okay," I said. "Brace yourselves." I projected myself into the hall so fast I heard the tail end of a high-pitched scream. Giving my disappearance an extra bit of time to sink in, I appeared back in the room a couple seconds later. Salaxia had moved out of her chair and was clinging to the twin with the buzz cut and button-up sitting on the bed.

The other twin with shaggy hair and a Green Day t-shirt started toward me. "What the heck is going on?" he demanded. "What are you?"

So much for making a good impression.

"He's like us, Dix," Lali told him. "He can project too."

Dix. If this one was Dixon, that meant the shorter-haired twin sitting on the bed was Ulyxses. I wondered if they purposely made themselves look as different as possible so people could tell them apart.

"That didn't look like astral projecting," Ulyxses mumbled.

"I know." Lali looked exasperated already. "It works differently for us. We don't have time to get into that now. I just need to know how your powers work. You might be able to help find Mom."

"Find Mom?" Oxanna gasped, her wavy hair falling around her shoulders. "How?"

"Is she in trouble?" Ulyxses asked. "Does this have something to do with why she left?"

Lali sighed. "That's what Kai and I have been trying to figure out."

My face burned with shame at their eager stares. I was surrounded by innocent kids I had turned into collateral damage, and all of them thought I was the solution to the problems I'd created. How much more screwed up could I be?

"Wait, where did he come from?" Oxanna asked,

throwing an arm in my direction. "How does he know about Mom?"

"I'll explain all that later." Lali looked up at me. "Everyone's power manifested differently. Oxanna's power is kind of like yours. She can appear and disappear. Dixon can project through time."

Project through time? Could he project me back in time to save Kala from being kidnapped in the first place? Would that even be possible?

"Salaxia can see thoughts," Lali concluded, bringing my excitement to a screeching halt.

"She can *see thoughts?*" I could have sworn my heart stopped. I'd just thought about the fact that I'd kidnapped their mom.

You just thought about it again!

I felt my temples throb. I had to get out of here before Salaxia figured out the truth. Lali turned to ask Ulyxses something, and my brain started going through a Rolodex of things to say in order to duck out without making anyone suspicious. My eyes shot to Salaxia, my new biggest threat. How could someone so small harness such a disastrous ability?

Lali was still talking to Ulyxses as I tried to work the tension out of my neck. I had to focus on something that didn't involve my moonlighting as a kidnapper. I could already feel beads of sweat forming along my forehead.

Turning to Lali, I blurted out the first thing that came to mind. "Why don't you stay here and help them figure out how projecting works for them? I'm going to see if I can get some answers from Delta."

"Okay," she said. "Hurry back."

I vanished without another word and dropped onto my unmade bed. What a disaster. If Salaxia could read my mind, how was I ever going to get any of them to help? I couldn't risk those kids realizing I'd had their mother this whole time. I would have loved to ask the girl to read Cade's mind for the sake of figuring out where the other transposers were, but there was no guarantee he wouldn't think something about Xiomara in the process and blow my cover.

Groaning, I pressed my fingers into my temples. Recruiting Lali's siblings to help had backfired, and following Lali back to Alea was out, thanks to my uncle's refusal to cooperate. I was going to have to do things Cade's way after all. I didn't have a lot of faith that Ori would know where to find Ursula, but any chance was better than nothing.

Cade was still in the kitchen when I appeared downstairs. "Okay," I said, pulling out the seat next to where he sat at the counter. "You win. Where can I find Ori?"

52

OPENING

It turned out that Delta knew where Ori worked. Apparently she'd slipped up and mentioned it in front of Solstice, who then told Cade. The problem was, Ori—or *Miss Jennifer* as her students called her—was a preschool teacher, and I couldn't exactly nab her in front of a classroom full of three-year-olds. The child care center where she worked in Wisconsin had a nice collection of photos online, so I'd been able to get there unnoticed. Pretending I was a soon-to-be teen father, I followed the center director around for a quick tour of the school.

In the preschool room, I'd been introduced to Ori and her two coworkers. Thankfully, Solstice knew Ori's fake name, and Ori was the only "Jennifer" in the classroom. It was easy enough to commit her wide face and long strawberry blonde hair to memory, but now I had to play the waiting game. Despite Cade's impatience, he'd agreed it was too risky to grab her in public. We decided I would preview Ori periodically until she got home.

In the meantime, Cade was back at Solstice's apartment with Delta. I was sure Delta was cowering in a corner somewhere, but Solstice and Cade were supposed to be figuring out the best way to get Ori to spill what she knew when we finally got her.

I told them I needed to get some sleep, but the truth was, I wanted to revisit my talk with Xiomara. Things were going to come to a head soon, and I was determined to get her to agree to keep Lali in the dark about the kidnapping.

"Kai?" she called out as I made my way down the stairs.

"Yeah," I replied, reaching the bottom of the steps. "I want to—" My phone buzzed in the pocket of my shorts, and I sighed as I dug it out.

Lali.

It had been over an hour since I'd let her and her siblings think I was trying to get answers from Delta. What was I going to say about it? And how was I going to make sure the little one didn't read my thoughts? Then again, what if Lali had checked the transposer and it was clear? The last time she called me and didn't get an answer, she ran off to Alea by herself. I had to see what she wanted.

"What's going on?" Xiomara asked.

"Just…hold on." I turned and headed back upstairs. Closing and locking the basement door behind me, I projected to Lali instead of wasting time calling her back.

"Hey," I said, frowning when I saw her. She was on

the wood floor, her hair wild as she reached under her bed. What was she doing?

"Kai!" She scrambled to her feet and hobbled over to me, holding her arm like it was hurt. "What the heck?"

"What? You called. I figured it was easier to come here instead of calling you back."

"That's not what I'm talking about," she hissed. "Why did I just hit a block? Were you in Alea?" She pushed something at me, its smooth surface sliding against my palm. I looked down to see the clear quartz I'd used to trigger her siblings' powers. *Crap.*

"And what is this doing here?" she demanded.

Good question. "Slow down," I begged, my brain racing to remember the last time I'd had it. I felt my breath seep from my lungs. I'd never taken it back home after I used it to awaken her siblings' astral energy. I must've dropped it that night when I tried to project to Lali and hit the block.

The block.

Oh, no. I'd been in the basement with Xiomara just before coming here. Lali must've tried to project to me and hit it. That was why she was on the floor. That was why she asked if I was in Alea.

"What block?" I blurted out, hoping I sounded confused.

Lali huffed. "I tried to project to you and went flying across the room."

My mind stalled, giving me nothing to work with as an explanation. Lame as it was, the best I could come up with was telling her that I didn't go to Alea. Her face told me she wasn't buying it, and I couldn't blame her.

"Then why did I bounce off a block?" she asked, studying me.

I glanced at the rumpled bed behind her and reached for a believable story. I came up short. "How should I know?" I hedged. "Maybe you tried to project to me at the exact same moment I projected to you."

Wow. There was no way she wouldn't see through that.

A low voice called her name, saving me from my bad lie. Dixon stood in the doorway. "Is everything okay in here?" he asked. His tight expression suggested he already knew the answer.

"Everything's fine." Lali's voice was a complete contradiction to her words, and I could tell her brother knew it.

"It sounded like the opposite of fine from the hall-way," he said.

"Just give us a minute," Lali replied, her tone pleading.

The kid narrowed his eyes at me before closing the door, and Lali stayed quiet for a moment. Now was my chance to smooth things over. It was stupid that we were fighting in the first place. We should have been figuring out how to get to Alea. If there was any chance for us to get back there before I had to kidnap Ori, I wanted to keep trying.

"Look, Lali." I tugged the quartz out of her hand and went with the first story that came to mind. "I came by with this the other night because I wanted to tell you what Delta and Solstice were attempting." Oh, that was good.

"But when I got here, you were gone, and I knew you'd gone after the portal again. When I tried to project to you, *I* hit a block."

I tensed, watching her closely to see if she was buying my explanation. "I must've dropped this," I continued. "But I forgot all about it. I panicked. I knew you'd gotten to Alea, and I was more concerned with making sure you were safe."

"Oh." Her face softened, and I had to fight to keep my expression from faltering. I still hated lying to her, but I was grateful she seemed to believe me.

"Listen," I said, eager to switch the focus. "I don't know about you, but I want to get one of those necklaces. Can you stop hating me long enough to check and see if they're still guarding the transposer?"

Letting out a sigh, she closed her eyes. A second later, her face smoothed into the peaceful expression that made her appear to be asleep on her feet.

Sure she had projected, I let out my own breath in a loud whoosh. I couldn't believe that fake explanation about the crystal had worked. Maybe I would be able to get her to believe a crazy story about what happened with her mom after all, especially if Xiomara went along with what I said. But after that, I was done lying to Lali. I pressed my lips together, making a silent vow of honesty once we got everything sorted out.

Tossing the quartz between my hands, I set it on her desk. I turned around and stepped back toward Lali just as her eyes snapped open.

"The coast is clear!" she cried.

My face went numb. This was it. "Then we have to go. Now."

She nodded, closed her eyes, and vanished.

53

STONE

I DROPPED TO THE GROUND WITH THE SAME SUDDEN JOLT I'd felt when I followed Lali to the transposer under the San Francisco Bay. A similar glowing ring hovered in the air above our heads, lighting up the silver dome around us. I rubbed my eyes. Was this really Alea?

Lali got to her feet, reminding me I didn't have time to gawk. She pointed at the dome's wall in front of me, and I turned to follow her finger. There was a thick rectangular outline carved into the metal.

A door.

"Let me look first," I breathed, pushing myself up. "It could be a trap." *And we don't need you getting caught again.* At least if something tried to snag me, I could disappear in an instant. I briefly considered taking Lali to her house, but knowing her, she'd project right back, make a scene, and draw attention to us. This was dangerous enough as it was.

I felt a gulp move down my throat, and I silently

assured myself that nothing bad was going to happen. I just had to get a look outside. Then we were out of here to come up with a plan of attack. Even with my attempt to reassure myself, my heart was trying to pound its way through my ribs.

"Stand back," I whispered. Lali stepped away so that opening the door wouldn't leave her visible to anyone outside. At the same time, I moved to the opposite side of the outline. Once we were both in position, I pushed the center of the door.

A fog of thick, hot air rushed in, and I nearly gagged as it traveled down my throat like a billow of smoke. How did anybody breathe here? I held my breath, waiting for someone to move or fire a weapon, but it stayed eerily silent.

Moments that felt like years passed, and my lungs burned with a need for oxygen. Not wanting to cough, I only allowed myself small inhales through my nose when I couldn't take it anymore. I looked across to where Lali stood, and I could see her cheeks were flushed. There was already a sheen of sweat over her skin.

Another minute of pure silence passed before I spoke. "I think we're good."

I hope we're good.

Peering outside, I did a double take. Countless white tree trunks big enough to fit three-car garages inside went on as far as I could see. Red and yellow grass grew at their bases, the combination of colors blending to appear orange. I realized in that moment that I'd never heard Cade describe what Alea looked like. From all the negative things he'd said about it, I pictured it as a dark and ominous place. But this was…beautiful. And bright.

I stepped toward the opening, and Lali caught my arm.

"Be careful," she urged. "This is where I got caught in the trap."

The small gesture sent a rush through me. I couldn't help the hint of a smile that hijacked the side of my mouth as I looked over my shoulder at her. "So you do care," I said.

She scowled. "Shut up and memorize a landmark." As unpleasant as I knew she meant to make those words sound, they reminded me of the first day I'd brought her to Lanai, when she told me she couldn't shut up and tell me if she could travel at the same time. We'd come a long way since then, literally and figuratively. I hoped that would be enough for her to want to keep me in her life when this was all over.

Focus! Pushing aside my rogue thoughts, I looked back out at the strange forest. I just had to get a good view of a tree branch big enough to support me. Then I could use the vantage point to look out on the rest of the place without being spotted, and appear whenever I wanted without alerting any guards.

At least, I hoped so.

I gazed up at the collection of branches tipped with red and yellow leaves. I meant to search for any distinctive feature that would work as a landmark, but I got distracted by the bits of soft, milky orange that showed between the tops of the trees. Was that the sky?

A blow from behind knocked me off balance. I hit the ground hard, and the added weight of Lali landing on top of me sent my chest slamming into the ground. I felt my lungs lose their limited air, and black spots danced in front of my eyes.

Before I could ask what was going on, metal clinked somewhere above me. Another clink, and Lali shouted my name. Facedown, I couldn't tell what was happening, but the panic in her voice told me I had to get us out of there fast.

I reached behind me, blindly grabbing until I found her arms. Sucking in a breath that felt like thick steam, I yelled, "Hold on!"

The first place I thought of was Lanai. The next second, I felt the sand against my face. Lali rolled off me, and I swallowed a deep lungful of salty air. It felt like a cool drink of water after the exhaust-like atmosphere in Alea.

"Let go of me!" Lali cried. Her body jerked beside me. I rolled onto my side, frowning. I was barely touching her.

Then I saw him. Moonlight sparkled off a transparent form clinging to Lali's leg. *A guard!* One of them had come with us in his astral form.

My body reacted before my mind could catch up. Springing to my feet, I launched myself at the intruder. His astral form was like a block of ice. My shoulder slammed into his, sending spikes of pain straight through me as we toppled into the sand.

He writhed beneath me, and questions rushed

through my head. How had he come with us? Could I project astral bodies, too? He shoved me back, putting just enough space between us for me to notice the long stone in the middle of his chest.

Every part of me froze. That had to be one of the crystals Lali was telling me about, one that allowed Astralii to break through astral energy blocks. I reached to grab it, but a frosty fist connected with my eyebrow. I fell sideways, my already sore shoulder crunching in the sand. I inhaled the shout that wanted to burst out of me.

Rolling over, I saw the silver form drift upright, as if lifted by an invisible board beneath his back.

No! I'd forgotten he would be able to fly. I couldn't let him get away with that stone. I dove at him again. Closing my fingers around his neck, I took him to the first enclosed space I could think of that would guarantee he couldn't float away from me so easily—Solstice's car.

Unfazed by projecting with me, he continued to thrash as I pushed him against the passenger side door. He threw his forehead into mine, sending a burst of sparkles through my vision. I landed a swift punch to his face, and my knuckles split open against his stonelike jaw.

He didn't even flinch.

Biting through the pain, I pinned his arms and reached for the purple crystal at the base of his throat. Closing my fingers around it, I pulled with all my strength. The chain popped, sending me backward with the stone in my fist.

My opponent kicked and shouted, but I hardly heard what he said. I didn't care. I had the necklace.

343

Grabbing for the door handle, I tugged it toward me and toppled onto the asphalt. Before he could come after me, I sprang up and shoved the door closed on the astral asshole.

His face slammed into the window, and I grinned at him from the other side of the glass. From what Lali had told me, these guys could permeate, too. I knew it wouldn't be long before he would focus and move through the car. Squeezing the stone in my palm, I quickly projected back to Lanai before he could touch me again.

54

CAUGHT

LALI'S EYES BUGGED OUT WHEN I APPEARED ON THE BEACH in front of her. "Are you okay?" she gasped.

"Peachy." I used my empty hand to wipe the beads of sweat above my mouth and tried to hide the smile that came at the concern in her voice. No matter how much she tried to pretend she didn't care, her body betrayed her. As excited as I was about the necklace hidden in my palm, I knew showing her would make her forget all about my injuries, and I couldn't bring myself to do it just yet. It was nice to have her fussing over me instead of at me for once.

She scanned me from head to toe as if looking for additional confirmation that I was okay. "What just happened?"

"The guard and I had a little disagreement." I shrugged, keeping my voice nonchalant. Maybe it was stupid, but I wanted to impress her. "You know, I've never fought someone who can't feel pain. I kind of impressed myself just now."

In truth, I didn't know for a fact the Astralis couldn't feel pain, but his lack of reaction to my fist hitting his jaw was evidence enough. I knew from experience how a feeling person would react—I'd been in my share of fights in middle school.

Lali rolled her eyes. "Why were you fighting in the first place? You should've just dropped him somewhere."

"Well, if I did that," I said, my excitement about getting the necklace finally bubbling over. "I wouldn't have been able to get this." I opened my hand to show her the stone, and her mouth almost hit the sand.

She stared at the crystal for a long moment, like it might disappear if she looked away. Her fingers trembled as she reached out to touch it. "How did you—" Her voice broke, and I felt a twinge of pride at having made her so happy.

"I have my ways."

She giggled. "I can't believe you got it."

"*We* got it, Lali," I corrected. She needed to know that I would never have been able to get the necklace without her. And now I was going to see Kala again. All Lali had to do was use the stone to project to my sister and find her way out of the lab. Then I could follow her instructions to get to Kala. I'd be able to appear and disappear quickly enough that I was confident no one would be able to catch me—especially when they weren't prepared for me.

"Kai," Lali whispered, breaking me out of my

thoughts. "Can we—" She met my eyes, and I immediately knew what she was asking.

"Oh." *Damn it!* Of course the very first thing she wanted was to be reunited with her mother. Now that she'd asked, I couldn't say no—not if I wanted her to project to my sister and figure out the route I had to take to get to her.

"Yeah, of course," I said, my palms starting to sweat. How was I going to get out of this? I couldn't take her to my basement—there was a chance she would recognize the house from when she'd seen Cade threatening Solstice with the gun. "We, uh, just have to get a new chain for this thing." It was a lame way to buy time, but it was all I could think of in the moment.

"I have plenty of chains in my room," Lali offered.

Naturally. "Yeah?" I shoved the necklace into my pocket, scrambling to think of something to stall her. But it was useless. I knew nothing I could say would stop Lali from wanting to go to her mom. There was nothing anyone could say to convince me not to go after Kala, either, and Lali was just as stubborn as I was.

You can pretend to hit a block. I was ashamed of myself for even thinking it, but I knew it was the only way to stop this disaster waiting to happen. I had to make Lali think the stone didn't work.

"Okay," I said, fighting the protests from my conscience. "Then let's go."

She took my hand, and I saw her lip tremble as she closed her eyes.

I was such a jerk.

~

I dove over to where Lali lay sprawled out on the wood floor of her bedroom, her face twisted in pain. "I'm sorry!" I shouted. "Are you hurt?" Shifting my hand under her to help her sit, I realized she had tears streaming down her cheeks. And it was my fault.

After my failed attempt to convince her to let me go after her mother first, I'd thrown myself backward to fake hitting a block. I'd at least had the foresight to lean forward and prevent my skull from cracking in the process, but Lali had no warning. I hadn't meant to hurt her, but from the looks of things, I had—emotionally and physically.

She made a rasping noise as I eased her upright.

"Hey, easy," I urged. I had to bite the sides of my tongue to stop myself from shouting out a thousand more apologies. She tried to say something but didn't quite manage.

"Lali, just breathe." I ran my hand in circles across her back and stared at her eyes. Her pupils didn't look dilated. That was a good sign, right?

"Why..." she gasped. "Didn't it...work?"

"I don't know," I lied, my mind already working to come up with more ways to deceive her. "Maybe the stones aren't the reason the guards can move through blocks. Maybe there's more to it." I could tell she wasn't buying it, and I didn't blame her. But I was running out of ideas.

"Or maybe it's because I don't have an astral form," I tried. "You said the Astralii were wearing them when they permeated the walls, right?"

Her face lifted. "Let me…try."

Well, that backfired. "How will you be able to wear it in your astral form?" I challenged, desperate to deter her. "You told me it repels things." Thank God she'd mentioned that back when she was trying to learn how to permeate.

Lali slumped forward, and I thought I had finally gotten her to drop it. Then she sucked in a breath and said, "Oxanna has an astral form." Naturally, now that I wanted her to be discouraged, she was a big bucket of optimism.

"But she doesn't know where your mom is," I reminded her.

Lali covered her face, and I forced down the lump in my throat. Getting what I wanted had never sucked so much.

"I'm sorry." I studied her rumpled comforter simply to avoid seeing Lali look so broken. "I really thought the stone would work, too."

"So, what? This was all for nothing? We just give up?" Her voice rose with each question. "I can't accept that, Kai. I won't."

"We're not giving up." *If you'd just let me go home, I could figure out a way to get you your mother.* Knowing there was no other way to get out of this, I said the last thing she wanted to hear. "We still have one option left."

She glared at me, picking up on my meaning. I didn't really want to go after Ori and Ursula, but I needed an excuse to go home.

"I know it's not what you wanted," I continued, "but it's the only way. If we can get all of them to release the energy inside the crystal, this will all be over."

"Yeah, for you," she burst out. "But they don't know where my mom is."

"Lali, look at me." Not surprisingly, she didn't. I moved closer, pressing my back against the wall as I sat next to her. "We'll find her. We'll find both of them. Whatever it takes. Just trust me."

Ha! Trust you? *Do you even trust yourself anymore?*

Lali still refused to look at me, and I couldn't take it. I had to go. I had to get her mother, get our story straight, and reunite the two of them. Then I'd let Lali try the crystal to find Kala. I'd have to backtrack on what I'd said about the crystal not working for Lali's astral form, but she'd be much more open to trying if she had her mother back. I was sure of it.

Giving Lali one last look, I projected myself home. I stopped in my room to drop off the guard's necklace, headed downstairs, and yanked open the door to the basement. "Xiomara," I called out, taking the steps two at a time. "Do you want to go home?"

She raced over, catching me just as I reached the bottom of the staircase. "What?" She brushed aside the short wisps of hair that had fallen into her face. "What did you just say?"

"I'm going to take you home. But only if you agree to a few conditions."

"Kai—"

"It's nothing bad. We just have to come up with an explanation for how I found you." She shifted uncomfortably, but I was determined to convince her. "We could say Solstice and Delta ended up having a picture of you, and I found you hiding out from the Eyes and Ears. That's easy enough, and Lali would believe it if you went along with the story."

"Kai, slow down. This is crazy."

"No it isn't. I don't want to hurt her anymore."

Xiomara blinked at me, the shock in her gray eyes reminding me too much of her daughter.

"Once Lali has you back, she can help me get to Kala," I said. "Then we can all move on with our lives."

"She's not going to Alea! Not again." Of course, now that I was trying to bring Xiomara back to her family, she was resisting.

I groaned. "She won't be in any danger. Her astral form is invisible. No one will even know she's there. All she has to do is project to Kala and find a way out of the lab. I'll do everything else on my own."

"You'll get yourself killed."

"Why do you even care?" I exploded, my whole body heaving. "Then you could all go on with your happy little lives without me ruining things all the time. Maybe everyone would be better off."

Xiomara's chin quivered, and she did the thing I least expected—she hugged me.

I tensed, squeezing my jaw as tightly as I could to fight the overwhelming urge to crumple into a ball on the floor. How could she hug me? After everything I'd done to her, how could she even look at me?

"It doesn't have to be like this," she whispered, her head resting on my chest. "You can redeem yourself. I know you have a heart in there." When she pulled away, there were tears in her eyes. "I've seen it, even when you didn't want me to. Just give yourself a chance to do this the right way."

A shaky breath made its way out of my nose. "There is no right way anymore," I moaned. "Not with this. I'll take you home right now. Just say you'll help me."

She studied my face, and I told myself she was considering going along with my idea.

"I'll take Lali to Solstice's apartment," I went on. "Solstice and Delta are already there. We can pretend they traced you somehow. Please. I just don't want Lali to hate me."

Xiomara stayed quiet for so long, my hope started to falter. Finally, she sighed loudly. "Okay, Kai."

My heart soared. "Really?"

She nodded, and before I knew it, I was hugging her again.

"Thank you." I let her go and grinned at her. "Thank you so much. Be right back."

Spinning around, I sprinted up the stairs and

projected back to Xiomara's house in record time. I appeared in Oxanna's doorway, feeling like I could fly.

Then Lali looked at me, and the horrified expression on her face erased every shred of excitement in me.

"What?" I asked.

Her shock transformed into rage in half a second. Charging at me like she was going to strangle me with her bare hands, she shouted, "You lying creep!"

...Hearing that come out of your mouth was like a shard of glass in my heart. Somehow, I knew you had figured it all out. I was sure I'd lost you, and I didn't know how to handle it. I was so ashamed, and so angry. Here I'd just gotten your mom to go along with my plan to reunite you two, only to have everything blow up in my face when I went to bring you to her.

As strange as this may sound, I found myself teetering between wanting to explain and wanting to make it worse. I didn't know if it was better to try and get you to understand, or to be the monster I was sure you thought I was so you could just hate me. The feelings between us were already complicated enough, and I didn't want to make things harder on you.

Unfortunately, no matter what I did, things just kept getting messier...

55

OUTED

I CAUGHT LALI'S ARM BEFORE HER FIST CONNECTED WITH my face. "*What?*" I gasped, even though my gut told me she knew everything. I fought it, telling myself that I was jumping to conclusions, that there was no way she could have figured it out.

"Where's our mom?" Dixon shouted, confirming my fear. He stormed toward me, looking just as murderous as his sister. Before he could complicate the situation more, I tightened my hold around Lali and projected her to Lanai.

She stumbled, fighting me as I held her upright by her forearms. "Where is she?" she screamed. "What did you do to her?"

"Lali, what are you talking about?" I knew I was grasping at straws, but I clung to the hope that she didn't know *everything*.

"Don't deny it! We saw you take her!"

I blinked twice. How could they have seen me take Xiomara? That was three months ago…

The time-traveling twins! One could go back to the past. Had he managed to go back to when I kidnapped his mother?

Lali strained against my hold. "Where *is* she?"

I sighed. There was no point in denying it. "She's safe," I said, wanting to bury myself in the sand blowing across my feet. "I haven't hurt her."

Seeming to find new strength at my confession, Lali jerked out of my grasp. "Let her go."

I was planning to. But now that Lali knew the truth, there was no way she was going to help me get to Kala willingly. I would have to hold her mom over her head to get her to cooperate.

Cade had been right all along; I should have taken that approach from the beginning. Now I understood why he'd been against involving Lali, against trying to befriend her. It was too messy. Going to all the trouble of lying was too much to keep up with, while threats made things simple.

"You know I can't do that," I said, that one small sentence hurting me as much as it must've hurt Lali. "Not until we get Ursula and undo this sink once and for all." *Well, Ursula* and *Ori.* I could project to Ori as soon as she got home, but we still didn't technically have her yet.

Tears ran down Lali's face. She looked at me with the fire of a hatred I'd never seen from her, like I was her arch nemesis. In a lot of ways, it seemed I was.

"How could you?" she sobbed. "I got you to Alea. I did everything you wanted."

"Lali—"

"Just let her go. I'll still help you, I swear."

Even if Lali meant that, I was sure something would screw it up. Xiomara would find a way to stop her from going to Alea or something would go wrong. Things never worked out for me, especially not when it came to Lali. It was like this was all some sick cosmic joke, with my happiness as the punchline.

Maybe it was better if she hated me and helped me out of fear. Otherwise, I couldn't depend on her. I couldn't depend on anyone except Cade. Once I got his ability back, the two of us were going to save Kala without anyone else getting in the way.

"Help me with what?" I spat. "The necklace won't work." There was no point in explaining that lie to her; I wasn't going to try and get her to use it anymore. "Cade is my only chance to get inside the lab, and he has to have his powers to do that."

Lali made a noise somewhere between a wheeze and a whimper. The look of devastation on her face put a crack in my resolve. Before I knew what I was saying, I was trying to explain. "Lali, you have to understand—"

"Take me to her. Please. I have to see her."

"That's only going to make it harder for you." *You* and *me*.

She dropped her face into her hands, and something tugged at me. How could I be so eager to make her happy one moment and so quick to crush her the next? I could hardly keep up with myself. But maybe if I gave a little, Lali would too. Maybe I should at least give her a chance.

"*Okay,*" I said, not sure if I was more disappointed in myself more for hurting her or for caring about her enough that seeing her hurt could hurt me, too. "Fine. But it can only be for a few minutes." Any longer than that, and there was no telling how I'd cave next.

"What? Why?"

I took a deep breath. She was going to try and make me bend more. I'd been in enough battles of will with her to know that. I had to stay firm. "Do you want to see her or not?"

She gulped.

I reached for her hand, but she hesitated. *Of course. She knows the truth now, and she's always going to hate you for it.*

I winced. Even if I tried to make it up to her, she was never going to look at me the same. "Come on," I huffed. "Before I think better of this."

I projected us to my house, and from the look on Lali's face, she recognized the space. "What is this?" she asked, frowning. "Where is my mother?"

"She's downstairs." I led her to the basement door and pulled it open. She poked her head through the frame slowly, like she thought I might lock her down there, too.

Before I could say anything, Xiomara called out, "Hello?"

Lali gasped. "Mom!"

"Lali?"

I stood frozen in place, listening to Lali's footsteps

thud down the stairs. The sounds of sobbing and comforting made my fists clench. When was it my turn to have a reunion? When was it my turn to be relieved to see someone I'd been missing? Lali got to reunite with her mother. There was never a question that she would be reunited with her, even if she didn't know it.

But my parents were gone forever, and I still had *real* obstacles to overcome to get to Kala. Lali had no idea how lucky she was that I was the only thing between her and her mother. She didn't know what it was like being forced into situation after situation where she had to do messed up things just to try and get someone back. Yet, here she was, judging me for it. She was *always* judging me.

A loud pounding noise snapped me out of my spiraling.

"What just happened?" Xiomara asked the question, but I already knew the answer: they hit the block.

I tore down the steps, fire racing through my blood. Sure enough, Xiomara was climbing to her feet, and Lali was sprawled across the floor. Lali had tried to project her mom out of here to get away—to get away from *me*— after I'd been kind enough to bring her here.

That was it. Screw being nice.

"I knew I shouldn't have brought you here," I said, more to myself than to Lali.

Xiomara stepped in front of her daughter as if I might attack her. Clearly, she'd already lost faith in me, too. "Then why did you?" she asked. "What's going on?"

"I had a moment of weakness." I studied Lali's face,

seeing the disgust there. "But I see you're trying to take advantage of it."

"How did you block this place?" she choked out. "You said the crystals to block astral energy were only in Alea."

"What?" Xiomara looked between us. "That's not true. Black tourmaline can be found here, too." Naturally, she had to blow that lie, too. Wasn't it enough for her that Lali knew the truth about what had happened with her mother?

"Did you tell me the truth about anything?" Lali hissed. Her question gutted me. Even though I'd had to lie about her mother, we'd spent so much time together over the last month that I actually felt close to her. I was honest with her about everything I could be honest about, and she wasn't giving me any credit for it.

"I asked you to guide her." Xiomara had the nerve to sound hurt. "Not fill her head with lies."

For crying out loud, I couldn't do anything right with these two.

Lali gaped at her mother. "You wanted him to—"

But Xiomara wasn't paying her any attention. "What are you trying to do?" she demanded, her gaze still fixed on me. "Why did you bring her here?"

"Good question," I growled. "It was a mistake. The kind people make when they let themselves start to care."

"*Care?*" Lali's mouth fell open. "You've been holding my mother captive for months! You *used* me!"

"Yeah, yeah," I grumbled. "I'm a heartless monster." *There. Is that what you want to hear?*

"What do you want, Kai?" Xiomara asked, the poison

in her voice telling me her earlier *I care* act hadn't been real. Nothing would ever be real when it came to these two.

"To take Lali home," I said. "I shouldn't have brought her here in the first place."

"I'm not leaving without my mother." Oh, now Lali was making demands? I'd already told her this would be a quick visit, but here she was trying to take advantage of me again. Well, I wasn't going to allow that. Not anymore.

"Then I'll have to pay your brothers and sisters another visit," I snarled. "I can't promise they'll all be there when you agree to go back." There. If she wanted to turn this into a power battle, I could play her game. She needed to remember that I still had the upper hand.

Lali shoved past her mom to stand right in front of me. "Why are you doing this? You're making us into enemies when we could help you. We don't even fully understand how my brothers' and sisters' powers work. What if one of them can help you find Kala?"

I narrowed my eyes. "Mind reading and body doubling isn't exactly what I need to find my sister."

"Your siblings developed their powers?" Xiomara gaped at Lali. "When?"

"I-I don't know," Lali stammered. "Today? Maybe last night. Delta and Solstice did some kind of crystal energy manipulation and—"

"Last chance to come with me," I snapped. I didn't have time for Lali to recap the day. I needed to check back on Ori and see what Cade and Solstice had come up with to get her to talk. "Or I go by myself, and it won't be pretty."

Lali looked back and forth between her mother and me, clearly debating which choice was safer. After everything we'd been through together, was it really that easy for her to believe I'd hurt her brothers and sisters? That ate away at me more than anything she'd ever said to me.

"Kai." She choked out my name like it hurt. "Let us help you."

I rolled my eyes. "Right."

"You still need to find one more person before you can undo the energy sink, don't you?" Lali pressed. I couldn't help but lift my gaze at her words. "I know how to find her."

56

TRADE

I FELT MY JAW UNHINGE. HOW COULD LALI KNOW WHERE to find Ursula? It didn't make any sense. But she said it with such conviction—the kind I knew she could never muster when she was lying. I'd seen her fail at being deceitful enough times by now.

"Xitlali!" Xiomara grabbed her daughter's arm, but Lali shook her off.

"Mom, it's the only way."

"And what way is that?" I asked, still suspicious.

"Let's just say it's my turn to offer you a trade."

What? Did Lali mean what I thought she meant? After she'd given me so much crap for everything I'd done, she was suddenly okay with trading people to get what she wanted?

Maybe there's hope for her to forgive you after all. The thought set off flutters in my stomach. If Lali felt desperate enough to toss her morality out the window for

364

the sake of her family, she would have to understand why I did the same thing.

"I mean it," Lali said. "You know me well enough to know I'm telling the truth." Well, she was right about that.

Xiomara spun her daughter around by the shoulders. "Stop this right now. You have no idea how dangerous—"

"What did you have in mind?" I asked, cutting Xiomara off.

Lali glanced back at me, overlooking her mother's objections, too. "If you want to know, you're going to have to do things my way."

"Xitlali!" Xiomara shouted.

I ignored her again and focused on Lali. "What does that mean? What do you want?"

"Bring my brothers and sisters here. They deserve to know our mother is okay. And that I'm okay. They're probably panicked after you hijacked me out of there." She hesitated a moment before adding, "But take me with you."

"Over my dead body." Xiomara pulled Lali close. "He's not taking you anywhere."

So much for her sappy *I know you have a heart in there* speech. Clearly that was her attempt to manipulate me into bringing her back to her family. I couldn't believe I'd trusted her.

"I'll be right back," Lali assured Xiomara. "I just want to let them know what's going on so they don't freak out." She stepped away from her mother and took ahold of my hand. Feeling the warmth of her skin only made the situation sting that much more.

"We have to go upstairs," I told her. "The crystals are lining the basement."

"If you hurt any of them…" Xiomara shot me a poisonous look. The threat in her eyes told me it was just as I suspected: she never thought I had any good in me—not if she so easily believed I'd hurt her kids after I'd left them alone this whole time. I'd been stupid enough to believe her act before, but not anymore.

Biting back all the profanities I wanted to shout, I turned to head upstairs. Even if Xiomara thought I was a monster, I couldn't give up on Lali—not when she was willing to help me find Ursula. I didn't know how she was planning to do it, but if she felt desperate enough to offer, I was sure she would understand that desperation had dictated my behavior, too.

As soon as we made it up the stairs, I closed the door behind us and turned to face Lali.

I could barely manage to whisper her name. "You know I never wanted it to be this way," I managed.

Her glare could've stopped a charging rhino. "Then you shouldn't have made it this way."

"Come on. You don't see the parallels here? You're doing exactly what I did—whatever it takes to get back someone you care about."

"This is *not* the same."

"It's *exactly* the same." How could she not see it?

"No," she snarled. "I'm going to ask for someone's help, not use threats and violence to force her into it. Now let's go." The venom in her voice nearly killed my budding hope of forgiveness, but I couldn't give up when it was so clear that we were doing the same thing here.

"You—"

"Do you want to find your sister?" Lali interrupted, looking at me like she wanted to throw me off a cliff.

I inhaled as deeply as I could and held my breath. She had to see that I was right; she was just being stubborn. But we could fight about it later—after we got everything sorted out with undoing the sink.

Taking her hand, I projected us to her living room. Gottfried saw us immediately and howled so loud I was sure they could hear him all the way in Alea.

"Lali!" Salaxia's stick-figure form followed the dog down the stairs, trailed by the others.

"Get away from my sister!" Dixon shouted from the middle of the pack.

I could only handle hatred from so many people at once. "Call me when you calm down the mob," I muttered to Lali, disappearing before her brothers and sisters pounced on me.

As tempting as it was to go to Lanai, there was no time. I needed to tell Cade that we had a way to Ursula, and I still had to see if I could get Ori yet.

I appeared in Solstice's apartment, and she and my uncle eyed me suspiciously. Delta sat rocking back and forth in the corner muttering to herself, seemingly oblivious to us.

"Where have you been?" Cade asked.

I straightened up. "Finding a way to Ursula." One of

his eyebrows quirked, and Solstice gaped at me. "Lali knows how to find her, so we don't have to worry about getting Ori to talk."

"No!" Delta shouted, apparently aware of what we were saying after all. "No, no, no!"

A low rumble came from Cade's chest. "Take us home. I can't deal with Delta anymore. Let her fall apart in the basement with Xiomara while we round up the others." It was harsh, but I didn't want to have Delta interrupting us, either—not when we were finally so close to rounding up everyone in XODUS.

I moved toward Delta as if she were a skittish cat, but she didn't resist as I projected her to my house and led her to the basement. She just sat at the top of the stairs while I closed the door against her back and locked it.

Don't feel bad. Do not *feel bad.* Gritting my teeth, I went back for Cade and Solstice. Just to be sure Delta didn't try to make a break for it, I brought them into the living room to explain Lali's offer to find Ursula.

When I'd finished, my uncle looked skeptical. "You expect us to believe that she wants to do things our way now?" he asked. "What's the catch?"

I glared at him for a long moment. "There's no catch," I said, not sure why I was defending Lali when she couldn't even admit she was doing the same thing I'd been doing all along. "She's just trying to get her mom back."

"See? Even your morally superior little girlfriend can be brought over to the dark side," Solstice muttered, flipping her hair. I inhaled slowly, feeling strangely vindicated that *someone* could see what I'd been trying to explain to Lali—even if that someone was Solstice.

Cade met me with a knowing expression. "It's just like I always told you: no one wants to help anyone unless they have something on the line. But if the girl really can lead us to Ursula, then we should be setting up the crystals in the transposer house."

"Why?" I asked. What did that matter?

"Because I haven't projected in twenty years," he replied. "I won't have enough strength to travel all the way to the portal from here."

"Okay." I didn't want to argue. He'd been right about everything so far, anyway. When all this was said and done, I owed my uncle a huge apology. "If Lali finds Ursula, we'll set everything up over there," I said.

Cade and Solstice exchanged a long look.

"But we still need to get Ori first," I reminded them.

Solstice clapped once, a loud, jarring sound. "Sounds like a plan to me. I'm ready to get this show on the road."

I couldn't agree more. I needed to keep my mind occupied, if for no other reason than getting Lali's betrayed expression out of my head.

57

GRUDGE

NOT HALF AN HOUR LATER, I FOUND ORI AT HER HOUSE. All it took was a threat to abduct her infant son to get her to come along without making a fuss. She left the baby with her teenage step-daughter, who remained unaware of my presence while I waited outside. I took Ori and Cade to the transposer house at the same time, just to be sure Ori wouldn't try to escape. Delta was still sitting where I'd left her at the top of the basement stairs, and I took her and Solstice over next. Unfortunately, that left me with Xiomara one on one, and nothing sounded less appealing.

Bracing myself, I called down to her. She came up to the living room wearing the same disgusted expression Lali had given me earlier. It was like they had mother-daughter training sessions specifically for making guys feel like scum.

"Where's Lali?" she asked, her voice quivering on the name.

"She's off doing exactly what I've been doing—hunting down someone she needs to get her family back. But somehow, it's okay when she does it, right? Because she's the good kid, and I'm just the evil orphan."

Xiomara sighed. "Kai—"

"Forget it."

"No. Listen to me. It's not okay for either of you. And I don't think you're evil. Cade has brainwashed you to act this way."

I scoffed. "Cade is the only one who understands me. You and your perfect little family will never understand what it's like to be in our shoes. You refuse to see it, even when your daughter is doing the *exact same thing.*"

Xiomara opened her mouth to argue but came up short. There was nothing she could say to negate it anyway. Cade had loved me unconditionally. He understood that I did what I had to do and never judged me for it. Lali was too judgmental to care about me unconditionally. She would only care when I lived up to her expectations.

My phone buzzed in my pocket, and I turned my back to Xiomara before answering it. Lali's voice came through loud and clear. "We're ready."

I hung up without a word. "Looks like your daughter is ready to give up Ursula," I said, turning to give Xiomara a smug look. "Even though Cade hasn't *brainwashed* her."

Xiomara's stunned expression gave me some satisfaction. That's what she got for patronizing me.

Once Xiomara was locked back in the basement, I

appeared in Lali's room. Silence hung between us like a thick fog as we headed down the creaky wooden stairs to where her brothers and sisters were waiting in the living room. They all looked ready to string me up by the ankles. I'd barely hit the last step when Dixon started for me, his mane of dark hair flopping wildly.

"Dix!" Lali caught his arm. "We're never going to get Mom back if you kill the only person who can take us to her."

"Where's our mom?" he yelled.

I inhaled slowly, doing all I could to stay calm. "She's fine. She has been this whole time."

"Maybe you should've told us that three months ago," Oxanna piped up. "You're one twisted—"

"Can we just get this over with?" I snapped.

Lali's face turned to ice. "Not until you give me your word that once this is all over, you will bring our mom back unharmed, and you and your uncle will leave us alone. Forever."

That last bit stung more than I wanted to admit. "Lali, you know I never had any intention of hurting your mom," I said, fighting to keep my tone even. "Neither did Cade."

"Yeah, well I don't exactly have a lot of faith in anything that comes out of your mouth." Lali waved her littlest sister over. "Sal, I'm going to need your help, okay?"

"Really?" Salaxia bounded toward us like an overeager puppy. "With what?"

Lali pulled her sister close. "I need you to read Kai's

thoughts. That's the only way I can be sure he's telling the truth."

I knew she was just trying to irritate me, but it was working. "Seriously?" I muttered.

"Yes." Was she sneering? "Now repeat after me: Once Cade has his powers back, I swear to leave the Yavari family alone."

I shook off the bite of her words. If that was what she wanted, fine. I didn't need her. It wasn't like I was in love with her.

Are you sure about that?

I tensed. I was *not* in love with her. And it didn't matter, anyway. She clearly loathed me.

Realizing Lali was still looking at me expectantly, I rolled my eyes. I knew I wouldn't get anywhere until I went along with her stupid little demand. Annoyed, I recited her words back to her. It was ridiculous that she even thought I'd keep bothering her family. I had no reason to involve them in anything else.

Salaxia nodded. "He's telling the truth."

Her statement jarred me. I'd almost forgotten she was standing there trying to read my mind like a creepy little cartoon character.

"Do you swear you won't hurt Ursula or any of the others?" Lali demanded.

I didn't let my face betray my disappointment that she felt she had to ask. "Of course."

"That's true, too," Salaxia squeaked, making me cringe again.

Lali sent her unsettling little sister away to sit with the

other three, who were all glaring at me from the couch like I was on trial for murder.

"Okay," I said, ready to get away from their accusing stares. "How do I get to Ursula?"

Lali met my eyes, but instead of the white-hot hatred from before, she almost looked ashamed. "I want to go with you." Swallowing hard, she reached into her pocket. "It will probably be less terrifying for her if I come along."

There was no point arguing about that. If Lali wanted to come with me, fine. It would be good for her to get a taste of what I'd been forced to do for the last few months.

She held out a scrap of paper, and I frowned. I didn't know what she'd been planning, but I was expecting a picture or something more significant. Taking the paper from her, I skimmed the scribbles across it. A name and an address in somewhere called Lincoln Park, New Jersey. I'd never even heard of it.

I didn't want to waste time trying to find a landmark, and then searching for a way to get there from that point. It had taken forever with Delta's house, and that was in a major city. Plus, there was no guarantee Ursula would even be home. I needed something faster, more concrete. Everyone was already waiting at the transposer house.

I told Lali I couldn't use an address in hopes that she had a better option. Her brothers suggested I look it up online, but I shot them down. We didn't have time for that.

"What if I project you with me?" Lali offered. I stared

at her. What was she talking about? "I can take you with me so you can see her face. I just did the same thing with Dixon a bit ago."

"You can bring people with you?" I felt my blood pressure rise. "Why didn't you tell me that after you saw Kala?" This changed everything. If we could find a way to get the stone on Lali's astral form, then she could project me with her to the lab. I could see Kala for myself, and then take matters into my own hands.

"I just found out today," Lali insisted. "Besides, it wouldn't have made a difference. We still can't break through the block."

I balled my fists so tight they started to shake. Another lie had blown up in my face. I couldn't tell her that I'd faked hitting a block. Now that I had her cooperating, I wasn't going to screw it up. We finally had access to all five members of XODUS, and I might as well get them to undo the sink. Then Cade could help me get to Kala, and I wouldn't have to deal with Lali or her family anymore. That was what she wanted anyway.

"Let's just get this over with." I made a point to avoid looking at her siblings even though I could still feel their eyes burning into the side of my face.

"Gladly," she said. "But the deal was you take them to see our mom first." She gestured to her brothers and sisters as they inched toward us. "They're going to have to sit around and wait for us anyway, and they deserve to see her, too."

I bit back my protest. "Fine." There was no point in arguing it now. "But I can only take two at a time."

Salaxia and Ulyxses came with me first, followed by Oxanna and Dixon. Standing at the top of the stairs, I heard their delighted shrieks as they reunited with their mom. Each served as a painful reminder of what I'd never get with my parents.

Once the four of them were all in the basement with their mom, I went back for Lali. Even after I'd just done what she'd asked, her face was still a firestorm.

I gave her a pleading look. "Lali."

"Don't."

"You're mad at me for doing the exact same thing you're doing now. Don't you see how irrational that is?"

"About as irrational as you expecting me to be okay with you *kidnapping my mother.*" There it was. No matter what I said or did, she'd never be able to get past that, even if she was doing the same thing herself. "Now do you want to undo this stupid energy sink or not?"

"Fine," I said, suddenly exhausted. "How does it work? Do I have to hold your hand to project with you?"

"Yes." Her voice came out clipped. "But first I want to make sure my siblings are okay."

"They're fine, Lali."

"I thought we established that I don't trust anything you say. Unless I have Salaxia here to read your mind, I'm going to have to see for myself."

Pressing my lips together, I inhaled slowly. She was purposely trying to upset me, and I wasn't going to play her game. When I projected her back to my house, she yanked her hand back and headed straight for the door to the basement. She stopped in front of it and leaned into the stairwell.

I crossed my arms, watching her impatiently. Was she eavesdropping? On her own family? Nice. And she talked about me and my spying.

Finally, she turned around and closed the door. Her face had gone slack, like she wasn't expecting to hear them down there or something. Ridiculous. What did she think I would have done with them? Project them off a cliff?

"Happy now?" I snapped.

"Very."

I took another deep breath, ready to find Ursula and get this whole thing over with. "Let's get moving," I said.

Lali stuck out her chin. "Fine by me."

POWER

"She's running!" Lali screamed, gaping after the red sedan taking off at full speed down the road. "She's running away!"

"Yes," I muttered. "I can see that." Lali's masterful plan to do things the nice way had failed miserably. At the mention of undoing the sink, Ursula had slammed the door in our faces. Her car peeled out of the garage a minute later, leaving us standing in the front yard watching taillights disappear.

Lali pressed her palms to her head. "What do we do?"

"I don't know about you, but I'm not letting her get away." I offered Lali my hand. "You coming with me?"

She hesitated but finally slid her fingers into my grip.

"Sit down," I instructed, already following my own orders. I'd never projected into a moving vehicle before, but I'd gotten a good enough look at Ursula's cat-like eyes, round nose, and mocha-colored skin to be able to project after her. As soon as Lali sat down next to me, I previewed Ursula, looked past her to the back seat, and aimed there.

The next second, Lali and I jostled as the car swerved and then jerked forward as the man driving hit the brakes. Judging from the ring on his left hand, he was Ursula's husband.

"What do you want?" he yelled once the car had stopped. He twisted around to shield Ursula from us, his birdlike face bunching into a glare.

"We want your help," I said, pinning him with a glare of my own. "And we're prepared to do whatever it takes to get it."

"We don't want to hurt you," Lali added. "Just help us. Please."

Ursula's black spiral curls bounced as she shook her head.

"It's not an option," I barked, hoping to salvage some of our intimidation factor after Lali just made us look soft. "We don't want to hurt you, but that doesn't mean we won't."

The man twisted further in his seat. "How dare you—"

I grabbed his wrist and projected us to Lanai before he could finish. I didn't bother explaining it to him. He was doubled over anyway, and I knew he wouldn't get far. I showed up in the car again to find Ursula screaming.

"Hey!" I shouted, snapping her out of her hysteria. "He's fine. *For now.* But I'd hate to have to drop him in the middle of the ocean. You get me?" The set of her jaw told me she did.

"What do I have to do?" she choked out.

I felt the corner of my mouth twitch. "That's more like it."

I took Lali and Ursula to the transposer house and went back for Ursula's husband. Projecting him to my living room, I locked him in the basement with Lali's siblings for safekeeping. Next, I took Xiomara to dig up the crystal she and Delta had buried under the tree back in Muir Woods, right next to where we'd waited for Delta to come for her ceremony for Brendan.

Back at the transposer house, it didn't take long to set up the space. I'd already gone to Solstice's apartment to collect the supplies from the ceremony that awakened Lali's siblings' abilities, and we moved some furniture to make room for everyone. Soon the ritual was under way.

Nothing about the situation felt real. The flickering candles made the home seem eerie, even with its fancy chandeliers and giant windows overlooking the San Francisco Bay. The view of the night sky was too peaceful for what was happening. But most of all, I couldn't wrap my brain around seeing all the members of XODUS sitting in a circle on the floor, together, after it had taken months to find them. Watching them prick their fingers and repeat chants to undo the sink all but short-circuited my brain. I didn't even want to blink, for fear they would somehow vanish.

Cade stood next to where I leaned against the bar

counter, his breathing as ragged as my own. He kept his gun visible just in case anyone got any ideas about trying to attack us. That, and because he'd had to threaten to shoot everyone to get Delta to snap out of her muttering and cooperate. If she wasn't messed up enough before this, she was definitely going to be messed up now.

I pushed the thought away, turning my focus to the clear stone in her hand. It hadn't glowed once, though it felt like they'd been at this forever. Was something wrong?

"It's not working," Solstice said, echoing my thought.

"Well, it won't work now," Ori huffed. "You broke the chant."

"Are we going to have to start over?" Ursula whined.

Solstice glared around the room. "Starting over won't matter. Something is wrong. It shouldn't take this long."

Everyone started talking at the same time, and Cade fired the gun. One of the windows shattered instantly. The rest of us froze as he closed the distance to Xiomara in seconds.

Lali took off to intercept him, but he spun around. "Stop right there," he ordered, leveling the gun at her.

My mouth went dry. I couldn't speak, couldn't take my eyes off Lali. The rest of the room faded until all I could see was her terrified face. I was vaguely aware of Xiomara speaking and Cade responding, but I couldn't hear her over my own thoughts.

He won't shoot her. He won't shoot her. No matter how much I repeated it in my head, my heart wouldn't stop trying to beat its way out of my chest. I started to inch toward my uncle, to encourage him to calm down. Anything to get the weapon pointed away from Lali.

"Don't even think about it, nephew," he boomed. "If *any* of you move without my permission, she's dead."

I swallowed hard. *He doesn't mean it. He's just upset.* Still, I wasn't going to set him off. He said not to move, but if he noticed me disappear, that was just as bad. This was what he'd spent twenty years waiting for, and if he thought it wasn't going to work, there was no telling what he'd do—especially if he didn't need Lali for it to work.

Or did he?

Delta's words played through my head: *Just trust me. I can connect them to the group and awaken their powers.* My gaze shot over to where she sat, her eyes darting around nervously. Was that why the ritual wasn't working? Had she purposely linked Lali and her siblings to XODUS to mess it up? Delta had been resistant to undoing the sink from the beginning, and I already knew she was good at manipulating the wording of intentions.

What had the women been chanting? *Release all the energy trapped inside. The blood of XODUS deems the time is right.* If XODUS now included Lali and her brothers and sisters, did we need their blood, too?

"Cade," Delta whispered. "Sometimes energy manipulation can't be undone."

Because you don't want it to be undone. My shoulders tensed. This must've been her way of making sure Cade wouldn't get his ability back. She was pretending she'd tried so he wouldn't hurt her, but she had sabotaged us on purpose.

Without warning, Cade fired the gun he still had aimed in Lali's direction.

"No!" I yelled over the rest of their screams. All the air seemed to leave the room as I whipped my head toward Lali. She stood with a dazed expression as my eyes flew over her body. She wasn't hurt, just stunned. My knees started to give out, and I nearly hit the floor. *She's okay.*

"Death can't be undone, either," Cade hissed. "So you'd better figure out a way to fix this. Next time I won't miss."

"We need the rest of them," I blurted out. I wasn't even sure I was right, but I didn't care. I just had to make Cade think we needed Lali to undo the sink. It was the only way to make sure she stayed safe. If what I said was true, it was the only way to make sure anyone in this room stayed safe. People snapped when they felt hopeless, and Cade had put everything he had into getting his ability back. If he thought it wouldn't work…

"We have everyone," Ori said.

I shook my head. "We need Lali's brothers and sisters. They're connected to this now."

"What are you talking about?" Cade moved his eyes to me.

"They got their powers after Delta and Solstice programmed a crystal to awaken dormant energy for XODUS," I explained quickly, hyper-aware that he still had the gun aimed at Lali.

His scar bunched below his eye as he glared at me.

"They programmed a crystal, did they? I see you've been doing even more behind my back than I thought."

I kept talking, doing all I could to convince my uncle we needed Lali and the others unharmed. "If their astral energy came out with the mention of XODUS, then they're a part of this now." I pointed at the clear quartz in the center of the crystal grid. "You need their intention behind releasing the energy inside that stone. You need their blood."

"That can't be true," Xiomara said, her voice quivering.

Delta gave me a hard look, as if she were upset I'd revealed everything. "It *is* true," she said. All my breath rushed out at her admission. "Kai's right; awakening their astral energy made them a part of this group—a part of XODUS. We need their intention to undo the sink." She said the last part like it caused her physical pain.

"Well, what are you waiting for, nephew?" Cade growled. "Bring them here."

59

BULLET

I BROUGHT THE REST OF THE KIDS OVER, DESPITE Xiomara and Lali begging me not to. There was no other option at this point. It was either bring Lali's siblings or watch Cade's sanity slowly crumble from thinking he'd never get his ability back. I was sure Cade wouldn't hurt anyone we needed to undo the sink, but I couldn't say I was sure he wouldn't hurt anyone if he thought things were hopeless. He already seemed to be teetering on the edge of snapping.

He kept the gun fixed in the direction of where the group of ten scrambled to get into the right positions around the crystal grid, but he and I stayed back by the bar counter. Seeing the crazed look in his eyes, I couldn't stop thoughts of calling the whole thing off from ricocheting through my mind. Everything about the situation felt wrong, and uneasiness weighed on me like a backpack full of lead. I'd been stupid enough to let Delta trick me into helping her drag Lali's siblings into this mess, even deeper than I'd anticipated. I'd never forgive myself if anything happened to them because of my gullibility.

I could project to get the gun away from Cade, and then I wouldn't have to worry about everyone's safety. But I knew my uncle. He was passionate and fierce when he needed to be, but deep down he was just desperate. We'd worked too hard and too long to get to this moment for me to screw it up because of a bad feeling. We were doing things his way, which meant we would do things his way to get to Kala. And in the end, it didn't matter how we did it, as long as we got her back.

I just had to focus on what was really important here and let go of the nerves knotting inside me. This would all be over soon, and it was going to work. It was going to work, and everything was going to be fine.

Xiomara kept her composure better than I expected as she and Delta went through the instructions for the ritual. Everyone was in place on the floor, the candles had all been re-lit, and the colorful crystals were lined up in their original pattern. Each kid had paired up with the adult who had the same initial.

"Everyone listen," Delta said, her gaze moving to each person in the group individually. "It is imperative that each pair place their blood onto the stone at the same time. And you'll have to speak the intention together."

Xiomara recited the intention from earlier and instructed her kids to repeat it until everyone had the wording and the pacing down. Then she nudged Lali.

"You and I have to go first," she said.

Lali moved her head up and down, but she was trembling so much, the motion hardly resembled a nod. I wanted to run over and comfort her, but I knew anything to do with me would only make things worse. She hated me now, and I was going to have to accept that.

Starting with Xiomara and Lali, everyone cut their fingers with the dagger and let their blood absorb into the stone with the same sizzling sound I should have been used to by now. I held my breath as they moved through the ritual, my heart slamming into my ribs so hard I was sure it was bruising.

It's going to work. It's going to work.

Everyone in front of me continued chanting, and wind tore through the room despite all the closed windows. Light shot out of the crystal and flooded everything with such brilliance I had to close my eyes against the glare.

Then everything went dark. No one spoke at first. No one even seemed to be breathing.

Finally, Solstice's voice rang out. "I think it worked."

Hearing her snapped me back into the moment. We hadn't won yet. They still had to test it. Something about that felt even more nerve-racking than the ritual itself. How long would it take them to relearn projecting?

I staggered over to the light switch and flipped it. "Well, we're about to find out." I wasn't sure if I was answering Solstice or replying to my own question. All I knew was I felt like I was about to hyperventilate.

Please, let it have worked.

I moved back over to Cade and took a deep breath to steady myself. "Did you feel anything? Can you—"

"Give me a minute!" Nerves shook his voice, making him sound more vulnerable than I'd ever heard him. He shut his eyes, his breathing so hard it made his entire upper body jerk.

A silver outline started to rise from where he stood, and my jaw nearly hit the floor. *It worked!* Before I could speak, another form flashed across my field of vision. Cade's astral form vanished as his physical body flew backward and slammed into the bar counter.

Somewhere in the commotion, something clattered to the floor.

The gun! He'd dropped it.

Lali, Solstice, Delta, and Ori seemed to register it an instant before I did. By the time I leapt forward, their bodies had already landed. Limbs were everywhere, grasping blindly, and then the gun went off. Everyone else froze when we saw its new wielder.

Solstice.

My body went numb. Of everyone here, I trusted her the least. I heard Lali scream something, but I was too busy running through my options in my head to make sense of it. I had to get the gun away from Solstice. I was right in her line of sight, and if I projected, she could get off a shot before I was able to subdue her.

I saw Lali dive toward her brothers and sisters, who were huddled in the center of the floor near Ursula.

Solstice followed the motion with the gun. "Don't you dare move. Any of you." Her arms twitched to point the weapon at each of us, as if to let us know she could take anyone down she wanted.

My chest constricted as it dawned on me that she could. There were too many people for me to project out of here. I couldn't possibly get all of them to safety without risking someone's life. I'd be lucky if I could save two of them.

Keeping the gun aimed in our general direction, Solstice moved to where Cade was just starting to sit up. "Are you okay?" she asked, kneeling beside him.

"Much better knowing you're the one who got to the gun first," he said as he slowly got to his feet.

Solstice cackled. "Mara's face still reads like a book. I knew she was planning to go after you the second she regained her power."

I could only stare. I knew my uncle trusted Solstice, but I wouldn't put it past her to shoot him at point blank range.

"Solstice," Delta whimpered. "What are you doing?"

"Ensuring the Eyes and Ears welcome me back to Alea with open arms." Solstice grinned wickedly. "Unlike all of you, I won't be at the top of their to-kill list."

What? I turned to Cade just as he moved behind the bar counter. The sound of a drawer opening and closing came from the other side, and he stepped out holding another gun.

What the—

"Nothing would make the Eyes and Ears more eager to welcome us back," he said, smiling at no one in particular, "than bringing them right to a pack of semmies and runaways."

My blood turned to ice. His eyes had lost all their emotion, and his whole demeanor seemed to have changed. Had this been his plan all along? No. It didn't make sense. There had to be something I was missing.

"Uncle Cade." I gaped at him. "What are you doing? You got your power—"

Solstice whipped her gun at me, and I barely had time to register the explosion before fire ripped through my chest.

60

LOSS

Burning spread through my torso as the room swam around me. I stared down at my shirt, watching blood soak through the thin fabric. *She shot me. Solstice shot me.* Pain clouded my mind, but that thought rang out loud and clear. Solstice wanted me dead.

My throat convulsed. She'd shoot again if I didn't drop to the floor. Closing my eyes, I let my knees give out, and the floor rushed up to meet me. The jolt of contact sent another knife of agony through me.

"Solstice!" Cade roared.

"Kai!" Lali screamed.

Everyone's shouts seemed far away. I heard feet shuffle, and someone fired another shot. My stomach rolled. I couldn't see who had pulled the trigger, but no one else hit the floor.

Yet.

"Nobody moves," Solstice ordered.

Squeezing my eyes shut tighter, I tried to breathe

through the pain. Every inhale only added to its intensity. But I had to overcome it. I had to stop Solstice before she hurt anyone else.

Or worse.

"What are you thinking?" Cade shouted. "He was useful."

Useful? A new fire rushed through me that had nothing to do with the bullet. Was that all I was to him? A means to an end? What about the fact that I was his only family in this world? He didn't call my name or come over to check on me. Did he even care that I could be dead? Had he ever really cared about me?

"He's also a threat," Solstice spat. "I don't need him appearing next to me and grabbing my gun."

I swallowed hard. Grabbing a gun was the only way I could help. But there were two of them, and I wasn't even sure I'd have the strength to project. Gritting my teeth against the pain, I arched my back slightly just to make sure I could still move.

Cade told someone to get up without a trace of emotion in his voice.

Over the throbbing in my head, I half-registered Xiomara saying her kids had nothing to do with this. But it was Cade's icy voice that made me freeze.

"They have *everything* to do with this," he said coldly. "You ruined my life, Mara. Now I'm going to ruin yours, and the lives of the people you care about most. The Eyes and Ears will have big plans for them, I'm sure."

The pounding in my head grew stronger. So that had been his plan all along. All Cade ever cared about was revenge. He didn't care about me, and he didn't care about Kala. Xiomara had been right about him using me, *brainwashing* me so I'd be dumb enough to do his dirty work.

I opened my eyes to slits, barely seeing the chandelier above me. I couldn't let him get away with it. If I could distract him long enough, one of the others would have to catch on and go after Solstice. She would be much easier to overpower than my uncle. I would take him down myself.

I barely heard the shouts around me anymore. I put all my energy into focusing my mind on Cade's face—the face of betrayal.

I managed to slip into a preview and targeted the floor a few paces away from where he stood in front of Xiomara. Both of them were so close to the broken window that sprinkles of broken glass surrounded their feet.

Still on my back, I appeared at Cade's side. Ignoring the searing heat in my chest, I rolled onto my hands and knees and sprang at my uncle before he could register my presence. One of the guns went off, but I kept going until my shoulder slammed into him. Spikes of agony shot through my upper body, ripping away my breath. The next thing I knew, broken glass rained around us. It took me a second too long to realize what was happening, and we moved through what was left of the picture window.

Then we were falling past the cliff face, toward the rocks below.

Darkness muted the view of the bluff as it sped past, and

everything seemed to happen in slow motion. Air forced tears to my eyes, making it even harder to see. I clung to the cotton of Cade's shirt with one hand and scrambled to find skin with the other. My fingers closed around his hand. Just as I shut my eyes and projected to Lanai, he slipped out of my grasp.

I hit the beach with a thud. Alone.

"No!" I screamed. The heave of my chest pushed fire through the rest of my body, but I couldn't stop the wails coming out of me. *I killed my uncle.* The last three years of my life blew through my mind like a tornado. I'd never be able to get an explanation from him, to unleash my fury on him for deceiving me—for the nights I spent telling myself I owed him everything for taking me in and actually feeling *grateful* that he did.

Every inhale was torture, and I felt my energy seeping out of me, but I pictured Cade's face. I tried to preview him, hoping he'd survived the fall somehow or managed to project to the transposer in time to switch to his physical body before hitting the rock.

But all I found was blackness. Nothingness.

My heart stuttered. Coughs racked my body, sending new waves of pain through me. My uncle was dead, just like the boy in the picture at Solstice's apartment.

Solstice.

Did she still have a gun, or had the others been able to subdue her? I had to make sure the rest of them were okay. Using every bit of strength I could muster, I projected myself to the transposer house. Part of me feared I'd find more death, but all I saw was Xiomara and

Lali staring in the direction of the broken window. Where was everyone else?

"Lali." I started toward her, my steps uneven. Her face went blank as she took me in. "Are you okay?" I asked.

Her eyes bulged, and then rolled back into her head. The next second, she was on the ground.

"Lali!" My outburst caused another wave of torture to tear through me as I stumbled toward her.

Xiomara crouched next to her daughter and cradled her head. She looked up at me when I knelt in front of them. "How are you—"

"Forget it," I said. "Where are the others?"

"They ran. Solstice went crazy and—" Xiomara let out a loud cry, her eyes filling with tears as they landed on something behind me. I followed her gaze to an unmoving body on the floor a few yards away. *Delta.* Blood pooled around her head, and her eyes were wide open and unblinking.

My stomach heaved. I fought to keep it from erupting as my brain flashed between the gruesome scene in front of me and the similar scene I'd witnessed with my parents.

"Kai, we have to get out of here," Xiomara whimpered. "Solstice could bring the Eyes and Ears back here any minute."

I shook my head, unable to look away from Delta. "We have to get her to a hospital."

"She's gone, Kai." Xiomara let her tears fall. "We'll

come back for her and give her a proper burial, I swear. But right now, we have to go."

I still hesitated.

"*Please*," she said. "Kids! Come out here. We have to go."

I took shallow breaths, praying I'd have the strength to project them all home. The burning in my chest was getting worse, and I was getting more and more light-headed by the second.

Lali's four younger siblings peeked around the door jamb one by one, followed by Ori.

"Hurry," Xiomara urged, waving them over with her free hand. They followed her command, though Oxanna was practically dragging Salaxia. Ignoring the head rush, I took the girls home first, followed by the twins.

When I returned to the transposer house a second time, Ori was covering her face, standing only a couple feet away from Delta's body.

Xiomara still sat with Lali's head in her lap. "Can you hear me?" She brushed her daughter's bangs out of her eyes.

Lali groaned as Xiomara slid a hand under her head.

"It's going to be okay, sweetie," Xiomara said. "We'll get you home." She looked at me. "Can you lift her?"

I shook my head. "I have a better idea." I sat beside them, took each of their wrists, and projected to Lali's bed.

Sliding off the side of her mattress, I staggered to my feet. Xiomara did the same on Lali's other side and tugged the crumpled comforter from the foot of the bed to cover her.

Promising myself I'd stay conscious long enough to take the other two home, I went back to the transposer house and found Ori helping Ursula step out of the tunnel below the house. She must've been hiding down there when everything went crazy. She'd been smart to run for it.

It didn't take long to get each of them home before I went to check on Lali. She still hadn't opened her eyes.

"Is she going to be okay?" I asked, grabbing onto her bedpost to keep myself from collapsing.

"Yes," Xiomara said, her gaze landing on my chest. "But I can't say the same about you." She pointed to the bloodstain on my shirt. "You need to get that looked at."

"It's a low caliber gun." Even as I said it, the room seemed to sway. I could feel the last of my energy draining.

"I don't care," she argued. "I'm driving you to the hospital."

Xiomara insisted on going into the emergency room with me. She pretended to be my mother and told them I'd been hurt in a hunting accident. The staff seemed to buy it. They rushed me into a room and went to work.

Turned out, the bullet had lodged into one of my ribs. I didn't need surgery, but they had to remove it and sew me up. The local anesthesia burned like hell, but after that, I barely felt anything as they cleaned and stitched up the wound. More than anything, I just wanted to go to sleep. Xiomara sat next to me, holding my hand the whole time as I slipped in and out of consciousness. I couldn't help but think of one of the few memories I had of my mother, of her holding my hand while Kala sat in her lap during story time.

But that family was gone, and now so was everyone else. Grandma Naida. Cade. My chance to find my sister. I had nothing left. That was the last thought I had before slipping into darkness.

...I woke up the next day, went home, and well, you know the rest. Sorry, this letter is turning into a novel. I wanted to explain everything in person, but when I tried, we got into a huge fight. You told me you wanted me out of your life forever, and I've tried to respect that. I haven't contacted you for weeks. Honestly, I was hoping that once you cooled off, you'd start to think about what I said and understand my mindset, ~~maybe even miss me,~~ but it's clear that you meant what you said.

But Lali, you're the only person I have left in this world, and I need your help. I've gone back to Alea countless times to search for the lab, and I can't find it. I might be projecting myself in circles—it's impossible to tell up there. Kala is still trapped, and I'm going at it alone trying to get her back. It's too much.

What I said to you that day in the cafeteria about not needing people—well, I was wrong. I know that now, because I need you. I understand that it's my fault you don't want to talk to me, but I hope this letter will help you find it in your heart to forgive me. I am truly sorry for hurting you, and I'll regret it for the rest of my life. I just hope that one day, you'll let me back into yours.

~~Love,~~
Kai

I set down my pen and skim the letter one last time. I've said all I can say. I just hope it's enough.

Folding the paper in half, and then into quarters, I write *Lali* across the back and gaze at the shiny black ink until it loses its sheen. I've never felt so pathetic. Now that

I've lost everyone in this world and I'm no closer to finding my sister in another, the loneliness is crippling.

Lali has to see that. Despite everything, I know she has a good heart—even if that heart hates me at the moment. Maybe this letter will be the start of me changing that.

Rubbing my fingers over the purple stone that hangs around my neck, I close my eyes and preview her. She's sitting with Nelson. His arm is around her shoulders. I ignore the stabbing feeling the sight gives me and pull out of the preview with a sigh. I can't show up when she's with him. Maybe I'll just leave the note on her nightstand and be done with it. *Like you should have done with the note her mother wrote to her.*

The thought taunts me, but I force it away. I have enough regrets as it is. I get to my feet at the same moment a silvery form bursts into my room. I leap back, but the shape follows me and stops inches from where I stand. The face is transparent and sparkly, but I'd know that sneer anywhere.

Solstice.

"Kai, how nice to see you," she jeers, her astral form hovering just above the floor. "How are things?"

"Get out," I snarl, but I know as well as she does that there is nothing I can do to make her leave. I should've paid more attention when Xiomara set up the block around the basement.

"That's no way to greet an old friend." Solstice crosses her see-through arms. "Especially one that could easily kill your dear sister."

All the air goes out of the room. I want to believe she's bluffing, but I can't be sure. If she's been back to Alea, she could have access to the lab.

"Funny how the tables have turned, isn't it?" she coos. "Now it's my turn to threaten you, to use you as my pawn the way you used me. Some would call that karma."

I feel my stomach twist. If Solstice really can get to Kala, I know she won't hesitate to hurt her. "What do you want?" I ask, dreading the answer.

"That's more like it." She locks her silvery eyes on mine. "I'm here to offer you a trade. Your sister in exchange for Lali and the rest of her little semmie siblings. I don't know if you intentionally kept me from learning where they live, but I'm sure you know how to find them."

I can't form words. All I can do is stare.

"It's not wise to waste time. I helped them awaken Kala's ability today, and they've decided it's not as useful as they had hoped. They were ready to dispose of her until I explained that she could be traded for five more semmies." Her smile is cruel.

My teeth clench as I think of the plan she and my uncle came so close to completing—the plan I came so close to helping them complete without knowing it.

"How long?" I demand. "How long were you and Cade using me like a puppet?"

She cackles. "It all started the first time you left me at Delta's house. Cade helped me realize that he and I had the same goals. And then when you and Delta tried to fool us with your little power-awakening ritual, it ended up working out even better. We had only planned to turn you over to the Eyes and Ears, but instead, we got five more semmies to use as bargaining chips."

I think I might be sick. It's my fault. All of it is my fault.

"Speaking of those little abominations," she says, cocking her astral head to the side. "Have them here in forty-eight hours, or your sister dies." She drifts up to me and pats me on the cheek with an icy hand. "Tick tock."

With that, she drifts over my bed and vanishes through my wall without a trace.

I stagger back and fall onto my bed. Is she bluffing? Could she really have access to Kala?

A gulp moves down my throat. I can't risk it. But I can't turn Lali and her siblings in to the Eyes and Ears either.

I force my hand through my hair. There has to be another way. Between all of our abilities, there has to be something we can do. Even if Lali hates me, I need her now more than ever.

Son of a—

ACKNOWLEDGMENTS

Here we are again! I can't believe how lucky I am to be able to pursue this crazy writing dream of mine, and to have such an amazing support system cheering me on as I do. I couldn't do this without you!

To my incredibly patient, kind, and loving life partner, Nefer Lopez, thank you for your constant encouragement (and for putting up with me) through another emotional roller coaster of a book. Having you by my side every step of my publishing journey means more to me than I can ever say.

To my wonderful family, thank you for still being excited about my books now that the novelty of my published author status has worn off and for understanding when impending deadlines threaten our FaceTime chats.

To Linh Nguyen, thank you for reading way more versions of this story than any one person should and for the late-night call that is probably the only reason I didn't give up on publishing this book eight months into writing it.

To Matthew Buscemi, thank you for continuing to believe in my work (and my obsessive, perfectionistic tendencies) enough to let me take the reins and still be a part of the Fuzzy Hedgehog family.

To Alissa Berger, thank you for being such an advocate for Kai's story even when I was only thinking about writing it, for your invaluable feedback, and your above-and-beyond spreadsheet-making to help me assess every scene.

To BJ Neblett, thank you for slicing and dicing the earliest versions of this story, for still being willing to read updated scenes even after reading said earliest versions, and for not being afraid to call me out when my writing gives away that I'm working myself to the point of exhaustion.

To my awesome Beta Readers, Patrick Hodges, Tiea McDonald, Elijah Shoemaker, and Ashley Tapper, thank you for your enthusiasm in sharing your thoughts on this story and for loving it even before I cleaned up all the typos.

To my Bainbridge Betas, Grace and Libby, thank you for being excited to dive back into the Astralis world (on your summer vacation, no less!) and for letting me know how Kai's journey moved you.

To Lindsay Tweedle, thank you for your fabulous editing that continues to both amaze me and help me sleep at night.

And finally, thank YOU, Dear Reader, for wanting to see Kai's side of the story and for venturing to understand him a little more. I know he appreciates it as much as I do.

About the Author

USA Today bestselling and award-winning author K.J. McPike lives out of a carry-on size suitcase and a backpack. After growing up in rural Virginia, she embraced the nomad life and has since lived in Spain, Thailand, Mexico, Indonesia, and Vietnam, as well as all over the United States. Somehow, she still hasn't decided where she wants to settle down.

No matter where she is around the globe, she is likely consuming too much caffeine and spending more time in coffee shops than her own apartment.

www.kjmcpike.com

Made in the USA
Middletown, DE
09 September 2020